A ROGUE COWBOY'S HEART

A Hart Ranch Billionaires Novel

STEPHANIE ROWE

COPYRIGHT

A ROGUE COWBOY'S HEART (Hart Ranch Billionaires). Copyright © 2024 by Stephanie Rowe

ISBN: 978-1-959845-13-3

Publisher: Authenticity Playground Press

Cover design © 2023 by Kelli Ann Morgan, Inspire Creative Services.

CHAPTER ONE

HER DAD NEEDED something to live for, or Maddie Vale was going to lose him.

She glanced over at her dad, Huck Vale, as she pulled into the parking lot of Winslow's Garden Center for supplies for their florist shop, Vale's Flowers. Huck was wearing navy sweatpants, a Vale's Flowers tee shirt, and old sneakers. His Diamond Lake hat was faded from the sun and the wind, and his salt-and-pepper hair was curling out from under it. He looked like he'd chosen all his oldest clothes, crumpled them for a few extra wrinkles, and then dragged them onto his weary, too-lean frame.

His physical therapy had gone fine today, but he didn't care.

She could see it in the slump of his shoulders, in the way he stared out the passenger window, seeing, but not seeing at all.

Her dog, Violet, a huge, rescue pit bull who looked terrifying but was actually the gentlest cupcake ever, was sitting between them, her chin resting on Huck's leg.

Maddie parked her pickup truck at the end of the lot, in

the shade. "I was thinking that it might be fun to sell baked goods at the shop. There's a woman in Birch Crossing who makes great cupcakes. I think it would be good—" She stopped when her dad looked over at her. "What?"

He cocked an eyebrow at her. "You're trying again."

She grinned. "I am. You're just so damned dull these days. I think getting you a sugar high would be great."

He cocked his brow. "Maddie, I'm an ex-FBI agent. I'm a complete badass. The level to which I don't need my adult daughter worrying about me is almost undefinable."

She laughed. "Emphasis on 'ex,' Pops. You're sitting in that seat like an old man."

He sat up taller, as she knew he would. "I'm not old, and I'm taking away your allowance for saying I am."

She raised her brows. "You never gave me an allowance in my entire life."

"And you're welcome. You'd be some wimpy girlie girl if I'd handed you money." He shot her a grumpy look. "You could thank me, you know."

She burst out laughing, so happy to hear him teasing her. It had been so long. "You want me to thank you for making me seal driveways when I was six so I would have enough money to buy cookies at the grocery store?"

He raised his eyebrows. "I'm waiting. Just once, to hear a thanks, one little thanks for anything, would be great."

Her smile faded. "Dad—"

"Oh, shit. No." His smile dropped off. "You know I didn't mean that. Don't ever thank me for that. You're my daughter. End of story. That's it."

She bit her lip. "I know you gave up a lot for me—"

"Nope. Conversation over. I'm not doing that." He folded his arms over his chest and closed his eyes. "I'm taking a nap. Go get the dirt."

Dammit. She'd lost him again. She'd been trying to get

past the wall of melancholy that had cloaked him since the car accident that had wrecked his knee and ripped his active life away from him. She was trying, but she kept failing.

He was her only family. She needed him. "I'm worried about you—"

"I can't hear you. I'm already napping. Snore. Snore. Snore."

She laughed and punched him lightly in the shoulder as she got out of the truck. "Men," she said. "Absolutely impossible."

His lips tightened. "Is that why you and Adam broke up?"

Her smile faded, and her stomach tightened. "Adam?"

He opened his eyes to look at her. "I'm not blind, Maddie. I know he hasn't been around, and you haven't been wearing your engagement ring. You want to talk about it?"

She pressed her lips together. What a fiasco her engagement had been. She'd trusted the wrong man with her heart, and she was still trying to put it back together. "Just sorting things out, Dad. It's good." Her dad had adored Adam, and she didn't want him to know what had happened. The choice she'd made. How both she and her dad had been fooled.

Her dad turned his head to look at her. "Lies," he said softly. "You know I'm trained in lies, right?"

She laughed. "I do know that."

"What happened with Adam? Do I need to shoot him? I haven't shot anyone in a long time. Might be fun."

Her dad and Adam had been great friends. Adam had been one of the lights in her dad's life. She'd tried to stay with Adam for her dad, but Adam had made that impossible. She couldn't make herself break her dad's heart by telling him what had happened. "No shooting necessary," she said as she got out of the truck. "We're working on things."

"Lies again."

She paused. "Dad. I'm not ready to talk about it, but I'm fine, okay?"

It was all she would give him. There was no way she was stealing what little joy her dad had by telling him what had happened with the man she'd dated for four years and agreed to marry last year. Four years, and she hadn't seen the truth about Adam, until it was almost too late.

But she *had* seen it before she'd married him, so three cheers for her.

Her dad sighed. "I'm here for you, Maddie. You don't have to handle this alone."

She grinned. "I have my friends. I'm never alone." Piper, Tori, and Keira were the funniest, silliest best friends a woman could have, and they'd been by her side the whole way. Their strength and support had enabled her to protect her dad, and she would always be grateful for them.

"Your friends?" He looked skeptical. "The ones you never go out with anymore because you're working at the shop twenty-four seven?"

She shrugged. "Someone has to keep all the brides in flowers," she teased. "If you got off your lazy butt and started coming to the shop, I could go party." But he wasn't entirely wrong in his concern. She did love their flower shop, and business had really taken off over the last year. It was great, but life was chaos right now, and she felt like she was struggling to stay afloat.

Which was fine. She could handle it, and she would handle it for as long as it took. She rolled down the windows and then turned off the truck. "I'm leaving the keys in case it gets too hot." She leaned over and kissed him on the cheek. "I love you, Dad."

He closed his eyes again and settled back in the seat. "I love you, too, Peanut."

Her throat tightened at the nickname he'd given her as a

little girl. He hadn't called her that in a long time. It scared her, like he was putting all his affairs in order before calling it quits on life.

She paused to look at him, napping in the truck. How did she get him to want to live again? He was only fifty-five. So much time, if only he decided he wanted it. She hit her palm on the door frame in frustration. "Come on, Violet."

The big, black rescue pittie hopped out of the truck, her therapy dog license and vest giving her the freedom to go into the store. Violet trotted next to Maddie as they headed across the lot, then suddenly, Violet froze and lifted her head, staring ahead.

Maddie's heart jumped, and fear clamped down on her as she set her hand on Violet's back. "What is it, girl?" She'd been so much more relaxed since she'd adopted Violet, being able to trust the huge dog to tell her when danger was near. Violet was her radar, and it had enabled Maddie to finally start to let down the constant vigilance that had consumed her for so long.

Violet was stock-still, staring at a man leaning against the side of the building. He was in the shadows, and he had a cowboy hat on, so his face was hidden. He was wearing jeans, a loose tee shirt, and cowboy boots. He was tall, muscled, and ripped, and fear caught in her throat.

"Is he dangerous?" she whispered to her dog.

Violet didn't move. She just kept staring at the man. Not growling, but alert.

Maddie tightened her fingers on Violet's leash. There was no way anyone could get to her with Violet by her side. She knew that. But she couldn't stop the rising fear, the raw terror that she hadn't felt for so long.

It was a busy Saturday afternoon. Plenty of people around. No one would grab her from a crowded garden store parking lot while she was accompanied by a dog who could kill an attacker in a split second.

Regardless of the man's intentions, she was safe.

And yet, her feet seemed to be stuck to the hot pavement. She couldn't make herself keep going. She glanced at the store, only a few yards away. Air-conditioned, safe, crowded.

He looked down at his phone and began typing onto it, not giving any indication that he was even watching her, let alone planning to abduct her.

And yet... "Come on, Violet. We're going back to the truck." She tugged her dog's leash, and began backing toward her truck.

Violet whined and tucked herself against Maddie's leg as Maddie turned and hurried back to her truck. She checked over her shoulder a few times, and he wasn't watching her. But still...a chill ran down her spine.

She needed to get out of there. Right away. She could feel it in her bones.

She was almost running by the time she got back to the truck. She opened the door and Violet jumped in. Maddie hurled herself into the front seat, started the engine, and rolled up the windows. Fast. Fast. Fast.

Her dad didn't wake up, which was both a relief and scary. Where was the FBI agent who would have known in his gut that something was wrong? She wanted to grab her dad and shake him awake, demanding he get his gun, but she didn't.

Because she didn't want him to see her scared.

She put her hands on the steering wheel, but they were shaking too hard to grip it.

Violet whined and wiggled onto her lap, pressing her face into Maddie's chest. Maddie wrapped her arms around the dog and rested her forehead against Violet's ear. "I'm still running scared, Violet," Maddie whispered. "I thought it would stop when I was eighteen, but it never will."

Her phone buzzed, startling her. She grabbed it and looked at it, half-expecting to see a text from an unknown number.

But it was a text from her friend, Piper Townsend. *Don't forget tonight! We'll pick you up from the shop at eight!*

Girls' night. She'd forgotten that Piper had invited them to a viewing of a band she was considering for one of her bridal clients. It was a black-tie event, and the foursome were making it a high-class girls' night, like the ones they used to have when they were all in their early twenties, broke, and sharing a loft. The nights where they'd pretended that they'd made it, that they had become the women they'd dreamed of being.

And yet, they were still having those nights, because none of them had become the women they'd planned to be, with the lives they'd intended to have.

Yet.

Yet.

It was the magic word. The word that kept them all going. They hadn't gotten there...*yet.*

Maddie took a breath. She didn't want to go out. She wanted to drop her dad off, then go to the shop with Violet, and work until she was too tired for fear and nightmares.

But she'd made a promise to herself that she had to start living. Her dad's response to the accident had showed her what her path would be if she gave up on fully living. Which meant she had to go.

She texted back. *Violet can come, right?*

There was a pause. *You're having one of those days, sweetie?*

Sudden tears filled Maddie's eyes, and she was so grateful for the friends who had never given up on her. She decided

1

not to tell Piper about the man. She was probably imagining things, and she didn't want to be that woman anymore. The scared woman. The one who had lived with three other women so she didn't have to live alone.

She took a breath and quickly replied. *I never have one of those days. I just want to turn Violet loose so she can knock over the dessert table, terrify small children, and shed all over the bride's dress.*

Hah! Perfect. Bring her along, then. She's one of us, baby, and we accept everyone as they are. Sending you hugs to tide you over until we can give you one in person tonight!

Maddie smiled and set her phone on the dashboard. "All right then, Violet. Let's go find you a gown for tonight." She glanced at the man in the cowboy hat as she shifted into drive.

He was staring right at her, his phone down by his side.

Chills shot down her spine again. "He must have noticed how I exude girl power," she said to her dog. "He's in awe of my awesomeness. Makes sense. I have that effect on people."

But as she pulled out, she was careful to stay at the far end of the parking lot so he couldn't get her license plate number.

Just in case.

Her tires bumped over the curb, jolting her dad awake. He sat up with a start. "Finished already?"

She didn't look at him, in case he saw the fear in her eyes. "Nope. Just getting started, Dad."

He frowned at her. "What are you talking about?"

She glanced in the rear-view mirror and saw the man with the cowboy hat watching her drive away. Did she tell her dad? Would it give him life or overwhelm him to know that a man had been watching her? A man she didn't know. A man who could be connected to the past they'd both been worried about since she was six.

She could use her dad's help.

But she needed him alive even more.

"Nothing," she said. "Nothing at all."

She was going to have to handle this herself.

Her and Violet.

CHAPTER TWO

MADDIE LEANED against the gorgeous bar, waiting for her water as she watched Piper, Tori, and Keira dance. The four of them had been dancing all evening, and Maddie was dripping with sweat. Her beautiful red silk dress was drenched, but her feet were happy in her sneakers.

She needed to be on her feet twelve hours a day at the store, and she'd learned years ago not to succumb to fashion at the expense of her feet. Violet was lying next to her, a crystal bowl of water between her massive paws.

The event was high class all the way, all the opulence lightened her mood. They were having such fun, like they used to back when they were all living together.

Piper looked over, waved at her, and then came bounding across the floor. Piper was unofficially on duty as a wedding planner, so she'd donned a subtle, but slightly sexy black dress that was drawing attention that Piper completely ignored. She was radiant, moving among the rich and famous like a woman who knew her way around a five-star life.

Only Maddie knew the truth about Piper, shared late one night when they were both tired, tipsy, and afraid. Likewise,

Piper was the only one who knew the whole truth about Maddie's past.

Some secrets were too dangerous to share.

Piper strode up, moving like a woman with purpose. "The band. What do you think?"

"Amazing."

Her face lit up. "Right? I think my bride will love them. I'm putting them on my list." She crouched down and ruffled Violet's head. "And I didn't forget about you, darling." Violet's tail thumped. "And just so you know, don't let your feelings be hurt by all the jerks who treat you like you're a monster who's going to eat them, okay? You are a big, smushy lovebug who takes special care of my bestie, and anyone who counts knows that. Okay?"

Violet slapped a big, smooshy tongue across Piper's cheek, and her friend laughed and stood up. "I love your dog."

Maddie's heart tightened. "You're not even a dog person."

"I know, right? Violet is magical." Piper sat down on a bar stool, and crossed her legs like a woman who knew how to use them, which Maddie loved for her. "Talk to me, girl. You've been scanning that crowd tonight like a woman on the run. I haven't seen that for a while."

All right, so maybe she hadn't quite moved past the afternoon's incident. Maddie glanced at the dance floor, but Tori and Keira were still dancing. "I saw a man in the parking lot at Winslow's Garden Center. I felt like he was watching me."

Piper gestured for a water from the bartender. "Was he?"

"I don't know. I can be paranoid, as you know."

"I do know." Piper smiled. "Remember that time when you thought you were being watched, and it turned out to be a bronze statue in the park?"

Maddie grinned. "Yeah, that was funny. I couldn't figure out why he wouldn't look away."

11

"You think you were being paranoid today?" Piper's question was casual, validating, and non-judgmental.

Maddie loved her friend so much. Piper's secrets gave her an insight into Maddie's past that no one else would have. "I don't know."

"Did you get a look at him?"

"He had a cowboy hat on, which put his face in shadow."

"A cowboy hat? We're in a suburb of Boston. Who wears cowboy hats around here?" Piper unscrewed the lid and took a long drink of the water.

"Stalkers?"

Piper pointed the water bottle at Maddie. "Many men with cowboy hats are loyal, honorable, and dusty. A cowboy hat doesn't make a stalker, necessarily. It could mean nights of romance, moonlight, and making love by waterfalls. Like those Harts. They're delicious."

The Harts were a billionaire ranching family of formerly homeless kids who had created a found family, given themselves the last name of Hart, and become reclusive, insanely popular celebrities. "I don't need a delicious man right now," Maddie said, rubbing her sneaker along Violet's back, both to love on the dog and to reassure herself that Violet was close.

"Au contraire, my darling." Piper had a sparkle in her eyes. "I think maybe you do need a delicious man, one who can show you that not all men are like Adam."

Maddie grinned. "So, then, that means you're also in the market for a delicious man to erase your recent trauma?"

"Me?" Piper barked with laughter. "My men problems can't be fixed by finding a yummy cowboy. They go much deeper than that, entwined into the very fabric of all my woman power."

"Ladies!" Tori Cardenas flung her arms around Maddie and Piper. "Isn't this party fabulous? I'm so glad the world decided to celebrate us by hosting this five-star bash for us! We finally get our recognition!"

Maddie grinned. It was the game they used to play when they were at their most broke, most desperate. They'd pretend they'd made it, that the world was at their feet. "A celebrity jeweler tried to give me a five-hundred-thousand-dollar diamond necklace to wear tonight, but who would wear something so gaudy?"

"Right?" Piper laid her open hand across her bare neck. "Nothing under seven figures ever touches this precious body of mine."

"We have to have standards," Tori said. "If we settle for hot dogs, cheap beer, and polyester clothing, we'll be eating hot dogs in used cars wearing our clearance-rack dresses for the rest of our lives. And who wants that?"

"Not me!" Maddie said.

"Hell, no." Piper raised her bottle of water. "Here's to standards!"

"Red silk rope, baby," Tori said. "No one and nothing gets past our red silk ropes unless we invite them." A red silk rope was their fancy, high-class way of referring to personal boundaries. It felt more elegant and concrete than just saying boundaries.

"Amen, sister." Maddie tapped her water against her friends' drinks. "If we don't create our life on purpose, then one will be created for us."

"And it might not be the one we want," Piper finished.

Her words settled deep, and suddenly the energy of the trio became more serious. They looked at each other, because they all knew that it was almost ten years later, and they were all still trying to create the dreams that hadn't seemed so far away back then.

"Are we too old for this?" Maddie asked. "For pretending like we made it?"

"No." Piper shook her head. "We're not giving up."

Tori nodded. "We keep going for as long as it takes."

Maddie took a breath. "Sometimes it feels like I'm going backwards." She held up her hand, which was no longer sporting an engagement ring. Not that being engaged was everything, but after her experience this afternoon, and her dad not doing well, she felt like things were getting worse, not better.

Tori held up hers, which had held a wedding band not too long ago. "I feel you, babe."

Maddie's heart tightened. She knew what Tori had gone through, and she squeezed her friend's hand.

Piper fluttered her left hand, which was also more barren than it had been recently. "It's our girl power time," she said. "We have each other."

Maddie raised her brows. "I love you, but I don't want to share a loft with you guys again," she teased, mostly because a part of her really did want to creep back into that old life, where she didn't have to face the harder truths of being ten years older and still being who and where she was.

Tori laughed. "We're not broke anymore, so at least we don't have to do that."

"I think Keira's broke," Maddie said.

"Yes, true. Keira might have to live in one of our closets," Tori said.

At that moment, the almost-broke member of their squad, Keira Kingsley, came running up. Her dark hair was curled in tight, sweaty ringlets around her face, and her light-brown skin was covered with a sheen of sweat. "You guys! I was in the bathroom, and I heard these women talking! They said that Lucas Hart is *here!*"

Maddie sat up and shot a look at Piper. The Hart men wore cowboy hats. What were the chances that Lucas Hart had been the one watching her today? "No," she said, at Piper's look. "No way."

"Yes, way." Keira missed the look that passed between Piper and Maddie. "Apparently, he was seen skulking around in the hallways."

"Skulking?" The word wrapped around Maddie's chest with much too much power.

Keira rolled her eyes. "That's what the Harts do. You know they hate publicity."

"Which makes them all the more interesting to all the paparazzi," Tori said. "Look! He must have walked in."

Maddie followed Tori's gaze, and she saw heads turning toward the rear of the ballroom. The buzz of conversation began to hum, and people paused, trying to see. A few people pulled out their phones to try to take a picture. "I could never live like that," she said. "In the spotlight all the time? This is a private event, and people are still trying to take pictures and bother him."

Keira put her arm around Maddie and kissed the top of her head. "Don't sound so worried, sweetie. No one's going to put you on their social media accounts just because Lucas Hart is here."

"I could get caught in the background of a picture." Only Piper knew the full truth about why Maddie never let her picture be posted anywhere on the internet, but she'd hinted enough to the others that they respected her choice.

"We'll shield you," Tori said, completely serious. "We're your human blockade."

"There he is," Keira whispered. "Damn. He is so tall in person."

"Smoking hot," Tori said. "That's unnatural."

Maddie kept her gaze on Piper, not wanting to look across the room. Afraid that the man she'd see was the man who had been watching her in the Winslow's Garden Center parking lot.

Piper met her gaze, her gaze understanding. "Why would Lucas Hart have been watching you? Why would he be following you?"

"I don't know," Maddie said. "You know I don't know." That was her problem. All her secrets, hidden even from her. She turned her back on the room, leaning on the bar. "I think I'm going to leave."

"No." Piper leaned in, putting her arm around her. "If Lucas Hart is following you, then he's found you twice. You need to know, because he'll find you again."

Fear gripped Maddie, and suddenly Violet was on her feet, nudging at her hand. She snapped her fingers and Violet stood up on her back legs, her paws on Maddie's chest, her big tongue flapping, her brown eyes gazing at Maddie like a promise to keep her safe.

"What's going on?" Tori turned back to them. "What's wrong, Maddie?"

Keira looked over, and then frowned. "Panic attack? Let's get you out of here."

Maddie felt tears burn in her eyes. She loved her friends so much. Their support was amazing. "There was a man in a cowboy hat earlier. I felt like he was watching me. It was creepy."

Tori and Keira's eyes widened, then they both looked across the room. "You think it was Lucas Hart?" There was no disbelief or doubt in Tori's question. Absolute acceptance that one of the country's most famous celebrities could be randomly stalking her friend.

Everyone needed friends like that, and she was so glad she had them.

"I couldn't see his face." Maddie continued to keep her back to the room. "I want to leave."

Piper shook her head. "You're safe here. If it's him, we need to find out what's going on right now, because you have all of us and a room full of people around."

Maddie bent her head.

"He's scanning the room," Tori said. "He looks like he's looking for someone."

Oh, God.

"Why would he be looking for you?" Keira said.

Maddie met Piper's gaze, at the secrets Piper was holding for her. "I don't know."

"Does this have anything to do with your panic attacks?" Tori asked. "He's looking at Violet right now."

Violet had been with her earlier. How many huge, black pit bulls wearing therapy vests were around? "Yes," Maddie said. "I..." She paused, and suddenly, she wanted to tell them her truth. She didn't want to hold it to herself anymore. "Squad promise."

It was their code for a secret that could never, ever, *ever* go beyond them.

Both Tori and Keira turned to face her. "Squad promise," they agreed, their faces solemn.

Maddie took a breath. "When my dad was an FBI agent, he was undercover trying to break up a drug ring." She talked fast, in case Lucas Hart was heading their way as she spoke. For some reason, she needed her friends to know. Maybe in case she disappeared after tonight. "He stumbled across me and a boy being held in a drug house. He bought me to get me out."

"Bought you?" Keira looked stunned.

Maddie nodded. "It was the only way. They couldn't find where this man got me from, so the courts allowed my dad to adopt me. I was six at the time. I don't remember my life before my dad, but I had night terrors for years and years, so it wasn't good." She looked at them. "I don't know where I'm from, and I've lived in terror my whole life that someone from my past will find me and try to take me back."

They all stared at her. "It could be anyone," Tori said.

Maddie nodded. "Based on what my dad said, he thinks I might have been stolen from another drug dealer and used to try to gain power. But we don't know." She shrugged. "Once I turned eighteen, I knew that they couldn't legally take me from my dad, and that helped a lot. But..." she shrugged.

"Holy shit, girl." Keira grabbed her and pulled her into a big hug, squishing Violet between them. "You need to tell us these things so we can help!"

"We love you so much." Tori also wrapped her up in a hug, and then Piper threw her arms around all of them.

"No one will get through us to you!" Keira said.

Maddie started laughing. "I'm sorry I didn't tell you. It was just...I guess I was scared that if I told anyone, then someone would overhear and then word would get back that the missing girl named Sienna is actually Madison Vale, living outside Boston and running a flower shop."

"Sienna?" Tori pulled back. "That's your real name?"

"No," Maddie said firmly. "My real name is Madison Vale. Sienna is a girl who used to exist." This was why she hadn't wanted to tell anyone. The statement that Sienna was her real name. The next one would be that Huck wasn't her real dad.

People who weren't adopted didn't understand how it worked. She was Maddie Vale. Huck Vale was her dad. The past was simply a story. A story that still haunted her, but a story nonetheless. A story that would someday not have any power over her anymore.

A story that she would take control over, starting now, by facing it.

Her arms still around her friends, she turned her head to scan the ballroom. She found Lucas Hart almost immediately. He was standing halfway across the room, tall, muscled, wearing jeans and cowboy boots at this black-tie affair, because he was a man who could do whatever he wanted.

His jaw was hard. His face sculpted. He was breathtakingly vibrant, his energy cascading across her even from a distance.

He was wearing the same cowboy hat as the man from the parking lot.

And he was staring right at her.

CHAPTER THREE

Lucas Hart had found her.

Madison Vale.

And she was a shock to his very core.

He hadn't known what to expect when he'd come after her. None of the Harts had. Until this moment, she'd been only a memory for his brother Jacob, and a name and address on a piece of paper.

And now...she was in front of him.

And he realized he hadn't remotely expected *her*.

The way she spoke to her friends was pure warmth and loyalty.

The way they hugged her showed how much they loved her.

The bond between the foursome was real and powerful, the kind of loyalty that the Harts lived and breathed every moment of their lives.

Madison was sexy as all hell in that red dress, and her sneakers made him grin. Her brown skin was insanely beautiful, and the intricate braids cascading down her back were a literal work of art. Sassy. Beautiful. Bold.

He liked her immediately, which surprised him. He didn't like many people. Trusted even fewer. But the energy between Madison and her friends hit right in the core of what made him get up every day. Love. Loyalty. Commitment.

She seemed like she had it all together.

His job was done. He'd seen her. He'd made sure she was all right. Now he was supposed to walk away and let her resume her life. His family was on alert. If Madison ever decided to unlock her past and started asking questions, the Harts would know and they would come forward.

But a family meeting had convinced the Harts not to confront her, because every single Hart had a past that they wanted to leave behind. Each Hart understood in their core that it would be cruel and brutal to force Madison's past on her unless she wanted it, because none of them wanted that to happen to them.

Jacob had wanted to come find her, but he'd asked Lucas to do it instead, not trusting himself to keep his distance once he saw her...also fearing that if Madison saw Jacob, she'd recognize him, and be sucked back into her past without the Harts even saying a word.

So, Lucas was here.

And Madison was fine.

Time to leave.

But he didn't move.

Because he couldn't take his eyes off her dog, and the bright orange Therapy Dog vest she was wearing.

They were at a black-tie affair in a five-star hotel. And yet Madison had a massive pittie by her side, even on the dance floor. She almost always had a part of her touching the dog, and the dog's vigilance to Madison was constant.

As Lucas watched, the dog suddenly rose to her feet and put her huge paws on Madison's chest, as if she'd sensed something was wrong with her owner.

Dammit.

At what point did he interfere? Madison's life was clearly fine. She had friends, a business, and a support system.

But that orange vest on her dog was a blaring alarm that all was not well with the woman who had haunted his brother for so many years.

Madison suddenly turned her head and looked right at him.

Lucas stiffened, shocked but also not shocked, by the jolt of electricity that shot through him when his gaze met hers. He already knew that he was drawn to her energy, but the eye contact felt like she'd fucking climbed into his chest and lit a fire.

Fuck.

Walk away?

Walk over to her?

He hadn't expected anything complicated, which had been incredibly short-sighted. He knew damn well what a traumatic childhood did to a person, even as an adult.

He realized that he'd hoped that she'd escaped unscathed, getting yanked out of that life at such a young age.

But the dog told other stories.

Madison said something, and immediately, her three friends all turned to look at him.

None of their faces were friendly, which he appreciated. He was accustomed to everyone idolizing him, wanting something from him, pretending to be his friend so they could get to his money or his family.

It was refreshing as hell to see four women studying him as if they were debating whether they needed to pull out their guns and take him out back into a dark alley.

Yeah. *Good job, Madison.* Friendship like that was everything.

The women didn't take their gazes off him, but he could

see their mouths moving as they discussed him. He wished he could read lips, but all he could do was watch their body language and their facial expressions to realize that they were deciding how to handle him.

He contemplated continuing to stand where he was and let them choose whether to approach him, but he was in the middle of a crowd. He didn't like crowds, and he didn't want his conversation with Madison to be overheard.

He shook out his shoulders, surprised to discover that his heart had actually sped up. Nerves? Anticipation? Didn't matter. His connection with Madison had been opened. He'd been careless enough to be seen watching her, and now he had to handle this.

What he was going to say, he had no idea.

But he'd spent his life in survival mode, adjusting on the fly, so he was in his zone of genius.

Except as he started walking toward Madison, and saw her stiffen, he suddenly felt like he was about to step into a world he had no idea how to navigate.

He didn't like that feeling at all.

At. All.

But there was no going back.

CHAPTER FOUR

"HOLY CRAP. Lucas Hart is coming over here." Piper hopped off the stool. "I'll handle him."

"No." Maddie put her hand on Piper's arm. "He hasn't taken his gaze off me. I need to know what he wants." She tightened her fingers. "Stay with me," she whispered.

"We'll never leave you," Piper said, moving to stand beside Maddie.

"What she said," Tori said, moving to Maddie's other side, standing so close that her shoulder was against Maddie's.

"You can handle him, but I need to shield you," Keira said. "People are taking photographs."

"Oh, God." Maddie's stomach churned. The idea of getting her face on the internet was even more terrifying than the man walking toward her.

"No worries." Keira shot her a smile. "We're on it."

Lucas walked up as Keira moved in front of Maddie, standing a few feet in front of her, so it looked to observers as if Keira was the one Lucas had come to meet.

He paused, looking in surprise at Keira. "Hi."

His voice was delicious. Low and deep, but it had a

warmth and gentleness that made Maddie want to sink down into it.

"What do you want?" Keira asked. Her voice was perfectly friendly, but there was a faint edge to it that made it clear she was protecting Maddie.

Damn, she loved her friends.

Lucas glanced at Keira, then looked over at Maddie. "I'd like to talk to Madison."

Maddie saw folks around them raising their cameras, so she turned her back on him and leaned on the bar, bending her head down. Keira would know what to do.

"You attract attention, Mr. Hart," Keira said.

Maddie watched him in the mirror over the bar, and saw his brows go up. "Call me Lucas," he said. "And I do attract attention," he agreed. "Is that a problem?"

"It is," Keira said. "Maddie is happy to talk to you, but she has zero tolerance for photographs."

"Maddie," he repeated softly, turning her name over as if it was a puppy he'd just met.

She met his gaze in the mirror over the back of the bar.

He smiled at her, a smile that was genuine and warm. Kind even. None of the airs or superficiality she would have expected from a man of his family, wealth, and celebrity. "My name's Lucas Hart."

She nodded. "Obviously. Why are you following me?" It sounded conceited to assume that Lucas Hart was following her, but she knew she was right.

He cleared his throat. "May we talk in private?"

"I don't hide secrets from my friends." Not anymore. Not after ten minutes ago, and that felt amazing.

He glanced at her friends. "I respect that," he said, "but as you said, I attract attention." He paused. "The manager's office is down the hall on the right. I will meet you there in ten minutes." He glanced at her friends. "All of you," he added, with just the faintest hint of amusement.

Then, before she could respond, he turned and walked away, taking the attention with him.

The minute he was gone, Maddie let out a shuddering sigh of relief.

"What the hell?" Piper hit Maddie on the arm. "He couldn't take his attention off you. What the heck was that?"

"Maybe he wants to hire Vale's Flowers for an upcoming wedding," Tori said. "I think one of the Harts is engaged. Maybe two of them."

Keira didn't laugh. Instead, her face was focused and intent. "Where were you living when your dad found you?"

Maddie knelt beside Violet and wrapped her arms around her dog. "Portland."

"Maine?"

"Oregon."

Keira let out her breath. "The Harts live in Oregon. They were homeless kids in Portland."

The four of them fell silent, digesting that connection.

"He must be here about my past," Maddie said softly, her fingers digging into the scruff on the back of Violet's neck. "I don't want to talk about my past. I don't want to go there." Her throat felt tight. She wanted to call her dad. Bring him in on it. Team up with the man who had swept in and pried her free of the life that wasn't meant for her.

But she didn't know what that would do to her dad. Would he freak out? Would he be energized? She couldn't take the risk.

"You can leave," Tori said. "You can walk away, and I'll tell him to stay away from you."

Maddie pressed her forehead against Violet. Her heart was racing, and fear was gripping her. "I've been running my whole life," she said. "I don't want to be scared anymore. Maybe this...maybe talking to him will help me."

Piper frowned. "You're sure?"

"No. Not at all." Maddie stood up. "But I'm going to do it anyway. I'm an adult. He and his family have no claim over me, no matter why he's here." She looked around. "You guys are coming, right? I can't do it alone."

They all nodded.

"Okay, then." She took a breath. "Let's go find a private, isolated room to meet with a strange, powerful man who might have ties to drug dealers and child traffickers. Good?"

Piper grinned. "It's what dreams are made of, baby."

Tori held up her purse. "I have Mace. If I scream 'watermelon,' everyone look away and cover their eyes, because I'm not great with weaponry."

Maddie grinned. "Watermelon it is. Let's go."

CHAPTER FIVE

THE MANAGER'S office was small. Too small.

Maddie felt claustrophobic and trapped, even with her friends there.

It had been nine and a half minutes, and Lucas wasn't there yet.

Was he coming? Should they have called the cops? What if he was rounding up a team of assassins? They couldn't stop that.

Piper picked up a porcelain art object and hefted it. "This would knock him out." She settled behind the desk. "No one get between me and him if I need to throw this."

A strangled laugh bubbled up. "You'll kill him with that."

Piper shrugged. "Defense of others is a legal defense. I'm good."

Maddie shook out her shoulders. "I can't do this. Let's leave."

Tori let out a visible breath. "Great idea. I've been freaking out inside waiting for him to show up. Let's go."

"Me, too," Keira said. "I feel like a little trapped bunny, and bunnies never win when cornered by wolves."

"Or coyotes," Tori said.

"Or even Corgis," added Keira. "Who wants to be a trapped bunny today?"

"No one wants to be a trapped bunny ever." Maddie stood up and patted Violet's head. "Let's go." Relief rushing through her, she bolted for the door, yanked it open, and ran straight into Lucas's solid, hard frame.

"Whoa." He caught her shoulders with a grip that was all support and no threat, but Maddie jumped back anyway, fear lodging in her throat.

Lucas stood in the open door, a frown etched on his face. "Change your mind?"

"We feel like trapped rabbits in here," Maddie said.

She expected him to laugh, but instead, understanding settled in his eyes. The kind of understanding that made sudden tears want to well up. "I hear you," he said softly, looking around at all the women. "How about if I sit on the floor at the far end of the room? That puts all of you between me and the door. If you need to run, I wouldn't be able to stop you from there."

She blinked. "You're treating us like traumatized children."

He paused. "Or trapped rabbits."

She couldn't help the giggle that wanted to emerge. "All right. I did claim that title." She took a breath and stood taller. This was Lucas Hart. A man who was in the spotlight all the time. If he was a serial killer, someone would have seen him do it by now. Plus, she didn't want to feel that scared. "You don't need to sit on the floor."

He shrugged. "I like the floor." He gestured to the room. "May I enter?"

Damn. The man was polite. Thoughtful. Gave her space to breathe. The protective energy of her friends and her dog surrounded Maddie, giving her the courage to continue with the meeting. "Yes."

"Great." Lucas flashed her a smile, then stepped into the office and shut the door behind him. He gave Violet a nod, but didn't try to touch her.

The office immediately felt small again, but this time, it wasn't the suffocating weight of fear. It was that Lucas Hart had a commanding presence that filled the space around him.

He looked around at everyone, then walked across the office and, true to his word, sat down on the floor on the far side. He set his cowboy hat aside, then leaned back, draped his forearms over his knees, and looked around the room. "Good evening, ladies."

All the women were standing, and he had to look up at them.

No one answered, because they were waiting for Maddie to take charge. This was Maddie's moment, and her friends would interfere only as needed.

"Why are you following me?" Maddie asked. She knew she wasn't being very polite, but this man *was* following her. Lucas Hart or not, that didn't earn him warm fuzzies. She'd be an idiot to succumb to his good looks, his reputation, and his visible attempts to make her feel comfortable.

Because he was breathtakingly attractive with his cowboy hat off. His hair was a gorgeous brown, short and efficient. His blue eyes were captivating. And he had lines around the side of his mouth that said he was a guy who liked to smile.

Lucas took a breath. "I was supposed to check on you and make sure you were doing all right, and then leave." He nodded at Violet. "But the therapy dog makes me think that it's not all good. So I have to ask."

She stared at him, trying to wrap her head around what he was saying. "Who wanted you to check on me?"

"Jacob."

She held out her hands in frustration. "Jacob who?"

He raised his brow. "Jacob Hart. My brother."

Maddie shrugged. "I don't pay much attention to gossip."

"He just got engaged," Piper whispered. "A single mom, I think, but the press doesn't have many details."

Lucas slid a glance toward Piper, a little resignation in his gaze that Piper kept track of his family.

Maddie didn't like that look. Piper had good reason to keep track.

"Hey," Maddie said. "You have one minute to tell me what's going on. That's it. Then we're leaving and if I see you again, I'm filing for a restraining order."

Lucas looked back over at Maddie, and respect flashed across his face. "I don't know how much you know about your past. I don't want to introduce things that you don't already have to deal with."

Her heart started to race, and suddenly, her legs started shaking.

Piper grabbed a chair and pushed it behind her.

Maddie sank down in the chair, and Violet immediately leapt up on her lap. "Are you here to try to take me away from my life?" She watched him closely as she asked, which meant she saw the look of startled surprise in his eyes.

"Take you? From friendship like this? From your dad? Hell, no. Never." He held up his hands. "Never in a million years would anyone in my family take you away from yours. I swear it."

She felt his truth, and the growing coil of terror inside her gut stopped twisting tighter and tighter. It didn't fade, but it went still, settling at the level it was at. She let out her breath. "I believe you."

He leaned forward, meeting her gaze. "Maddie, every one of the Harts grew up in hellish situations. We know what a shitty past is like. And we know the relief when you find a family that will stand by you. I know where you are. I get it. That's why I didn't want to stick myself into your life. We just wanted to know you were all right, but I don't know that yet, so I have to ask."

"I'm fine," she said automatically.

His eyebrows went up. "What's your dog's name?"

She hugged Violet tighter. "Cujo."

He grinned. "You don't seem like the type to name your dog after a horror novel."

"You'd be surprised at the level of paranormal terror I inflict on unsuspecting innocents on a regular basis."

His smile widened. "I gotta agree with you on that. I thought you were a bad ass, powerful woman doing a hell of a job in her life, not a deadly poltergeist."

Badass. He'd called her badass. Her dad called her badass, too.

"Well, you just never know, right?" She took a breath. "How are you connected to my past?" The moment she asked it, her heart started to race. Not from fear, but from anticipation. For her whole life, she'd hidden from her past, but she was beginning to trust Lucas. Maybe that meant that the information he had about her past might not be dangerous.

He met her gaze, accepting her question and not challenging her as to whether she really wanted to open that door. "What do you know?"

"I know that my dad bought me from some terrible man. No one could find out where the man had gotten me from, so the courts let my dad adopt me. I don't know anything else."

He nodded. "The man's name was Ivan."

"Ivan?" Her dad had never given the man a name. "Was he biologically related to me?"

"No, but he's the biological father of my brother, Jacob."

She sat up. Was that why Lucas Hart had an interest in her? Not because he was going to abduct her? But because his brother had come from the same hellhole she'd passed through? "Really?"

Lucas nodded. "Ivan sent Jacob out one night on a job with the bastard's friends. When Jacob got back, you were gone. He's spent his whole life since then looking for you. We found you last week."

"Oh. *Oh.*" Her chest tightened. "My dad said there was a boy there with me, but he couldn't get him out."

Lucas nodded. "That's Jacob. Do you remember him?"

She shook her head. "I don't remember anything about that time. Sometimes I dream of bad things, but I don't know what's real or not." She paused. "Is Jacob my brother?"

"In his heart, yes. Biologically, no. But no one in the Hart family gives a shit about biological family." He paused. "Jacob didn't come because he thought you might recognize him. He didn't want to bring back trauma into your life. So I came, because I'm subtle and you wouldn't notice me." He gave an ironic smile. "That worked out well, right?"

She couldn't help but smile. "You're the antithesis of low visibility."

He shrugged. "I do my best." He paused. "Would you like to meet Jacob?"

Beside her, Piper sucked in her breath, and Maddie did the same. "Is he *here?*"

"No. He's in Oregon. But I have a private jet—"

Keira held up her hand. "I hate to interrupt, but before you sweep Maddie up into some little Hart web, I'd like to ask if you guys have found where Maddie came from before she got to Ivan's house. Basically, is there any chance that someone out there is still looking for her, someone she *doesn't* want to show up in her life? What about Ivan?"

Maddie shot an appreciative smile at her friend. This was why they were there with her: to notice things she was too emotional to remember.

"Ivan is dead," Lucas said.

"Dead." Weird emotions shuddered through Maddie, ones she didn't understand. But suddenly she couldn't breathe. If Ivan was the monster in her dreams, would he go away now? Would he be gone?

Lucas frowned at her. "You okay?"

She held up her hand. "Fine," she lied. "Keep talking. What about before Ivan?"

He watched her carefully, clearly not convinced. "No. We're looking, but we haven't found anything."

Keira leaned in. "So, I take that to mean that if the press gets pictures of Maddie with the Harts, and finds out that she is this long-lost family friend, then someone from her past could see that, put the pieces together, and decide to come after her?"

He ground his jaw. "Yes, that's possible. Unlikely, though. She was a child back then with a different name."

"*You* found me," Maddie said. "You tracked me right down despite everything my dad and I have done to sever all ties to Sienna. Maybe your attempts to find me sent a ripple out there that someone is going to pick up on." Oh. God.

Lucas's eyes widened. "We're very good at what we do—"

"Would you stake your life on it?" Maddie asked.

He paused. "No."

Piper stood up. "I think you've done enough, Mr. Hart. We love our Maddie, and you don't have a right to put the Hart spotlight on her."

Lucas didn't move. He continued to sit on the floor, his arms draped over his knees, like he had all the time in the world. "Maddie," he said quietly, as if she and he were the only two people in the little office. "Jacob is a great guy. Losing you has eaten away at him since that day. He would love to meet you. Every Hart has an ugly past, so we know security. We would commit to protecting you."

Maddie stiffened. "I don't want a life where I need protection," she said. She stood up. "I love my life. My friends. My dad. All I want is to be able to walk down the street and not flinch whenever a car slows down too close to me. I want to go to bed at night with the windows open, and know I'm safe." A year ago, she would have added wanting to be able to sleep at night without fear, but since she'd gotten Violet, she'd learned to trust the dog to keep her safe, and she'd finally been able to sleep well and hard, which she loved.

She didn't want to lose what progress she'd made. "Tell Jacob that I'm fine, and I have a great life. He doesn't need to worry about me." She stood, suddenly restless. "Thanks for stopping by, Mr. Hart. Have a great flight home."

He watched her for a moment, then stood up. He grabbed a pen and paper, and jotted something down. He left the paper on the corner of the desk. "If you need anything, ever, call me."

He walked toward her, and she stiffened, stepping to the side as he neared. He paused near her, searching her face. There was so much emotion in his eyes, so much complexity. She could tell he wanted to say more and do more, and a part of her wanted him to.

There was something about Lucas Hart that made her feel safe in exactly the way she'd yearned for her whole life.

But he brought with him a whole new set of dangers, so she said nothing.

He nodded at her friends. "All of you are welcome to my phone number. Don't share it anywhere else, but if any of you ever need anything, call. We consider Maddie under our protection, and therefore all of you are as well." He glanced at her. "And your dad and your dog, of course."

Maddie put her hand on Violet's head. "Thanks."

He nodded. "Good luck, Maddie. With everything."

Then, without waiting for any further response, he walked out of the office and shut the door behind him.

Maddie let out her breath and sank down onto a chair while Piper locked the door.

"Holy crap," Piper said. "That man is electric. Am I the only one who felt it?"

Maddie wrapped her arms around Violet while Tori and Keira agreed with Piper.

"Maddie?" Piper sat down next to her and put her arm around her. "You all right?"

She lifted her chin. "I'm great. It's good to know I have the Harts' protection, if I want it, right?"

"I'll get his number," Tori said. "I'll text it to all of us."

"Yes," Piper said with a frown. "But are you all right?"

Maddie laughed softly. "The most compelling man I've ever met has dumped himself into my life, past and present."

"He told you Ivan's dead, though. So that's good." Keira grinned. "One down."

"Right." Maddie was tired, but she managed a smile. "Well, at least the worst happened, and I survived, right? Someone from my past showed up, and it was all right."

"Yes, it was," Piper said, firmly. "Keep telling yourself that when you can't sleep tonight, right?"

She patted Violet. "I'll sleep fine. I just need to process, that's all." She stood up. "Party is still young, ladies. Let's go have some fun."

For a moment, her friends said nothing. They just looked at each other, and then at her.

She rolled her eyes. "Oh, for heaven's sake, ladies. I'm fine. Let's go! I want to dance the night away with my girls!"

Piper narrowed her eyes, then nodded. "All right. No better way to clear the shadows than having fun with the girls. Maddie sandwich!" She dragged Maddie into a hug, and

Tori and Keira threw their arms around them both, squishing Maddie in the middle.

By the time the hug was over, she was laughing, and felt better already. "Let's go!"

The foursome headed out into the hallway, and Maddie couldn't help but look around. She didn't see Lucas anywhere, and she almost laughed at her disappointment. The last thing she needed was a man, especially one who was tied to the past she did her best to leave behind.

As she followed her friends down the hall, her phone beeped. She glanced at it and saw it was the text from Tori with Lucas's phone number.

Her finger hovered over it to delete it, then, she changed her mind and added him as a contact.

Not that she would ever call him.

But...just in case.

CHAPTER SIX

LUCAS HAD JUST SAT down on one of the Hart private jets when his phone rang.

He looked at it immediately, half hoping that it was an unknown number, maybe Maddie calling him.

It was his brother Dylan. He ran a private detective agency, and he was the one who had found Maddie.

Lucas tried to reach Jacob earlier, but his brother hadn't answered the phone.

He wasn't going to give the report on Maddie to anyone until he'd spoken to Jacob, but he never silenced a call from his family. "What's up?"

"How's Madison? Did you see her?"

Maddie. She was beautiful, courageous, funny, and had cultivated an incredible group of friends. She was also carrying the weight of her past in a way Lucas was all too familiar with. He'd wanted to talk to her, to offer advice, to do whatever he could to help, but he'd felt her walls and knew she wasn't interested in his help.

And he fucking loved that. His life was built around people who wanted things from him and his family. It was refreshing to be around four women who wanted nothing from him except to get out of their way.

He respected the hell out of that...and it made him want to go right back into that office and demand they let him help. "I want to give the report to Jacob first," he said to Dylan.

Dylan paused. "I need to talk to you before I talk to Jacob about something."

Lucas leaned forward, gripping the phone. "We never hold secrets from each other." It was part of the Hart family bond, started by Dylan, the oldest. They weren't allowed to keep secrets from each other, stemming back to the days when they were all living under the bridge together. Secrets meant isolation, and the only way they'd survived was by sticking together.

The rule against no secrets had continued to this day. So, what the hell?

"I found out that Ivan had a partner. His name is Les Shipman. He supplied drugs to Ivan. He disappeared when Ivan got arrested back then, and stays off the radar."

Lucas bit his lip. "And?" What did this have to do with Maddie?

"He's Ivan's half-brother. They were close, but he was the mastermind. Ivan was the labor, Les was the strategy. Les spent twenty years in prison for shit you don't want to know about."

Lucas's leg bounced restlessly as the plane began to taxi for takeoff. "He's alive?"

"When I was looking for Maddie, I found trails he left behind. I've been following those trails, and that's how I found him. He's been looking for her, too."

Fuck. The plane began to speed up, rolling down the runway. "You think she's in danger?"

"Until I find him, we need to keep an eye on her."

Lucas swore as the plane's wheels caught air. "I just took off. I'll have to circle back."

"Do it." Dylan paused. "I don't know whether to tell Jacob."

Jacob had had a brutal childhood, and they all tried to protect him when they could. "You have to. If Les is after Maddie, he might also be looking for Jacob. He's got Annie and Phoebe to protect now. He needs to know so he can take precautions."

Dylan swore. "I'll go over to his house. Talk to him in person."

"Do it. I'll cover Maddie out here. Let's stay in touch." Lucas hung up the phone, told the flight attendant to redirect the pilot, then leaned back in his seat, thinking.

Maddie didn't want him involved in her life.

He got that.

He thought about Les.

He thought about Violet.

He thought about the way Maddie's eyes flashed with humor, courage, and fear.

How was he going to get in there to protect her without fucking up what she'd done to keep herself sane, safe, and happy?

CHAPTER SEVEN

LURKING in the shadows like any good stalker, Lucas stood across the street from Vale's Flowers the next morning, watching as Maddie set up the sidewalk display.

Her dog shadowed her constantly, and Maddie took twice as long setting up because she kept pausing to love on her pit bull.

He watched as customers came into the store, lighting up when Maddie greeted them.

He grinned when an irate bride raced into the shop, her hair still in foils, and he marveled at Maddie's ability to soothe her.

He saw an old man slump into the store, and walk out with a dozen roses, and a twinkle in his eye.

Maddie was great with people, and she had an inner sparkle that lit up everyone around her.

But at the same time, he noticed how much she looked around, checking her surroundings, pausing to watch whenever a man went by.

He knew that way of living, because he'd done it too. So had all of his siblings.

Still did sometimes, out of habit.

It was no way to live, especially for a woman. His brothers had had it tough enough, but his two sisters had taught him that women had to deal with vulnerability in a way that was very different than men.

Lucas spent most of his time trying to protect his family, not just from actual threats, but from the shadows that haunted them. Trying to build the protections that would help them feel safer, able to breathe, free to laugh.

And the longer he stood there watching Maddie, the more Lucas found himself wanting to bring Maddie into his circle of protection.

But she didn't want him, his family, or the memories he represented.

He got that.

She stopped suddenly, shielding her eyes to stare across the street. It appeared as if she was looking right at him, but he knew he was hidden in the shadows.

She pulled out her phone, tapped the screen, and then held it to her ear.

His phone rang.

He pulled it out and saw it was an unknown number. He hit the screen. "Lucas Hart," he answered.

"Tell me it's you across the street being all creepy and secretive in the shadows, and that it's not some paid heavyweight coming to get me." Maddie's voice rang out clear and strong, but with the faintest edge of fear.

Damn. He liked her voice. And she'd kept his phone number. He grinned. "It's me," he admitted. "No nefarious intentions at all."

"Get over here." She hung up the phone and walked back into her store.

Lucas chuckled as he shoved his phone in his pocket and

headed across the street. He loved that she spoke to him like he was a normal person, not a celebrity.

Maddie had solved the problem of how Lucas was going to approach her. Next step, getting permission to shadow her, without having to scare the hell out of her by telling her that Ivan's half-brother was looking for her.

MADDIE HAD MADE it behind the counter by the time Lucas walked in, his dominating frame and engaging smile seeming to envelop the entire store the moment he stepped across the threshold.

Lucas Hart was dangerously compelling. She needed to remember that.

"Hey," he said. "You look beautiful this morning."

She heard the hitch in his voice, and she paused, surprised. "You mean that." She was wearing her work clothes, because she hadn't yet had time to change into her dealing-with-customers attire yet. Old jeans. Boots. A baggy Vale's Flowers tee shirt that was already wet and dirty. The circles under her eyes showed the effect of sitting up all night, listening to the creaks of her house, trying to decide if any of them were footsteps.

Even Violet hadn't been able to help her sleep last night.

"I do," he said. "Beauty radiates from within. You have that." His matter-of-fact tone did more to make her heart go mushy than if he'd been all lovey-dovey.

She wouldn't have trusted lovey-dovey.

But matter-of-fact felt safe. "Well, thanks. Come in back with me."

He cocked an eyebrow at her command, but shrugged. "Sure."

Maddie was viscerally aware of Lucas behind her as she

pushed through the door to the back of the shop, which was four times the size of the front. It was stuffed with beautiful flowers, most of which had arrived that morning. She had so much to organize, and her dad had once again said he didn't feel up to coming in.

Lucas stopped. "Hell. That's a lot of flowers."

"I know. I have two weddings I need to prep for. I don't have time to stand around and chat, but I can see the front door if anyone comes in." She hurried over to the white roses that she'd already trimmed and set in water to open last night. "You need to go back to Oregon." She picked up several vases, and then glared at him when he went to pick up more. "I can do it."

"I'm sure you can, but help isn't a bad thing." He set the vases next to the ones she'd carried. "Don't you have assistants?"

"It used to be my dad and me, but now it's just me. I need to hire someone, but I don't like strangers." She grimaced at his sideways glance. "I mean, strangers are fine. It's just that I have a certain way of doing things, and I want someone who will make less work for me, not more."

"I get that. Want me to bring the rest over?"

She sighed. "You're ignoring me. I said you need to go back to Oregon."

"I will. How can I help you?"

She put her hands on her hips. "I'm not an idiot, Lucas. I'm well aware that you're ignoring me. I don't like it."

He turned to look at her then, his face serious. "Fuck. I didn't mean to make it feel like I wasn't respecting you. That's not my intention. It's just—"

He stopped.

Her heart tightened and fear started to creep down her spine. "It's just what?" She moved her foot so her left leg was pressed against Violet, who was right next to her, as always.

He swore under his breath. "I'd like to stick around for a few days."

She stared at him. "Stick around? Me?"

"Yeah. Help with the store. Maybe watch your house at night so you can sleep better. We don't have to talk about your past. I just want to be present for you." He met her gaze with full candor, allowing her to see his expression.

But she couldn't read it. "Why?"

"Jacob wants me to make sure you're good."

Her stomach flipped. "That's a lie. You just lied to me." Oh, shit. She'd just been starting to trust him. She stepped back. "You need to leave—" Her foot caught the table leg, and Violet shoved her to the side, knocking her out of the way as the table tipped, and the vases they'd just brought over tumbled. "Crap!"

She lunged for the nearest vase, but it hit the floor and shattered. The other two also fell, and both broke as well. "I can't use those flowers. They'll have glass in them—"

The front door jingled, and a voice rang out. "Maddie," Piper called out. "We're here. We're a little early."

Oh, crap. Piper was there with a new bride already? "I'll be right out." She spun around looking for her mop while Violet ran out to greet Piper, her tail wagging.

"No, it's fine, she's super friendly," Piper explained to the bride, who was no doubt running for the nearest exit at the sight of Violet.

Lucas grabbed the mop. "I'll clean it up. You go do your thing."

"But—"

He raised his brows. "Go."

She hesitated, torn, but he waved the mop at her. "It will do my protective soul good to be able to sit here and help you while you go make someone's day brighter. I got this."

When she still didn't leave, he put down the mop and walked over to her. "Maddie."

She stood taller as he neared. "What?"

He stopped in front of her, not quite in her personal space, but dancing at the edge of it. And weirdly, she was okay with him being there. "I got you," he said softly. "You can go."

Sudden tears filled her eyes. God, she needed help, and she'd just gotten an angel with a cowboy hat dropped in her lap. She'd sort it out later, but right now, all she could do was accept it. "Okay. Thanks."

At his nod, she turned and bolted to the front of the store, where Piper and her newest client were fawning over her bridal display, always set out and ready for the brides that kept her business booming.

She met Piper's gaze, and saw her friend look meaningfully toward the backroom and raise her brows.

"My new maintenance guy," she said.

"He's very attractive," Piper said.

"What? Who?" The bride peered around Piper and looked in back. "He looks like Lucas Hart, doesn't he?"

"Lucas is much better looking," Piper said with a snort. "Plus, he'd never be *mopping*."

Lucas turned his back on them, clearly overhearing the conversation, but not before she saw him grin. His smile made her chuckle.

"I'm sure Lucas Hart would never raise a finger for such mundane things as mopping," Maddie said.

"Right? That man is a national treasure," the bride said. She smiled, her brown eyes radiant with joy, her brown skin glowing like a woman who was so in love she could barely contain herself.

Maddie felt herself grinning. This was why she loved the flower business. Because flowers made people happy, so she got to see the best in people, day after day. She thrived on that energy, and she let it lift her up every day.

Plus, for right now, she didn't have to worry that someone was going to sneak in her back door, because it was currently being guarded by an attractive, stubborn cowboy who seemed to think he had a life debt he had to repay to her.

Who was she to argue with fate?

She was going to enjoy every single minute of feeling safe for as long as she had that chance. She held out her hand. "My name's Maddie Vale," she said. "Let's get started."

CHAPTER EIGHT

AT NINE O'CLOCK THAT EVENING, Maddie finally locked the shop door after the last customer, then turned around to face the Hart rancher who had stayed the entire day and helped her.

Lucas was wiping down the counter, whistling to himself, his biceps flexing as he wiped.

He had made himself completely at home in her shop, and she'd been too busy to argue with him or make him get out.

But now... "Lucas."

He didn't look up. "I know."

"You know what?"

He kept scrubbing. "I know I have to tell you why I followed you around like your dog today."

Maddie looked over at Violet, who had curled up on her bed in the corner. She was napping, but her ears were up, listening for any hint that Maddie needed her. "You know, I *was* thinking about you as a dog all day," she said.

He finally looked up and grinned. "I could tell. That time you told me to sit and stay was a dead giveaway."

She finally smiled. "You're so sassy."

"I know, right?" He tossed the sponge aside. "I'm a pain in the ass that way."

"Sassy is fun. I'm okay with it."

He flashed her a grin. "Great. Then you won't mind if I stick around for a while then?"

"What's a while?"

"A week. Maybe two. Maybe three."

Something inside her fluttered, something that she didn't like at all, because it was a mushy, girly feeling that she had no space for. "You want to follow me around like a dog for three weeks?"

He gestured to the immaculate store. "I do great work. And I even stayed out of sight. No one knew Lucas Hart was your assistant today."

Dammit. The man was so disarming. "You have all the right words, don't you?"

His smile faded. "I'm not trying to be suave. Just trying to...do right by you."

"Do right? Jacob owes me nothing. My life is great." She shrugged her shoulders, trying to ward off the sudden chill. She didn't even like saying Jacob's name. "So I have some anxiety. It's fine. It's not his fault."

Lucas swore under his breath. "What if I asked you to simply trust me? To say, 'sure, Lucas, hang around. I need help.' And call it a day?"

Maddie stared at him, a sudden sinking feeling in her gut. "Oh, no," she whispered. "Something has happened. I'm not safe? That's why you're here today?" She immediately stepped away from the window, and Violet leapt to her feet and bolted over to her.

"Shit. No." Lucas stepped around the table and caught her arm.

She instinctively spun around, twisted out of his grip, and

launched herself out of his reach, her hands up protectively as she whirled to face him, feet braced.

He went still, his hand in the air where it had been on her a second ago. "Damn," he said. "That was a great move."

"My dad was FBI. He taught me a lot of things." She lowered her hands, appreciating that he didn't treat her like a freak for overreacting. He was even impressed, and that made her feel good.

"Can you shoot a gun?" he asked.

"Of course."

He cocked an eyebrow, studying her.

"What?" She asked. "You think that just because I can handle myself physically I shouldn't have anxiety?"

"Nope. I don't think that at all." He laughed softly. "Every Hart has trauma. Your ability to take care of yourself doesn't necessarily erase lessons from childhood."

She took a breath and nodded, sudden emotions clogging her throat. She tried so hard to hide her vulnerability from her dad, because she didn't want him to feel like he hadn't done enough for her, but Lucas had caught her off guard.

So, now he knew she wasn't entirely all right, at least a little bit.

Maybe that was good. Maybe it was good not to have to hide it. She took a breath, and then sat down on the rubber floormat to hug Violet. "What's going on?"

Lucas immediately sat down on the floor as well. He leaned back against the side of the counter, taking up the same relaxed position as he had in the manager's office. She wondered how many times in his life he'd taken up that unassuming position to make someone else feel at ease. Maybe a lot, given what he'd said about his family.

He said nothing for a moment. He simply studied her face. She could almost hear him analyzing his possible responses and which one he would give her.

"Just tell me the truth," she said. "Otherwise, my imagination will create something that I can almost guarantee will be worse. Spill it, Hart."

He grinned. "All right. When my brother, Dylan, was looking for you, he ran across the trail of someone else who was also looking for you. He called me last night and said he'd finally traced the digital footprints and he knows who it is."

Maddie's heart began to race. She wanted to crawl into her closet, curl into a ball, and close her eyes, like she'd done so many times as a kid.

But she wasn't that girl anymore. She needed to get free of her past, and she was ready to face it. "Who is it?"

"Ivan's half-brother."

She blinked. "Ivan had a brother?"

He nodded. "Not a good guy. He's been in jail for a while and recently got out. He's been looking for you, and for Jacob apparently."

She started scratching Violet's head, focusing on the feel of the silky fur beneath her fingers. "What does he want?"

"I don't know. But the Harts, myself included, are unwilling to leave you unprotected. You might have passed through Jacob's life for only a short time, but that's all it takes to get in our circle."

"Wow." She almost started laughing. "I've spent my life worrying about someone coming to get me, and telling myself that I was safe, and then it actually happens."

Lucas was watching her carefully, maybe wondering if she were going to freak out. "Maybe he's not coming to get you. Maybe he wants to give you a billion dollars for the hardship of having to know his brother."

She grinned. "I'd like a tropical island. Do you think he has one he wants to give me?"

Amusement twinkled in Lucas's eyes. "Probably. I'd ask

for cabana boys before you accept. Who wants to get their own drinks when you're on a tropical island?"

"Good point. I'll make a list so I'm ready when he shows up. Has he found me?"

Lucas didn't even hesitate at her pivot. "Not that we know of. Dylan is trying to get to him before he finds you. That's our plan."

"So, you hanging around me is just a precaution?"

"Yep. Plus, I like playing with broken glass, so that's an added bonus for me."

"Men and their toys," she teased. "So, what now? You really want to shadow me for a few weeks?" She didn't think she liked the idea. But at the same time, a little part of her was curious. What would it be like to feel safe? It was weird to feel safe when there was someone hunting her, but Lucas was capable.

He leaned in. "I want to be your bodyguard 24/7 until this is over."

Oh, boy. "And if I say no?"

His jaw flexed. "Please don't."

"Please don't?" She started laughing again. "Why is that so funny?"

"I'm trying to respect your boundaries." He didn't smile. "But the thought of walking away and leaving you unprotected is making me crazy, and I haven't even left yet." He paused. "I met Ivan. He was a cold-blooded sociopath who fucked up my brother so badly that he can't function normally in society. Even as an adult, Jacob almost went..." He paused. "Jacob had a tough time. This is the man who held you. This is the man whose brother is looking for you. I don't know what he wants, but I saw the aftermath with my brother. Don't fucking say no, Maddie. Let me help."

Maddie closed her eyes and pressed her face to Violet's

neck. She imagined what it would be like if she went home alone tonight and tried to sleep.

There would be no sleep.

Not ever.

Not until Lucas called her and told her that this man had been handled.

"Maddie?"

She didn't open her eyes. "On the plus side, at least this isn't anxiety. It's genuine fear of an actual sociopath who might want to kill me. I feel very validated. It's like years of my mind running in circles in constant panic has resulted in an actual, clear threat that I can address."

He chuckled softly. "There's always a plus side, right?"

"Absolutely." Without lifting her head from Violet's, she opened one eye and peered at Lucas. "You want to sleep in my house?"

"I won't sleep much, but yeah."

"Ride in my car?"

He grinned. "Yep."

"Walk my dog with me?"

"You bet."

"And what if the world notices Lucas Hart following me around?"

"Then the man after you will know you're not an easy target."

She thought about that. "I have an extreme aversion to my face on social media. I can't do it."

He paused. "All right. I'll disguise myself."

"You? You're like this walking billboard of sex, charm, and fantasy. No one is going to fail to notice you."

He raised his brows. "Sex, charm, and fantasy?"

Oh, damn. She tried to ignore the heat in her chest. "Or so I've heard. I just see you as an annoying nudge who is good with a mop."

He smiled. "The Harts have managed to go a lot of places without drawing notice. If we're out in public, no one will know it's me."

She highly doubted that. Lucas Hart exuded an electrifying charisma that was impossible to conceal. Even if he dressed up as a clown with full makeup, his essence would glisten through.

But at the same time, she was warming up to the idea of having Lucas keep her safe while a sociopath was looking for her. "All right. I'll let you bodyguard me on one condition."

Relief flickered in his eyes. "Anything."

"If someone recognizes you, and I get caught in some photo of you, you have to hunt down that photo and destroy it, and pay me a billion dollars for every photo of me that hits the internet." A billion dollars could buy her a lot of security. It was a trade she could live with.

"A billion dollars per photo?" He looked amused.

"Yes. I am already envisioning the jewelry I'm going to buy myself." She fluttered her hand. "I'll be that girl who buys herself and her friends diamonds."

He cocked his head. "You don't seem like the diamond type."

"No? What do I seem like?"

He studied her for a moment. "I'm not sure yet. But I'm interested in finding out."

Her heart fluttered at his low undertone. "That sounds like you're flirting. Are you flirting with me? Because that changes the vibe here."

He studied her thoughtfully. "How would you feel if I said yes?"

Why did that make her stomach do a little flipflop? "I would have to fire you. I am very committed to being single at the moment. No flirting allowed."

Amusement flickered in his eyes. "Got it. I'm not flirting,

then. I'm just interested in knowing you because you seem like an interesting person. I like interesting people."

She narrowed her eyes. "Holy crap, Lucas. You're lying to me. You *are* flirting with me!"

He had the grace to incline his head. "I'm not trying to flirt. I find you genuinely fascinating. I do want to get to know you. But I respect your boundaries. I'm an impartial bodyguard. I won't attempt to get you to kiss me even once."

"Kiss you?"

He grinned. "If I kiss you first, I feel like I would wind up in the hospital. So you'll have to make the first move."

"I'm not making a move."

"Then we're good. Just friends. Shall we head out? Grab some food and then go to your house?"

She bit her lip. Did she really want to do this? Despite her claims to the contrary, she found Lucas insanely compelling. He was sexy, yes, but there was also so much more to him. She wanted to know about his past. About how he managed it. About his family.

And she wanted him to kiss her.

There were a plethora of reasons why she needed to tell Lucas she'd hire her own bodyguard if she needed one.

Except, how would she know she could trust a paid one?

Lucas cocked an eyebrow, waiting for her, clearly aware that she was processing, and he was okay with that.

Dammit. She trusted him. He made her feel safe.

She didn't want anyone else.

She wanted Lucas Hart, even if she did want to kiss the man. "All right," she said. "Let's go. But no flirting."

The smile that lit up his face was positively endearing.

Why did the man have to be so freaking appealing?

CHAPTER NINE

IT WAS AFTER MIDNIGHT, and Lucas was still wide awake.

He was sitting on Maddie's couch, the pile of blankets he'd been intending to sleep under still folded on the end.

Maddie had gone to bed as soon as they'd gotten home.

She'd been quiet, and he'd given her space.

He was still reeling from the day. From her. From—

His phone rang, and he saw it was Jacob finally calling him back. He answered it quietly. "Hi."

Jacob wasted no time with small talk. "How is she?"

"She's solid."

The sigh of relief was audible. "She's good, then?"

Lucas looked at the photos on the coffee table. Her friends. Her dad. No boyfriend. "She's got a great dad. Great friends. Successful business." He paused, then decided to be honest with Jacob. "She has shadows from her past, but she doesn't remember any of it. What do you remember about her time at Ivan's?"

Jacob let out his breath. "Shit. It was bad. It was bad for all of us. I protected her as much as I could, but when you hear or see the violence, it's almost as bad as if it actually gets to you."

Lucas rubbed his eyes wearily, his heart heavy for the shadows Maddie was carrying. She might not actively remember what happened, but her soul knew. "I don't think she wants to know what happened."

"No need," Jacob agreed. "It's a bunch of crap anyway. Should I come out there?"

Lucas grimaced, but the Harts didn't keep secrets from each other. "She doesn't want to see you. She doesn't want to go back to the memories she's hiding from."

"I get that," Jacob said, his voice quiet. "Tell her that I'm here for her, in any way she needs or wants. She'll always be my sister in my heart, even if she never remembers who I am." He paused. "Dylan says Les doesn't appear to have found her yet, but thanks for watching out for her."

"You got it." From Jacob's comment, Lucas figured Dylan had talked to him. "You doing all right?"

"Yeah. I'm keeping Phoebe and Annie close, and I let Dylan put a few men on us. I hate having them around, but it's not about me anymore. Phoebe and Annie are everything to me, Lucas. Every fucking thing."

Lucas smiled. "I know. They're lucky to have you." The entire Hart family, Jacob included, would never have believed that Jacob would wind up with a woman and a child. He just couldn't handle people in his space, even his own family, for long.

But Phoebe and Annie fit him, and they were giving him life and freedom that he'd never had before.

Lucas was jealous. Not jealous, so much as inspired. If Jacob could find someone who fit him, who could get past the demons and the nightmares, then all the Harts had a chance. Even Lucas. "I gotta ask you something."

"What's up?" Jacob sounded curious.

Lucas stood up and paced across the room, away from the bedroom door. "Maddie's radiant, Jacob. She literally lights up any room she's in. She sasses me, and she and her friends don't give a shit that I'm a Hart. She told me I would owe her a billion dollars for every photo of her that winds up on the web because of a paparazzi shot of me. She's funny. She's irreverent. She's tough. And at the same time, she's so fucking vulnerable."

Jacob was quiet for a sec. "You like her."

Lucas let out his breath. "Yeah."

"You want to know if I'm okay if you date her?"

"Yeah." Lucas paced across the kitchen, surprised that his heart was actually racing.

"Hell, bro. You know my answer."

"I need to hear it."

"Since when did you turn all soft like that?" Jacob said with a chuckle.

"Since I met her."

"Ah...it's like *that*." Understanding softened Jacob's voice, a timbre that had been reserved only for horses until Phoebe and Annie had taught him that people needed him, too.

"Yeah," Lucas said.

"Like Annie and Phoebe?"

Lucas had been there the moment Jacob had driven up with Annie and Phoebe for the first time. The mom and little girl had jumped out of his truck and raced across his lawn. Lucas had expected Jacob to be spiraling, unable to handle them in his space.

And then he'd seen the look on Jacob's face. Peace. Serenity. Expressions and emotions he was pretty sure Jacob had never experienced before in his life. Emotions that he was pretty sure Jacob hadn't even understood.

Lucas hadn't understood them either. Not really.

But now he did, because Maddie had awakened a softness

that he hadn't known he was capable of. "Yeah. It's like Annie and Phoebe."

Jacob let out a low whistle. "Then I wish you all the luck in the world, bro. I hope you find what I found."

Lucas closed his eyes. "So, you're good with it? With me and her, if it works out?"

"I've known you since I was a teenager. Lost, fucked up, and scared shitless. I know who you are. I know how you treat people. You're the one who takes care of everyone. Makes sure we're okay. You've held me together so many times when I thought my mind was going to explode and shatter. Maddie would be lucky as all hell if she wound up with you. And I mean it."

Lucas felt his throat tighten. He knew that Maddie meant everything to Jacob. She'd haunted him since the day she'd disappeared. The fact that Jacob would trust Lucas with her was...a statement. "Thanks."

Jacob's voice was equally rough. "I love you, bro. I believe in you."

"Thanks. Love you, too."

"If she's the right one for you, it's worth it. It's worth hanging in there. But it's not easy. It'll scare the shit out of you more than anything you've experienced in your life."

Hell. Lucas had experienced a lot. "Yeah." It had been a very long time since Lucas had been drawn to a woman. He'd been burned badly, and the lesson had branded itself into the fiber of his being.

Until now.

"I'm not sure what to do about it, Jacob," he admitted. "Maddie wants her distance."

"Give it to her. Phoebe gave me the distance I needed. That's why I was able to handle what I was feeling. Give her time. Patience."

Lucas laughed softly. "You're the people expert now?"

STEPHANIE ROWE

"Nope. Just a man who hated people, until he met the one he'd been waiting for all this time."

Lucas lightly punched his fist against the cabinet. "Fuck. I'm so happy for you, Jacob."

"Yeah, me, too. I want to go back to them now. We good?"

"Yep."

"All right." He hung up abruptly, making Lucas smile.

He knew Jacob so well. When Jacob's ability to connect reached his limit, he had to retreat. Suddenly. Completely. But at least now, he was retreating to Phoebe and little Annie.

Lucas hung up the phone and tapped it against his chest.

How did he go forward with Maddie? The last thing he wanted to do was push her. He'd never push her. But—

"Lucas?"

He spun around, his chest tightening when he saw Maddie standing in her bedroom doorway. She was wearing plaid pajama bottoms, a loose sweatshirt, and fuzzy socks. She looked tired and tense, and he had to force himself to lean back against the kitchen counter instead of striding across the small house to pull her into his arms. "You okay?" Obviously she wasn't, but he wasn't going to make her admit anything she didn't want to reveal.

She hugged herself. "I can't sleep. Usually Violet is enough, but my mind is going crazy."

Something inside him softened. Tough, independent Maddie. He loved that she'd been honest with him. "How can I help?" Did she want him to sit in her room? Hold her while she tried to sleep? Sleep on her floor? He was down with any of that.

"Pizza."

He started laughing at himself. "Pizza?" Not him being some heroic presence in her bedroom, cradling her. *Pizza.*

Fuck, he loved that. Maddie had powerful boundaries, and he respected that.

"And ice cream."

He grinned. "You bet. Got a favorite place?"

The corner of her mouth quirked. "What do you think?"

"I think you're a woman who knows her pizza and ice cream."

Her smile made it to her eyes. "A gold star for Lucas Hart tonight."

"You want me to go pick it up?"

"It's too late for delivery, but we can go together." She held up her phone. "I already put my order in. Do you want anything?"

"You bet." He walked over to her and accepted her phone. Their fingers brushed, and he met her gaze. For a split second, Lucas saw interest flash in her eyes, and then she looked away.

But he'd seen it.

Maddie was as aware of him as he was of her.

He had a chance.

CHAPTER TEN

"WE CAN'T DO THIS," Maddie said. "It's one in the morning!" But she was laughing as she scrambled out of Lucas's rental car, a big, badass Cadillac Escalade that had enough room in the back for Violet to do sprints.

"We have to. It's a full moon. It'll be great." He grabbed the food out of the backseat while Violet scrambled into the front seat and bounded out beside Maddie.

She shut her door and then paused as the night settled around them.

Lucas had suggested that going home to eat the pizza in the place where the panic had hit her wasn't her best option. Instead, he'd convinced her to go to a nearby park that he'd noticed earlier, so they could have a picnic in the moonlight.

Moonlight.

Maddie looked up at the sky, sucking in her breath as she surveyed the vast night sky. Full moon. Endless stars. She breathed deep, inhaling the fresh night air. "This is the difference between men and women. Men can do things like go to a park at one in the morning for a picnic. Women can't."

"I know. I have two sisters." Lucas walked around the

front of the truck, carrying their food and two bottles of water. "Just so you know, I could drop a man twice my size, no problem. Plus, I'm armed. You're extremely safe."

She looked at him. "What if we got jumped by a gang?"

He shrugged. "I spent my childhood fighting for my life. I learned how to fight dirty and successfully. Then, once I hooked up with the Harts, I got serious about being able to protect myself and my siblings. When you're rich, you have the time and money to do whatever you want, and I spent many years trying to become the next superhero so no one I cared about would ever feel unsafe again, including me."

She put her hands on her hips, startled by his statement. "Did it work?"

"Yes and no. On a physical level, I'm safe, as is my family. But turns out you can't make people feel safe just by ensuring their physical safety."

She smiled. "I feel so seen."

"Right? Traumatic pasts bond us. You'd fit right in with the Harts." He jerked his head at a nearby hill. "Up we go, Ms. Vale."

"Away from the truck?"

He raised his brows. "We can sit in the truck. It's fine. Let's do that." He began to turn, but she touched his arm.

He stopped immediately, his gaze going to her hand before snapping to her face.

She didn't pull her hand away. Touching him made her feel grounded. Connected. *Safe.* "If you really can keep us safe, no matter what happens, I would like to have our picnic on the top of the hill." Eating outside at one in the morning felt terrifying, but at the same time, the taste of freedom was intoxicating.

She wanted to go up that hill.

She burned for the sense of power and freedom that being up there in the dark would give her, after a lifetime of always looking over her shoulder, even when she was in the middle of crowds.

"You sure?" Lucas moved a step closer, so she didn't have to reach so far to continue to touch his arm.

She nodded. "I need it."

Understanding flickered in his eyes. "Then let's do it." He handed her the pizza. "I'll get a couple blankets from the back."

"You packed blankets?" She frowned as she took the box. This wasn't his way of seducing her, was it? She didn't want to think he was playing her.

"I thought I was going to be sleeping outside your house for the next few weeks, so I came prepared when I showed up at your store this morning." He tossed her a grin as he pulled two red plaid blankets out of the back of the SUV. "This is a much better use for them."

She took a breath. "All right."

He nodded at the grass. "Lead the way. Turn around if you want. You're in charge."

She sighed deeply, the panic easing. Lucas Hart seemed to know exactly what she needed from him. He made it easy to relax around him, especially since she didn't have to hide her past from him. She could just be herself, and not try to pretend all her shadows weren't real. She whistled for Violet, who was sniffing the grass at the edge of the parking lot. "Let's go, girl."

She and her dog headed for the grass, with Lucas following behind her, just slightly off to the side so she could see him out of her peripheral vision.

The hill was steeper than she thought, and they were both laughing when they arrived at the top. She was panting a little, but Lucas wasn't. Which was good. No bodyguard should ever get out of breath. He had to be unstoppable.

Lucas pointed behind her. "That's the view I wanted to see."

She turned and saw they were up above the town far enough that she could see for miles. The lights of houses. Streetlights. Headlights. And just space and freedom and earth. "Wow." She breathed it in. "I feel like I'm standing in the middle of the freedom I always dreamed of."

"Glad you appreciate it. I thought you might." Lucas sounded pleased as he spread the blanket in front of her, and then set the ice cream and their drinks on it. "Your table is set, my queen."

"Awesome. I'm actually starving." She set the pizza on the blanket and sat down, grinning as Violet dove into the grass and rolled, grunting with delight. "This is so much better than sitting in my bed, listening to every sound, wondering if I'm going crazy."

Lucas sat down next to her, stretching his long legs out with a relaxed leisure that was contagious. "Not going crazy," he said easily. "Trust me on that."

She looked over at him as he opened the pizza box and handed her a paper plate. She wanted to ask him what his story was, what his past was, why he understood her so well. But a part of her didn't want to open that door. She was still on edge, still a little nervous being exposed on the hill. His secrets weren't good, she was sure of that, and she didn't have the capacity to handle it right now.

But she liked Lucas. She wanted to connect with him. "Are you dating anyone?" *Holy crap.* How had that come out of her mouth? She felt her cheeks heat up when Lucas looked over at her. "I mean, whatever. Just you know, wondering if anyone is worried about you playing bodyguard. Do you need to go home to Oregon? Because it's fine if you do. I'm fine. Like, whatever—"

"Nope."

She paused. "Nope, what?"

"Nope. Not dating anyone. My family would care if I had to sacrifice myself, but no one romantic." He was watching her, the smallest smile playing at the corner of his mouth. "You?"

She looked down at her pizza. "No."

"No, you're not dating anyone?"

"That is correct." She took a big bite, grateful to stuff her mouth with food to keep her from saying anything else.

"Ever been married?"

She started laughing, and then had to cover her mouth to keep from spitting her food out. Of course he would ask her right when she stuffed her face.

Lucas grinned. "Mouth full, eh?"

She nodded, trying not to choke.

"I'll wait. It's a good question."

She finally swallowed. "Is it? Why is it a good question?"

"Because I find you interesting, which makes me want to know more about you. So, married?"

"I was engaged until a few months ago," she admitted. "You?"

Curiosity flickered in his eyes, but he let her shift the topic away from herself. "Never married or engaged."

"In love?" The question was bold, but in the moon-light, she felt connected to him. She couldn't find the walls she usually lived behind to keep people at a distance.

He nodded. "Fell in love when I was eighteen. Loved her family. Loved her. Thought she was my ticket out of my hell. Then she stole something, said I did it, testified against me, and got me put in jail for eight months. Never trusted a woman again."

Maddie stared at him, her pizza halfway to her mouth. He'd said it so casually, as if he'd recited it so many times that it didn't even matter anymore. But his words suggested different. "Seriously?"

"Yep."

"That's a long time for that to still burn."

He looked over at her. "Yeah, it is."

"Jail?"

"Yeah." He shrugged. "I was a menace to society growing up. In some ways, it was inevitable that I would end up behind bars. I was one of the ones who benefitted from incarceration. I learned a hell of a lot about the power of the choices we make and the people we trust." He took a bite of his pizza, cutting off the rest of his speech.

"You learned to trust only your family."

He shook his head. "I trust a fair number of people, actually, on some level. It was a conscious choice because I didn't want to end up struggling like Jacob. But inner circle is different. Inner circle is by invite only."

She smiled. "I know what you mean. My friends are amazing. I would do anything for them."

"But romance?"

She smiled. "I thought you were giving me space on that one."

"I did. I was proud I waited that long to circle back. It shows incredible self-discipline."

She laughed then, cocking a look at him. He was stretched out on his side, looking so relaxed and delicious. "Adam was my fiancé. I knew him from high school. I thought I really knew him. I didn't."

She escaped into her pizza, thinking that Lucas would ask more questions.

But he didn't. He rolled onto his back, clasped his hands behind his head, and gazed up at the stars. "Someday I would like the details of that," he said. "It sounds like I might have to put him on my shit list."

Maddie burst out laughing, his humor easing the tension that had started to build inside her. "I thought you were my bodyguard. You're stargazing. How will you see anyone coming?"

He didn't turn his head. "Violet is off to our right, playing in the little duck pond. There's a couple on a blanket about a hundred yards to the right, and two women walking three dogs past our truck right now."

Maddie looked around and saw he was right. "How did you know? You aren't even looking."

"The magic of a misspent youth," he said. "I learned to always know everything around me. Always. I can't turn it off. Don't particularly want to. It keeps me and whoever I'm with safe." He patted the blanket beside him. "Watch the stars, Maddie. It fills the soul."

"I can't."

"Why not?"

"I have to keep an eye on what's around me."

He sat up then. "I'll watch. You stargaze."

"I'm good." She reached for the ice cream and a spoon. "Tell me—" She looked over at him, and her stomach tightened at the way Lucas was watching her. "What?"

"You're safe with me. You know that, right?"

She nodded slowly. "Yes."

"My primary goal is to keep you safe until we sort this out. That's why I'm here. You know that, too, right?"

"I do." She stuck her spoon in her ice cream and set it down. "Why?"

"I don't want you to get the wrong idea when I tell you that I really want to kiss you right now."

She sucked in her breath and her heart started racing. Anticipation coiled in her belly like warm sunshine.

"I didn't bring you up here to seduce you. I brought you up here to help you. But sitting here with you, watching you in the moonlight, hearing your stories...." He took a breath, meeting her gaze. "I can't stop thinking about kissing you."

Maddie swallowed. "I hadn't been thinking about it," she said.

His brows shot up. "No?"

She almost laughed at the comical look of surprise on his face. "I think you're wildly attractive, but I'm not interested in dating. I have an emotional block around dating right now. So I wasn't thinking about you romantically at all."

He seemed to hear the subtext she was saying. "But now?"

"You put that image in my head of you kissing me, and now I'm thinking about it."

He smiled. "Welcome to the party, then."

Silence settled between them, silence that was taut with anticipation and possibility.

"I already told you I wasn't going to make the first move," he said. "I can't break that promise."

Oh, God. "I release you from your promise."

"Well, hell." His voice dropped about a thousand octaves, and he took a breath. "All right then." He didn't move. "It's been a very long time since I kissed a woman that I was genuinely interested in. Give me a sec to remember how to do this."

She burst out laughing. "You forgot how to kiss?"

"I always thought I was a king with the ladies when I was a homeless truant. Then I became old and boring. I don't want my kiss to bore you."

Her heart was racing now. "I don't think there's anything about you that could be boring."

"Oh, I am. Very boring." He moved closer, until his hip was against hers. "Excruciatingly boring, Maddie. If we started dating, you'd fall asleep by five every evening. We'd have to start eating dinner at three because you wouldn't be able to keep your eyes open."

She giggled. "Well, I'm not boring. I'll be my own excitement while you're being boring."

"An independent woman. I fucking love that." He touched her jaw with his fingers. "Skin like temptation."

Goosebumps prickled down her spine. "A touch like an angel," she whispered.

"Devil in disguise." He leaned in, his gaze searching hers. "Your eyes are gorgeous in the moonlight. They look black, but I know they're brown."

He knew her eye color. How sweet was that. "Yours also look black."

"They are black."

"They are not. They're blue."

He smiled. "We both noticed each other's eye color. That's a good sign." Then, before she had to come up with an answer, he leaned in and brushed his lips over hers.

Her whole soul seemed to shiver at the touch of his mouth. His kiss was melt-worthy-tender with an undercurrent of passion held in strict check. His fingers still lightly rested on her jaw, connecting them, but not threatening.

She kissed him back, and he leaned in, deepening the kiss. Electricity seemed to jump between them, igniting a part of her that hadn't been alive in so long. Kissing Adam had never felt like this. She wanted to tackle Lucas. Literally, grab his shoulders, tackle him, and kiss him like a woman who had waited her whole life for this man.

The idea of doing that to him was intoxicating, and she couldn't help but smile under the kiss, so happy that she loved kissing him this much. She'd thought she'd never want to kiss a man again, but then—

Violet suddenly let out a loud bark, and they turned to see the pit bull racing toward them, teeth bared. "Oh, no! She thinks you're attacking me. No, Violet, no!" She scrambled to her feet, trying to block her dog.

Lucas stayed sitting. "She's fine. Let her come."

"What? No! She'll kill you."

"No, she won't." Lucas whistled softly and held out his hands, palm up. "We're good."

"I'm not letting her kill you!" Maddie lunged for her dog, but Violet sidestepped her, and launched herself at Lucas. "Violet!"

Lucas didn't move. He simply held out his arms. "Hey, sweet girl," he said softly. "We're good."

Violet hit him in the chest with both paws, but he didn't flinch. She stood on his chest, staring down at him, a low growl emanating from her chest. "Violet—"

"Let her be. We need to work this out," Lucas said softly, his gaze fixed on Violet. "I'm on your side, sweetheart. We're good."

Violet didn't move, and Maddie's fingers twitched with the need to grab her collar. "I can't afford to pay the bills if your family sues me."

"My family honors animals. They'd never blame the animal. They'd probably pay you for traumatizing your dog with my presence."

She relaxed slightly at his absolute lack of concern. "Well, that's good at least. Anything that winds up with me and Violet richer works for me."

"Right? It's fine." Lucas continued to stare down her dog. "You know I'm all right, don't you, Violet?" He kept his voice kind and gentle. "Otherwise, you'd already have bitten me. I do like her protectiveness," Lucas said to Maddie. "And I'm even more impressed with her control. She doesn't want to bite me, but she wants to send a message."

Maddie put her hands on her hips, biting her lip as she watched the exchange between man and dog. Violet was wet and muddy from playing in the stream, soaking Lucas.

He didn't seem to care.

71

He seemed like a man who would be happy to negotiate with her dog until dawn, if that's what it took.

"Hey, Violet," he said again. "I won't hurt Maddie. We'll protect her together."

She whimpered and laid down on his chest, her full body weight pinning him to the ground.

Maddie smiled. "That's her love language, lying on you like that."

"She wants to make sure I know she's the one in charge of you." Lucas slowly reached and scratched Violet's head. "I'll take the number two spot, pup. We'll protect her together."

Violet's tail thumped, and she slathered a big, slobbering kiss across his cheek, making him laugh. Then she groaned, rolled over, and fell off him. She landed beside him with a thud, then rolled onto her back, asking for a belly rub.

Lucas obliged, grinning as he scratched her. "I knew we'd be fine," he said.

Maddie sat down next to them, pulled her knees to her chest, and rested her chin on her knees, smiling as she watched her dog grunt for more pats. "Violet chooses her people carefully," she said. "That speaks highly of you that she decided to trust you."

He looked over at her. "Come kiss me while I'm patting her. Show her that we're good."

Her belly tightened. "I thought I'd made it through the kiss unscathed."

"You did. But there's always more." He held out his hand and raised his brows.

Maddie bit her lip and didn't move.

Lucas grinned. "Are you overthinking?"

"Yes."

"If you weren't overthinking, what would you do?"

She took a breath. "Probably kiss you."

He nodded. "Thinking can be a bitch sometimes."

"Totally." Suddenly, she didn't want to be in her mind anymore. She didn't want to have a million "what if's" running around in her head. She just wanted to feel like a normal woman, on a moonlight picnic with a normal guy, feeling all sorts of zings and allowing it.

She quickly unfolded her body, scooted across the blanket, and then leaned over the dog and man, and kissed the man.

He slid his hand through her hair, drawing her down toward him. His touch sent delicious shivers down her spine, and his mouth was warm and tantalizing. Violet whined, and Maddie put her hand on her dog's belly, her fingers brushing against Lucas's while they both soothed the dog.

With his free hand, Lucas angled Maddie's head, deepening the kiss. His tongue tasted like chocolate ice cream, and his lips seemed to send magic sparkles all the way through her body, to the tips of her toes.

She relaxed on top of him, loving the feel of their bodies touching. His was so strong and solid, and his hand was a gentle caress as he drew her more tightly against him. She braced her elbows on either side of his head, fully putting all her weight on him, delighting in the sensation of being in control, of being the one to decide to stop, start, continue.

Except she wasn't in control. Her body was coming alive in the most amazing way. She wanted more of this man. She wanted to kiss him under the moonlight until she fell asleep in his arms, safe, protected, and nurtured.

She felt like he gave her freedom, both by the way he treated her, and because he knew her past. She didn't need to hide it, or conceal the toll it had taken on her over the years.

She wanted more—

Her phone suddenly rang, startling her. She pulled back. "That's my dad's ring. I need to take it."

Lucas nodded, his gaze hooded as he propped himself up

on his elbows, watching her as she pulled out her phone and answered it. "Dad? What's up?"

"Croissant." Her dad gave her the code for asking if she was safe.

She laughed softly and snuggled back down beside Lucas. "Lollipops." She gave him the code back.

Her dad let out a breath. "That scared the shit out of me, seeing you in that park at this hour," he said. "You're always home at night. Why are you there?"

Wow. That was depressing. She was almost thirty and she was home every night, and her dad was still checking on her? "I'm having a picnic."

"What safety precautions are you taking?"

"I have a personal bodyguard."

Her dad was silent for a second, and she knew he was trying to decide if she was joking. "Put him on."

Ah... of course her dad could tell when she was telling the truth. He always had. She put the phone on speaker. "Lucas, my dad wants to talk to you."

Lucas put his arm around her shoulders and kissed the top of her head. "Yes, sir."

"Name."

"Lucas Hart."

"Social security number."

He paused. "I don't hand that out."

"Smart man. Home address."

He paused again, and Maddie knew he didn't give that out either. But then, to her surprise, he answered. "I live on the Hart Ranch." He gave out the street address.

Maddie patted Lucas's chest, appreciating that he'd been willing to accommodate her dad.

Her dad was quiet for a moment, and they could hear clicking sounds while her dad ran a background search on him.

"Lucas Hart? Of the Hart homeless-to-riches chosen family?"

"Yes, sir."

"Why are you, a billionaire celebrity, playing bodyguard to my daughter?"

Lucas raised his head to look at Maddie, asking her how much she wanted to share.

What a question. She didn't have the answer. She and her dad never talked about the past he'd ripped her from. It caused them both stress, so it had become a taboo topic.

"Maddie?" Impatience rippled through her dad's voice. "Talk to me."

She thought of her dad, wilting away to nothing. Not caring. Maybe he needed something to live for. Maybe it was time for them both to stop hiding from the past that neither of them forgot. "Do you remember the boy who was at that house with me when you found me?"

Dead silence on the phone.

"Lucas Hart is his brother."

More silence.

"Dad?"

"Bring him here. Now." Then he hung up.

CHAPTER ELEVEN

Lucas was on edge.

Tense as hell.

He stood back as Maddie and Violet ran up the steps to the small ranch house that her dad lived in. The neighborhood had modest houses, but they were all neatly kept, almost military neat.

Twenty minutes ago, Lucas had been lying under the moonlight, sandwiched between Violet and Maddie, kissing this incredible woman, feeling things he hadn't allowed himself to feel in a very long time.

And now he was dealing with a pissed-off dad.

The last pissed-off dad he'd met had gotten him sent to prison for eight months.

This was why he didn't date. Because women came with family, friends, colleagues, a life before him. A life that he didn't trust.

Maddie flung open the door and raced inside, calling for her dad.

Lucas sat on a wicker chair on the porch and faced the

street. He braced his elbows on his thighs and scanned his surroundings, watching for any threats.

He heard Maddie talking in a low voice, and he heard a man's voice talking back. The man's voice was elevated with tension, but there was no hint of violence or anger in it. Maddie was safe, which meant Lucas didn't have to go in.

After a moment, Lucas heard footsteps coming toward him. He clasped his hands between his knees and focused on the street.

He felt the moment Maddie's dad stepped onto the porch. His energy was elevated and tense, and Lucas had to look over just to make sure that he wasn't about to be attacked.

Huck Vale was mid-fifties, his gray hair cut short and precise. He was wearing old sweatpants, and a Vale's Flowers tee shirt. His feet were bare, and he was favoring one leg. He looked older than his years, especially if Lucas looked into his face. But there was an energy to Huck that made it clear that he had a history of competence, control, and power. He held himself like the FBI agent he would always be, and Lucas instantly became wary.

Then Lucas noticed all the emotional weight in Huck's eyes, enough that Lucas rose to his feet and faced him. "Mr. Vale," he said quietly. "My name is Lucas Hart."

"I know."

Maddie came out onto the porch, standing between them, not picking sides. Violet sat next to her, clearly picking her side with Maddie being the winner.

Lucas appreciated that dog. He liked that Maddie always had a champion, no matter what.

"What's the boy's name?" Huck asked without preamble.

"Jacob" Lucas knew what boy he was referencing. "Jacob Hart."

"Jacob." Huck suddenly sank to his knees and pressed his face to his hands. *"Jacob."*

"Dad!" Maddie knelt beside him and put her arm around his shoulders. Violet whined and rested her chin on Maddie's thigh.

Huck looked up, his face stricken. "Can I talk to him?"

Lucas blinked in surprise, unsettled by the intensity of Huck's reaction, by his request. "On the phone?"

"Yeah. Now."

Maddie frowned, and Violet wiggled closer to Maddie.

"Jacob doesn't usually answer the phone, but I'll try. I have to ask him first if he wants to talk to you. He doesn't like to talk to people." Lucas stepped away and pulled out his phone. He wasn't sure about this, but he called Jacob anyway.

To his surprise, Jacob answered. "Maddie okay?"

Wow. Jacob was keeping his phone nearby in case there was an issue with Maddie. Lucas felt like he was standing in the middle of a situation that was about so many people other than him. Was he an intruder? Maybe. "So, I'm here with Maddie's dad—"

"Is he a decent guy? Did he take good care of her? Is she all right with him?"

"I haven't talked to him yet. He wants to talk to you."

There was silence for a moment. "Me?"

"Yeah."

"Why?"

"I don't know."

"Ask him."

Of course Jacob wouldn't be willing to walk blindly into a situation that involved other people, even if it was only a long-distance phone call. He looked at Huck. "Jacob wants to know why you want to talk to him."

Huck shook his head. "Only for him."

Lucas grimaced. "That's not going to fly with Jacob."

Huck shook his head and held out his hand. "Phone." His voice was thick with emotion.

Lucas turned away, needing to break the grip of the emotions pouring off Maddie's dad. "He won't tell me," he said to Jacob. "He says he has to talk to you."

Jacob didn't hesitate. "No."

Of course that would be Jacob's response. "Give me one sec." He turned to Maddie. "Jacob will not speak without context..." His words faded when he saw the stricken look on Maddie's face. She had backed up toward the door, and she was gripping the door handle. Violet was pressed against her legs, staring up at her.

Jacob wasn't simply about her dad.

Jacob was about Maddie as well, and Lucas could tell that Maddie wasn't ready.

"I gotta go," he said to Jacob. "Talk later."

"Yep."

Lucas hung up the phone and shoved it in his pocket. "Jacob's not available at this time," he said to both of them.

Maddie nodded once, relief in her eyes, but tension still gripped her body, while her dad bent his head and braced his hands on the porch flooring. He looked up at Lucas. "Is he all right? What happened to him? I went back for him, but he was gone. Never found him."

Was that guilt in Huck's eyes? Loss? Something more? Lucas wasn't sure, but it was an emotion that he felt uncomfortable with. It was intense to have a stranger feeling such strong emotions about a member of Lucas's family. "Jacob found us when he left," he said, being intentionally vague. The Harts protected each other from strangers, and he didn't like the way Huck was probing for Jacob's details. "He found his family. Us."

Huck searched his face. "And he's all right?"

Jacob carried the weight of a billion burdens in his soul,

and it showed. But he had the Harts, and he had Phoebe and Annie, and his rescue horses. "He's good."

"Tell him I'm sorry," Huck whispered. "I wanted to tell him myself, but tell him I'm sorry."

Lucas stiffened. "What did you do to him?" Hell. Had this man abused his brother somehow? If so, he was taking Maddie away from him right then, and never letting her go back, no matter how much of an asshole, controlling move that was.

"I left him," Huck whispered. "I was so scared for Maddie. I had to get her out fast. She was so little. Ivan was willing to sell her, but he wouldn't part with the boy. I tried, but then I realized I had to get Maddie out before I blew the deal. Once I got her out, I went back for him, but he was gone. I was so scared he was dead. Or worse. I...just..." He covered his face with his hands and broke into sobs. "He's all right," he whispered. "He made it."

Lucas's throat tightened with unexpected emotion as Maddie knelt beside her dad and wrapped her arms around him. Violet sat next to Maddie, leaning against her, giving her comfort and strength as only a dog could do.

Lucas felt the authenticity of Huck's emotions. Huck had spent his life worrying about Jacob in the same way Jacob had spent his life worrying about Maddie.

He didn't understand how Huck could feel so strongly about a boy he'd barely met, but the feelings were gritty and real, and more than he wanted to handle.

But at the same time, Lucas had experienced Jacob's stress over it. He knew the guilt was real, and he knew it would eat away at Huck.

Lucas wanted away from this situation and this emotion, but the man in front of him was too much like Jacob, suffering the same way. And this man was suffering for Lucas's brother. He had to honor that.

Summoning strength he wanted no part of, Lucas walked over and crouched in front of Maddie and Huck. "If you had taken my brother, he never would have found us, the family he was meant to have. Me. My siblings. The Harts."

Huck looked up, his eyes red-rimmed. He said nothing, but his gaze searched Lucas's, desperate for comfort, for words that would fill the gaping wound that had been festering for so long.

Lucas knew from experience that he couldn't heal Huck's wound, but he offered the words he would have given Jacob if he'd been able to, if he'd known what had happened to Maddie. "Jacob left the day after you took Maddie. He'd stayed only for her, to protect her, and when he lost her, it broke him, and he bolted. He's been worrying about Maddie all this time in the same way you've been worrying about him."

Huck kept looking at him, waiting for more.

Lucas knew he was waiting for the words that would set him free from all the pain, but he knew from his own experience that no words could do that. It was so much bigger than a few words.

But maybe he could help.

"Jacob's engaged to an amazing woman who gets him. She has a daughter and a maniac dog. They make the perfect family. I'm grateful every day he found her."

Tears broke free and trickled down Huck's cheeks. "Tell him I'm sorry."

"No. Nothing to be sorry about. You took care of Maddie for him. He's grateful for that." Lucas looked over at her. "We all are."

Her eyes were glistening with tears as well, and her arm was tight around her dad's shoulders.

So much emotion. It was so overwhelming that it was difficult for Lucas to breathe. But he had one more thing to say, one more thing that might help. "Jacob would not have gone with you," he said. "He didn't trust anyone. He was fifteen. He didn't want a dad. He wanted to be free, to be safe, to control his own life. He needed us, not you. But the day he found out that Maddie was alive and safe, a part of him that had been bleeding his whole life finally stopped bleeding. It's starting to heal, and now you can, too."

It was all Lucas had to say. All he had to give.

He needed to step away now. To get away. To breathe.

"You guys need some time. I'll stay out here." He looked at Maddie. "Get your dad inside. He needs to be away from me." He wasn't sure if it was because Huck needed space or Lucas needed distance, but he could feel the need to step away burning in him.

Maddie's cheeks were wet with tears, and Lucas suddenly found himself reaching out. She met his gaze as he brushed his finger across the tears, brushing them away. She closed her eyes and leaned into his touch for a brief moment that connected them both, and something inside him settled.

He took a breath and nodded once as he pulled his hand away.

Jacob had found his anchor with Phoebe and Annie, and it seemed like Maddie did that for Lucas...whether that was good or not, he didn't yet know.

Maddie took her dad's arm. "Let's go inside, Dad."

She helped the older man to his feet, and both father and daughter looked back at Lucas as they went into the house, a thousand emotions and stories in their eyes. They took that intensity with them as they went inside with Violet and shut the door.

Leaving him alone.

Lucas sank down on the top step and leaned his forearms on his knees, forcing himself to breathe.

He reserved his energy for his family, not for strangers.

He hadn't allowed someone outside his family to get under his skin for a very long time, but the emotions of Maddie and her dad were like a pulsating ache in his chest.

It wasn't what he was looking for, this complicated family dynamic.

He didn't want it.

He didn't want it.

But he'd made a commitment to protect Maddie, so he wasn't going anywhere.

Because that's what Harts did.

CHAPTER TWELVE

"SHUT UP! YOU KISSED LUCAS?" Piper smacked Maddie on the arm.

"Shh!" Maddie waved at Piper to be quiet, glancing at the counter in the café where she'd met her girls for breakfast, as they always did on Monday mornings. Vale's Flowers usually had a late opening or was closed on Mondays, the only day of the week she gave herself a break. "He can hear you!" He'd gone to get coffee, but the café wasn't very big, or busy.

"Oh my God! Lucas can hear me?" Piper's eyes widened. "Does he not know you guys kissed each other? Crap. Sorry. I blew that one."

Maddie started laughing. "You're such a dork." It felt so good to be out with her friends, feeling their warmth, their laughter, and their bond. Last night at her dad's had been so intense. She'd wound up sleeping in her old room with Violet, while Lucas slept on the couch. Her dad had been so emotional, but he'd refused to talk about Jacob, same as always.

She hadn't had a chance to talk to Lucas last night, and this morning had been a little awkward. There had been a faint undercurrent from the kisses the night before that neither of them had brought up as he'd taken her home to change and then driven her to breakfast.

It was a lot, and she needed the light of her girls so much.

Violet was under the table at her feet, Piper, Keira, and Tori were all there, and Maddie had her favorite croissant sandwich, coffee, and chocolate muffin in front of her.

Friends, coffee, and food. Exactly what she needed.

Keira waved dismissively at the counter. "Lucas is giving us space. No one takes that long to get coffee."

Maddie glanced over. Lucas was leaning against the counter, his elbow resting on it. He was relaxed, sipping his coffee. He'd ditched his cowboy hat and replaced it with a Boston Red Sox cap, dark sunglasses, and a Red Sox sweatshirt. He was wearing old sneakers, had shaved his traditional stubble, and his jeans were ripped. He looked nothing like a celebrity billionaire, and everything like a local Sox fan out for a coffee.

He looked so approachable, normal, and sexy. Like pure, untamed male without any airs at all. The look suited him, and she loved it.

When he noticed her watching him, he shot her a goofy grin, wiggled his eyebrows, and raised his mug in a silent toast.

She couldn't help but smile. The man was too compelling for anyone's good, especially hers. And his playfulness felt good after all the intensity of last night and the morning.

"Oh...look at your face," Piper said, clapping her hands. "You like him!"

"I do not." Maddie pulled her gaze away from him. "He's my bodyguard. That's all."

"A bodyguard you're kissing," Piper pointed out.

Maddie rolled her eyes. "I know."

"Well, how was it?" Tori leaned in eagerly. "Are you going to kiss him again?"

"I don't know." Lucas was watching her so closely it made Maddie wonder if he could read lips. The thought made her laugh for some reason. Lucas eavesdropping on her girl time? She suspected that he wanted nothing to do with it. What man would?

"Do you want to?" Piper asked. "Kiss him again, I mean."

Maddie sighed. "It's so complicated."

Piper let out a whoop of delight. "That's a yes. Ladies, we have a yes!"

Maddie grabbed Piper's arm. "Ssh!" But she couldn't help laughing. "Stop!"

"No way, girl. We need to celebrate this moment for all of us," Tori said, looking delighted. "You give us hope, Maddie. I thought none of us would ever kiss a guy again. If you did it, then maybe we all have a chance to heal enough to want to try again."

Piper held up her hands and leaned back. "No, I'm out. I can't do that again." She was wearing a navy suit, and she looked gorgeous, stylish, and ready to win over any bride. No one looking at her would ever guess what had happened to her.

Keira shrugged. "Honestly, I'd love to fall in love with the right guy. I believe love can be wonderful, even if none of us have figured it out."

"It's not love," Maddie said. "I kissed him once." But as she said it, her gaze swiveled to Lucas again. She barely knew him, but she felt safe around him in a way she never had with Adam. He made her want to be more, to try more, to trust more.

"It's a start," Tori said. "I'm excited for you."

Maddie drew her gaze off him, and back to her friends.

"Well, let's get through this little situation before we worry about me kissing him again."

Piper's smile faded. "How dangerous is this guy Les?"

"I don't know."

Tori frowned. "You can't hide forever. What if he's always out there in the wind somewhere? Are you going to have Lucas shadowing you 24/7 for the rest of your life?"

Maddie bit her lip. "No, of course not—"

"Did you tell your dad about why Lucas was really here?" Piper was leaning back in her seat, eying her.

"Not really. He was so upset about Jacob—"

"Maddie!" Piper smacked her hand on the table, making their coffees slosh. "Your dad had guilt for decades about some boy he never met because he wasn't able to help. How do you think he'll feel if you're in danger and he doesn't get the chance to protect you? What if something happens to you, and he realizes that you never told him you were in danger because you were trying to protect him?"

Maddie grimaced, but lifted her chin. "Nothing will happen to me—"

"What if it does? What if someone comes for you? What if this guy comes after your dad? If he finds you, he'll find your dad, and your dad is the one who snatched you away from him."

Maddie stared at Piper, alarm creeping down her spine. "I never thought of anyone going after my dad. It was always me I was scared for."

Tori pressed her lips together. "I hate to bring negativity into this situation, but I think Piper has a point. Your dad could be in danger, and he needs to be ready."

Maddie looked at her friends, alarm rising. "Les hasn't found us yet—"

"Once he finds you, there may be no time to prepare. No warning," Keira said.

Maddie's dad was her whole world. She'd never thought of him as being in danger. He'd always been indestructible to her, the foundation that she was so scared she would be ripped away from.

It never occurred to her that someone could rip him away from her.

Piper put her hand on Maddie's. "Sweetie, your dad's a freaking FBI agent. He doesn't need protecting right now. He needs a heads up."

"Like *right* now," Tori agreed.

Keira picked up the bill. "We got this. Go get him, Maddie. We love your dad."

"Okay." Maddie shot to her feet, her heart racing. Lucas saw her move, his brows shot up, and then he ditched the coffee and headed straight for her, his hand on his hip, like he was ready to pull his gun. "Lucas—"

Piper grabbed her arm, pulling her attention back to the table. "Maddie." Her voice was fierce. "You stay safe. Do you understand? We love you, and we need you." Then she threw her arms around Maddie.

Emotion clogged Maddie's throat. "I'll be fine—"

"I know. But I have first-hand life experience that things can go bad fast when dealing with bad people." Piper pulled back, searching her face. "You want me to call my brothers?"

Holy crap. What an offer. Piper had run from her brothers and her life years ago. She'd hidden herself to keep them from coming after her. But her brothers were the kind of people who knew violence, which was why Piper had offered.

She hugged Piper. "Never," she whispered. "Never in a million years would I let you make that sacrifice for me. I have Lucas."

Piper whirled toward Lucas. "You keep our girl and her dad safe. Do you understand?"

His eyes narrowed, and he glanced around at the table of women staring at him. "I do understand," he said. "What happened to make everyone so worried?" His voice was casual, but there was an edge to it. He was a man ready to take action, and Maddie was glad for it.

"Piper pointed out that if Les finds me, he'll find my dad. Since my dad was the one who took me from his brother, he might be in danger. Maybe even more than me."

Lucas's eyes widened ever so slightly. "Hang on." He immediately turned away and pulled out his phone, speaking quickly as soon as someone answered.

Tori and Keira were on their feet now. "I feel like we should all hang out at the store today," Tori said. "Just in case you need us."

"No!" Maddie shook her head quickly. "Look, I'm sure we're all overreacting. Lucas's brother is working on it, and I have Lucas. We just need to hang on for a couple more days until Dylan finds him." She tried to take a breath, but panic was closing in. Violet whimpered and licked her hand, but she didn't want to sit on the floor with her dog in the middle of a café.

She wanted to be normal and capable right now, not collapsing under a panic attack.

Action always helped. She lifted her chin. "Okay, I'm going to go find my dad. Lucas?"

He shoved his phone into his pocket. "I have someone going to his house now. He lives nearby. We'll meet him there." He put his hand on Maddie's lower back. "Shall we go?"

"Yes, let's go." She hugged her friends again quickly, and then almost ran out of the café. Her heart was racing, and she could feel she was spiraling. "Where's your truck? I forget." She spun around, searching.

Lucas caught her shoulders with his hands, pausing her frantic spiral. "Maddie."

"We have to go!"

"No, we don't. I have someone on his way who is very capable. He'll be there in five minutes. Your dad will be safe."

"Lucas—"

"Take a step back."

"What? Why?" She could barely process what he was saying.

"Take a step back. Literally. Now." He dropped his hands from her shoulders.

She stared at him.

He stood there and waited.

Finally, she took a step back.

He nodded. "Say 'breathe.'" His tone was autocratic and unyielding, but there was a softness and understanding that broke through her resistance.

"Breathe." As she said it, she felt herself take a big breath that seemed to go all the way to her soul.

"Say 'settle.'"

"Settle." Again, as she spoke the words, she felt her weight sink into her feet, and her body seemed to connect with the ground.

"Now, listen to whatever thought comes up. What is it?"

The first thought that popped into her mind was, "Everyone I love is going to die and be ripped from this earth, tortured, and destroyed." She stopped, surprised. "No wonder I feel panic. That's a very aggressive thought."

He grinned. "It needed to be heard. Do it again."

She cocked an eyebrow. "So I can discover I also have thoughts about aliens coming to Earth and stealing my dog?"

He shook his head. "Do it again."

"All right." She took a step back, and then said. "Breathe."

The same thing happened. Her body pulled in a huge amount of air, and she felt her mind ease.

"Settle."

Again, she felt her feet sink into the ground, and her shoulders lowered.

She listened for the first thought that popped into her head. "Capable." Well, that was a surprise. And better.

He raised his brows. "And?"

She paused, continuing to listen to the thoughts that wanted to pop up. "My dad is capable. I'm capable. You're capable."

He nodded. "One more time."

She took a step back. "Breathe."

Her body instinctively inhaled a long, deep breath.

"Settle." Again, her feet seemed to sink into the ground. Her shoulders relaxed. Her mind quieted. And she listened to the next thought. "Fun." She looked at Lucas. "Fun? I just thought this is fun. An adventure."

"How does that thought feel?"

She paused. "Honestly, it feels good. I like adventures. My dad and I used to go on adventures in the woods all the time."

He smiled. "So, now you're thinking that we are all capable, and this is fun."

She rolled her eyes. "That sounds so stupid. I should be panicking. But I feel a sense of lightness now."

"That's because you let your brain and instincts find the thought that would help you settle in that moment, instead of trying to force what you think will work." He grinned. "You'd be amazed at some of the thoughts the brain will come up with when given free rein to help. Sometimes, it's a color. Just blue. Or a question. Or a statement of what's bothering me, and I just need to hear it so I can let it go. I've been doing it for years. It works for me."

She felt calmer now. Able to think. And she felt the truth

of the thoughts she'd had. She was capable. So was her dad. So was Lucas. And it was so much more fun to think of it as an adventure, not a terror-filled hunt where she and her dad were the prey. "How many times do you do it in a row? Always three?"

"As many as it takes. Sometimes once. Sometimes I do it thirty times in a row, although not so much anymore. The 'step back' is critical because it tells your brain you're stepping out of the cycle. Not trying to stop it. Just stepping out of it." He grinned. "Glad it worked for you. It doesn't always help everyone."

The panic attack wasn't coming. She could tell. "You're amazing."

His smile widened. "Just a guy who has seen a lot." He opened his car door. "Your chariot, my ladies."

Violet hopped in, but Maddie didn't move.

She just stood there in front of Lucas.

He raised his brows. "What's wrong?"

"Nothing," she said softly. "I feel like for the first time in a long time, nothing is wrong. Which is ridiculous because everything is crazy, but I just feel lighter. I feel empowered. Not scared. Not like I'm sitting around waiting to become a victim of some terrible event." She didn't have words. "Thanks."

He smiled. "You bet."

The moment became still. Silent. Full of just them.

Maddie wanted to kiss him. She wanted to connect with him. She wanted more of this insanely handsome man who was beginning to feel like her soul's guardian angel.

His smile faded, he cocked an eyebrow, and he slid his hands along her jaw.

Her heart started to race, and she stood on tiptoe as he leaned down to kiss her.

His kiss went from gentle to sizzling in a split second. It

was as if all the emotions of the last twenty-four hours had unleashed themselves into the kiss. She wrapped her arms around his neck as he pulled her against him.

Her breasts hit his chest, and awareness poured through her. She wanted more of this man. More with this man. More of everything Lucas. He was so intense, and at the same time, he got her, and he helped her see herself.

He let out a low groan, and angled his head, deepening the kiss until she felt like her insides had caught fire. His arms were strong and solid around her, holding her against him, encircling her like walls of steel and kindness.

The kiss became more. More electric. More complex. More irresistible. More unstoppable.

He backed against the car and sat down in the passenger seat, pulling her between his thighs, shielding both of them behind the door of his truck. The brim of his hat bumped her forehead, and his sunglasses brushed her nose, but neither of them stopped.

His disguise gave them freedom for this moment, out in a parking lot, out in public, and yet, no one cared what they were doing because they were nobodies.

Just a man and a woman, jumping into a connection that had been drawing them in since they'd met.

This man was a billionaire. A celebrity. A homeless kid who had fought his way to family, wealth, and kindness.

And yet, in his arms, Maddie felt like he was simply a man who had already healed a hole in her soul that had been there since she was tiny, maybe forever.

Violet put her head on his shoulder and licked their faces fiercely, pushing Maddie's head to the side. They both laughed, and she let go of Lucas to pat her dog. "No growling this time," she teased her dog. "I guess you and Lucas really did sort it out."

Lucas kept his hands looped around her waist, and he

pressed a kiss to the side of her neck. "I feel like I could kiss you forever and still want more."

She pulled back to look at his face, and her heart got soft at the expression on his face. "It wasn't just me?"

"Hell, no." He slid his hands through her hair and leaned in to kiss her again. "This is insane, Maddie," he said after another long kiss, his lips brushing over hers while he spoke. "I don't react this way to women. I don't allow it."

She clasped his wrists. "Well, I was finished with men and dating for the rest of my life. I don't want a man. I don't want to be attracted to anyone. I don't want this." But as she said it, she tightened her grip on his wrists to make sure he didn't pull away.

He raised his brows. "You might not want anything to happen between us, but I do."

CHAPTER THIRTEEN

I DO.

Lucas swore under his breath when those two words popped out of his mouth. What the hell?

Maddie stiffened instantly and released his wrists. "I love kissing you, Lucas. It's awakening all sorts of emotions in me, but I truly don't want anything more. I can't. I don't have space for it in my heart. Or my life. I shouldn't have done this—"

"Maddie." He fought to right himself. The comment had surprised her, and it had stunned him. He'd been thinking of Jacob and Phoebe, and his two other brothers who had found their soulmates. He'd been thinking of their relationships while he'd been kissing Maddie, and he'd been thinking about how he wanted what they'd found, too.

How Maddie was making him burn for the kind of romantic connection he'd believed he didn't want.

And how that was scary as shit, but it also stoked a fire inside him that lit him up.

He could see from Maddie's response, that "scary as shit"

was the only response his words had evoked. He had to pull back, and fast. He forced a soft chuckle. "I'm not asking for anything from you. Not now. Not ever. I love kissing you. That's all."

She gave him a skeptical look. "That's all?"

He nodded. "My job is to protect you. I would never do anything that would interfere with that."

"It felt like..." She paused. "I don't want to hurt you."

Fuck. He was so into her already that she could rip his soul out of his body and eviscerate it. He could feel himself falling hard for her, and the way Maddie was reacting made him think she sensed it, too. He had to fix this fast. "Maddie. I'm a grown man who has been through hell and back. I can take care of my own emotions. It's not your job." Truth.

"But—"

He shook his head. "My emotions. My job." He meant it, and he let her see it.

After a moment, she took a breath. "Okay."

He cocked an eyebrow. "Okay, what?"

"I don't know." She laughed softly. "I guess just, okay?"

He smiled. "One more kiss, then? No emotions involved. Just raw, hot, sexual attraction that will wind up with us having sex in the back of my truck in about two minutes."

She laughed, and heat sparked in her eyes. "Raw, untamed sex that has no emotional baggage?"

"Yeah." He pulled up his tee shirt. "I have a six-pack. Does that tempt you?"

Her gaze shot to his torso. She stared for a second. "Holy crap, Lucas. What is that?"

"It's my magnet to attract women. I work hard at it. Does it work on you?"

"Um, yeah." She laid her hand on his stomach, and his muscles tensed under her touch. "You're a gym rat."

"It's all the ranch work. Hauling hay bales around is a great ab workout."

She cocked her head, studying him with open curiosity. "Don't you pay someone to haul hay bales around?"

He shrugged. "We don't like strangers much in our space, so we try to handle everything ourselves. There are nine of us, plus a few friends that are like family."

"That's what my dad and I do at our store," she said. "Sometimes one of my friends helps out, but we try to just be us. It's getting more difficult now that business is taking off, so I'm not sure how much longer I can do it alone, though." She smiled. "It's a good problem to have, right? Being successful?"

"It sure is." He kissed the back of her hand. "You and I are perfect for each other. Antisocial animal lovers who are devoted to family. We should have hot sex to celebrate."

She laughed, amusement dancing in her eyes. "I only kiss cowboys. I never sleep with them."

"Damn. Then I better make these kisses worth it." He pulled her in for a kiss that went from hot to boiling pretty much instantly. He smiled to himself when Maddie leaned into him, fully surrendering to his kiss.

He liked the surrender not just because it felt fantastic to have her body against his, but because it showed she was learning to trust him. He'd learned enough about Maddie to know trust was the foundation of everything for her, and she didn't give it out easily.

He wasn't going anywhere.

She could lean on him all she wanted, and he was going to be there.

Even if it was only for kissing, but he sure as hell hoped it became more than kissing.

More than sex.

More than friendship.

Even though the idea of going all-in with Maddie scared the living crap out of him, it didn't matter. He'd spent his life facing down fear, and it didn't stop him anymore.

Because everything good was on the other side of fear, at least for him.

And he wanted Maddie.

CHAPTER FOURTEEN

WHEN LUCAS DROVE up to Huck's house twenty minutes later, there was an Escalade parked in the driveway. "Tell me that's your guy," Maddie said. Were they too late? If her dad got killed because she'd been kissing Lucas—

"It's my friend, Declan," he said. "It's good."

"Thank God." Maddie jumped out of the truck with Violet the second Lucas parked the car. She bolted up the steps, with Lucas right on her heels. The front door opened as she reached it, and a man about Lucas's age appeared in the doorway. He was wearing jeans and a tee shirt splattered with white paint, and his boots were the same. He even had paint in his dark hair.

His shoulders were broad, and he carried as much muscle as Lucas.

He looked like a complete badass, and she was startled to realize she recognized him. "Aren't you Piper's landlord?"

"Piper?" He frowned, looking at her more closely. "That's right. I've seen you over at the carriage house sometimes." Piper lived in a carriage house on Declan's property. Declan wasn't the most social guy, but Piper had a charming little cottage with a patio, so it was perfect.

After what she'd been through, Piper deserved a beautiful space, even if her landlord was a little grumpy. Maddie had never noticed how attractive Declan was, though. Maybe Lucas was making her notice men now. She wondered if Piper had noticed how insanely hot her landlord was. Probably not. Piper was fully committed to being single. "I'm Maddie Vale."

Declan nodded at her. "Declan Jones. Your dad's in his office, preparing for an assault. Apparently, he has a vault in there."

"Yes. His gun vault." She hurried inside as Declan stepped to the side to let her pass, slightly favoring his knee, like her dad was doing. Injury? Surgery? She wondered what had happened to him.

She heard Lucas thank him for helping out, and Declan respond as she strode to the back of the house. She hoped she'd find the fiery dad of her childhood, not the man who had been limping around so dejectedly of late.

She flung the door open, and then grinned when her dad spun around, a gun in his hand. His eyes were clear and focused, and his shoulders were set. He looked capable, just like she'd told herself in her little panic-handling-therapy moment with Lucas.

"Hi, Dad." She felt like dancing. Her dad was back!

Huck glanced behind her as the two men followed her in. "Declan didn't give me details, but when an ex-cop shows up at my door and tells me that Lucas just called him to be my emergency bodyguard, it makes a guy wonder what the hell his daughter and her new boyfriend aren't telling him."

Ex-cop? Declan was an ex-cop? And Lucas was her boyfriend? So many things to address in that one statement, but Maddie focused on the most pressing one. It was time to stop protecting her dad. The threat hadn't weakened him. It had fired him up, so she knew she didn't have to hold back. "Ivan, the man who sold me to you, has a half-brother named Les. He was in prison for a long time, and he's looking for me."

Huck stared at her. "How long have you known this?"

"Since yesterday." She nodded at Lucas. "Since he showed up."

Huck shot a hard look at Lucas. "How long have you known?"

"About eight hours longer than Maddie." Lucas sounded cool and focused, almost defensive, making her glance over at him.

His feet were spread, and his hands were on his hips. He looked like a man ready for a fight. With her dad? What did he think her dad was going to do to him? Shoot him? Challenge him to a duel at dawn?

Maddie turned her attention to her dad, trying to get his focus off Lucas. "I was worried that if Les found me, he'd find you, and he might be mad at you for your involvement," Maddie explained to her dad. "He might come after you. That's why Lucas sent Declan over."

Fire flashed in Huck's eyes, and he held up his gun. "I would fucking love for Les to come after me."

She blinked. Her dad never swore. Ever. "Um..."

"Tell me everything you know," Huck said, gesturing to the couch. "All of you. I need full information." As he spoke, he walked to the window, nudged the curtain aside with his gun, and peered out.

Maddie had to bite back laughter. Her dad looked like he was in a movie with all his drama. It was fantastic. She hadn't seen him so lively in a long time. She definitely needed to get stalked more often, apparently. It was great for her dad's psyche.

"I don't have a lot of info," Lucas said. "My brother Dylan

is the private investigator. He's working on it. He is trying to find Les before Les finds us. Right now, we're simply in a holding position of protecting you and Maddie in case he shows up."

Huck looked at Lucas for a long time, then swore. "How good are you?"

"Unstoppable."

Maddie almost laughed again. The men were so dramatic. "Unstoppable? Really?"

He looked over at her. "Yeah. I am."

His absolute confidence made her belly tighten. Why was confidence so freaking attractive in a man?

"All right," Huck strode across the room. "We'll split shifts. I'll take the nights. You take the days. Declan, you can jump in for a few hours every morning. Twelve-hour shifts are too long to stay alert."

"No." Lucas leaned against the doorframe and folded his arms casually across his chest. His body language presented him as utterly relaxed, but there was a stubbornness in his jaw that indicated otherwise. "Declan doesn't do this for a living. He was simply doing me a favor this morning. And I'm 24/7 with Maddie."

Huck drew back his shoulders. "You think I can't protect her?"

"I think you can. But Jacob asked me to stay with her, so I will. I answer to him, not you." There was just the slightest edge to Lucas's voice.

At Jacob's name, her dad visibly winced, but then he lifted his chin. "Maddie and I have done just fine without anyone interfering." He looked at Maddie. "We're leaving town. Shut down the store for a while—"

"Shut down the store?" While the men battling for dominance was mildly entertaining, Maddie had long ago stopped being the little girl who was controlled by men.

Huck nodded. "Absolutely. Safety is our priority. We—"

"I'm not shutting down the store." Maddie lifted her chin. "While you've been sitting in your recliner feeling sorry for yourself for the last six months, I've been busting my butt with the store. It's doing well, and I'm not walking away from it. We'll lose all the momentum. Plus, I have weddings that I'm providing the flowers for. I won't let the brides down."

Her dad narrowed his eyes. "Madison—"

"No, Dad." Somehow, the fact that her dad was up and functioning the minute that there was a threat was starting to bother her. "For all this time, I've been taking care of you, and worrying about you, and protecting you, and now, the minute some man comes in and tells you there's danger, you're fine? Does that mean that all along you've been fine? I've been so scared of losing you, but the only thing that's wrong is that you've been feeling sorry for yourself?"

"I'm not fine! My leg still hurts—"

"That's a bunch of crap, Dad! So what if your leg hurts? That doesn't mean you have to lie around in that stupid recliner all day giving up on life!" Violet whimpered and leaned against Maddie's leg, but Maddie didn't want to be comforted.

She wanted to be angry.

"Did you know I have anxiety? Panic attacks? Because of my past, and because I couldn't talk about it with you, because every time I brought it up, you changed the subject! I couldn't talk about it with anyone because you told me my past was a secret, because someone might find me."

Her dad's eyes widened. "You have panic attacks?"

"Why do you think I have a dog that wears a therapy dog vest?" She was so frustrated. "You know, Dad, I'm sorry that you feel guilty that you left Jacob there, but guess what? You didn't leave me there. You had me, and I needed your help to process my past. That's why you never talked about it, right?

Because you were feeling so guilty about some boy that you met a handful of times?"

"I'm aware I had you." Her dad narrowed his eyes. "I gave up everything for you, Maddie."

"I know. I know that. Trust me, I know that. You gave up the career you loved, and I've spent my life trying to be good enough to make you glad you made that choice. Trying not to be a burden. Trying to be a bright shining light. Trying to deserve the gift you gave me."

The words were pouring out, words that she'd never articulated before, but suddenly were tumbling out of her as if they were coming to life on their own.

Huck stared at her. "I love you, Maddie."

"I know! And I love you, too! But I'm so angry at you for being a victim for so long when you're actually fine, and you're just broken because you don't run around and catch bad guys anymore! Flowers, Dad! You do *flowers*, and you hate it! This gun-wielding badass is who you are! This is the dad I wanted!"

He snorted. "You wanted me to go back to work and maybe get shot and killed?"

The question made her pause. "What? No—"

Her dad walked over to her. "I chose my life, Maddie. You don't need to be or do anything to be worthy of it. I'm your dad. You're my daughter. I would choose to walk away from my career for you a thousand times over. Again and again and again. And it's not your job to feel guilty about it or to earn it. It simply isn't."

Tears filled her eyes. "I needed help, Dad. I needed to talk about the danger. My past. Us. The boy."

Huck nodded. "I know. But I couldn't talk about it. I saw his face every time I went to sleep. My soul ached with grief for the fact I couldn't get him out of there. I knew the kinds of things that could happen to a teenage boy trapped in that life. I knew it. And I replayed that scenario a thousand times, the night I got you. What could I have done to free him, too? I planned to get both of you that night, but he wasn't there, so I decided to get you out and come back for him. And then it was too late. He was gone, and Ivan wouldn't tell me where he was."

She watched the guilt on her dad's face, and her heart sank. Despite what she'd just told him, he still couldn't let go of his guilt over Jacob. It was still about the one he'd left behind, not the daughter he had.

She wasn't enough for him.

Suddenly, she felt exhausted.

"I'm going home," she said.

"What? No." Her dad grabbed her arm. "You're staying right here, Maddie, where I can keep you safe."

She twisted free, needing her space. "Safe from what? From a guy who is looking for me and might never find me?" She shook her head. "I've lived under your umbrella of fear and guilt my whole life. I can't do it anymore. I love you, but I need to go home right now." She'd been so stupid to rush home to protect her dad. He might have chosen to make himself small, but he wasn't. He was a freaking FBI agent who came alive at the idea of fear and danger. He could protect himself a lot better than she could protect him.

She held out her hand to Lucas. "Keys, please."

He didn't hand them over. "I'll drive you."

"I don't want to talk to anyone."

"I won't talk. I'll just drive."

She was too tired to argue. "Fine. Come on, Violet."

"Maddie, wait—" Huck reached for her, but this time, she stepped aside, out of his reach.

"Dad," she said softly. "I love you, but I need space right now."

"I'll keep her safe," Lucas said to her dad. "You watch your own back."

"I can stay," Declan said quickly.

She looked at Declan. "Thanks."

Then she turned and walked out, leaving the men behind. If Lucas didn't catch up to her by the time she got to his truck, then she was going to keep walking.

He caught up to her just as she reached the passenger door. He pulled the door open, and she and her dog got in.

The minute she was in, Maddie leaned back in her seat and closed her eyes, refusing to look and see if her dad came after her. Her heart ached, and she didn't want to get dragged back into a discussion with him. If she saw him, she wouldn't be able to leave, and she needed to.

Lucas started the truck. "Home?"

"No. The store."

"I thought it was closed today."

"It is, but sitting home idle isn't going to help me. I need to work."

"Got it."

Lucas didn't say anything else. He simply shifted into gear and started driving.

She waited for him to start talking. To try to make her feel better. To do that man thing of trying to interfere and make everything better.

But he didn't.

True to his word, he said nothing.

But he was there beside her. With her. Asking for nothing.

He began to sing under his breath as he drove, and she recognized the tune as that of Tatum Crosby, a famous pop star who was married to his brother Brody.

Lucas had a wonderful voice, and it was funny to hear him

singing the pop tune that millions of teenage girls had in their playlists.

Tatum Crosby was his family now, and apparently Lucas was going to sing her songs.

It made Maddie smile.

CHAPTER FIFTEEN

MADDIE WAS A WOMAN ON FIRE.

Lucas knew all about working so hard that he didn't have the energy to think of the shit he didn't want to think about, so he knew exactly what Maddie was doing.

They'd been at the store for ten hours, and Maddie hadn't stopped.

She'd been arranging flowers for a morning pick up, reorganized the display coolers, and gone over receipts.

She didn't talk to Lucas at all. Even her dog gave up getting attention and went to nap on a cot that Maddie had in the back room, undoubtedly so she could have a place to crash when she worked until she dropped.

He had a feeling today was one of those days.

He'd brought them lunch, and she'd eaten that while working.

No break.

No talking.

A woman trying to outrun her demons.

She'd erected a wall around her that she didn't plan to let anyone get past.

But he had siblings who did the same things. He was used to it.

He also had a lot of experience getting around it.

He finally walked over to the cot and sat down with Violet. The huge pit bull thumped her tail and licked his hand as he patted her.

He stretched out beside the dog and closed his eyes.

Waiting.

It took only a few minutes. "What are you doing?" Maddie asked.

"Napping."

"What if someone comes to get me?"

"I can hear in my sleep."

"Can you see in your sleep?"

"Violet can."

"Seriously? You're going to take a nap and let my dog protect me? Why are you here then? What's the point? Why don't you just leave?"

He smiled to himself. Those were the first words she'd spoken to him since they'd left her dad's house. "I didn't like how I reacted to your dad." The minute he said it, he swore under his breath. He hadn't meant to say *that*.

There was silence, and he hoped he'd pissed her off by bringing up her dad.

But he wasn't so lucky.

"What do you mean?" Maddie asked. "I mean, I did notice that you got very tense when you were talking to him. Why? Did you think he was going to shoot you?"

"No."

"Then?"

Lucas grimaced. How far was he willing to go to connect with Maddie? Shit. Shit. *Shit*.

"Lucas?"

"Your dad seems very protective of you."

"He is. So?"

"I had a little PTSD moment." He let out his breath. There. He'd said it. Moving on. "How are you doing? Want to talk about Jacob?"

"PTSD?" There was a moment, then she made a noise of understanding. "You mean, the girl and her dad who got you put in prison?"

"Yeah. I don't like dads." He decided he'd gotten her talking, so time to move on to something he didn't mind talking about. "You want to get some dinner?"

The cot sank as she sat next to him. "Lucas."

Fuck. He didn't want this to be about him. His fault for bringing it up, yeah, but he still didn't want to be in this conversation. He opened his eyes, and then his smart-ass response faded when he saw Maddie looking at him.

There was kindness and understanding in them, and suddenly he felt like a fucking baby. "It's fine." He sat up. "It's good. I'm fine."

His move put him sitting shoulder-to-shoulder with Maddie, literally pressing against her.

It felt good, so he stayed where he was.

She didn't move either.

"My dad would believe me if I told him you did something wrong to me," she said quietly. "You're correct."

He felt his body tense, and he swore and stood up, pacing across the back room. "Look, Maddie, I'm fine—"

"But I don't use him to solve my problems."

He braced his hand on the metal table and took a breath. Shit. He hadn't been in this place for a long time. Maddie made him vulnerable, and he didn't like that. "He couldn't touch me now," he said. "I have power."

"He has power, too, and you know that. That's why you're tense."

He swore again. The old man did have a fire in him. Lucas

had felt that. But Huck's power came from his love for his daughter. That could drive a man to lengths nothing else could. "It's stupid. It's fine. I don't think you're going to try to get me put in jail."

What the fuck was wrong with him? Why was he spiraling like this? He was a tough, rich, powerful man. No one could touch him. Not even Huck.

He knew that.

He *knew* it.

So, why was he losing his shit?

"Lucas."

The way she said his name hit a chord. That tone. That kindness. His whole body responded, and he suddenly knew why he was freaking out.

It wasn't that he was afraid she and her dad would toss him in jail.

It was because the last time he felt this way, he was betrayed.

He was afraid of giving Maddie the power to betray him. He was afraid that he was falling for her. The last time he'd trusted a woman with his heart, he'd been destroyed.

Fuck.

He was falling in love with her.

He barely knew her, but his soul knew who he'd found.

His soul wasn't giving him space to breathe, to catch up, to make sure it was safe.

Son of a bitch.

He spun to face her, bracing his hands on the table behind him. "Maddie."

She was watching him. "What?"

He couldn't tell her what he was feeling. She'd bolt and run, and there was nothing she could say to help him. If she said she'd never betray him, he could still choose to believe her or not believe her.

He had to find his way himself.

Could he trust his heart with a woman who had clearly stated she didn't want his heart and she would never give him hers?

That felt like a great fucking plan.

"What's going on with you?" she asked. "I'm not going to put you in jail."

"I know." He did know that. No one was going to put him in jail. Not ever.

"And my dad doesn't matter." She laughed softly. "He fell so in love with my ex that I still haven't told my dad what my ex did. I don't want to break my dad's heart. But I guess I should, huh? Getting him fired up to save me seemed to work wonders."

Lucas was glad for the distraction. "What did your ex do?"

Her face shuttered, and she shook her head. "It doesn't matter."

But it did matter. Lucas could see the way her body tensed, and her jaw hardened. Pain and fear settled in her eyes, and for a split second, she looked vulnerable and fragile, not the tough Maddie she tried to be.

And that's when Lucas realized that her refusal to trust him or hope for more with him was because she, too, had been eviscerated. She had no trust left to give to a man.

Which meant that if neither of them got brave enough to trust, they would never get anywhere. Never have a chance.

One of them had to take the leap.

Fear. Fuck it.

He'd survived a wrecked heart once.

He could survive it again.

But he wouldn't survive allowing fear to keep him from trying.

He shook out his shoulders, then walked over to Maddie.

Her eyes widened as he neared, but she didn't move away or tell him to stop.

He dropped to his knees in front of her. The cot was low, so they were almost level. He put his hands on her knees. "Maddie."

She cocked an eyebrow. "It's about time you learned my name. After all the great times we've had together."

He grinned. Sass. He loved it. "I'm a quick study." He moved in between her knees and slid his hands along her thighs. "Your cot is bored."

"It's bored?" Her eyes met his, and he saw the heat in them.

He didn't want to complicate anything with talking. He simply wanted to connect in whatever way she'd let him. Words would scare her. But a kiss? Maybe not. As long as he didn't let her know what the kiss meant to him.

"Yeah." he said. "Your cot is definitely bored. No one is doing anything fun on it. Cots are meant for action." His hands reached her hips, the magnificent curves of her hips. He watched her reaction carefully, ready to back off the instant he got a hint of her discomfort or reluctance.

"Cots are meant for sleeping." But she put her hands on his shoulders.

Hell, yeah. "Not this one." He leaned in, slowly, ever so slowly, to give her all the time in the world to stop him.

She didn't. She just waited, anticipation dancing in her eyes.

So he kissed her.

The minute his mouth touched hers, Maddie locked her arms around his neck and pulled him in. Her response wasn't surrender. It was claiming.

Maddie was claiming *him.*

It was he who surrendered to her, allowing her to take over the kiss. She pulled him close, and he rose, following her back onto the cot. They had only a small place for their feet, with Violet refusing to give up her spot.

Lucas was good with that. He loved animals, and he appreciated how Maddie treated her dog like family.

She kept her hands locked around his neck as he lowered himself onto her. The moment their bodies were touching, he felt something inside him settle. Being with Maddie felt right. He knew he was where he was meant to be.

Lucas rolled onto his side, drawing Maddie into the curve of his body. She came willingly, tucking herself against him. When he draped his leg over her hip, enclosing her into the circle of his protection, it felt amazing.

They kept the kiss going, deepening and expanding. The heat between them was electric, burning through their clothes. "I want to feel your skin against mine," he whispered between kisses.

Maddie immediately put her hand on his forehead. "Good?"

He laughed, the chuckle starting deep in his chest and rolling through. "Yeah, that's exactly what I meant."

"That's too bad. I was hoping to get a closer look at your chick-magnet abs." She shrugged. "Oh, well."

"Yeah, I can't share those with you. I want you to stay sane. It drives women crazy."

"So, you're holding me to the same lower standard as other women? I can handle them." She pushed back at him. "Shirt off, cowboy."

He grinned, loving that Maddie was taking control. He was a man who was used to running everything. The man who held shit together. So to have Maddie taking control of the situation was unfamiliar, and intoxicating as hell. He knew she needed to feel in control in order to feel safe, and he was all right with that.

So he sat up, ripped his shirt over his head, and tossed it aside.

Maddie raised her brows and placed her palms on his torso. Her touch sent sparks shooting through him. Awareness. Heat. *Need.* He wanted to lock his arms around her and drag her against him, shower her with kisses until she was on fire for him.

But he didn't make a move.

He waited for her to decide what was next. His cock was hard, but it could stay that way for all he cared.

This moment wasn't about having sex. It wasn't about what they ended up doing.

It was simply about acknowledging their connection and building trust with Maddie. Showing her that he was the guy she could have faith in, no matter what.

Which meant that when she leaned in and pressed a kiss to his stomach, he didn't react.

All he allowed himself to do was lift one hand and lightly trail his thumb and forefinger along her hair.

She looked up at him, her eyes wide. She was still on her side on the cot, and he was sitting up. "What do we do, Lucas?"

"About what?"

She took a breath. "I want to kiss you."

He grinned. "Best news I've heard all day."

"You're..." She paused.

He waited, his fingers still gently playing with her hair. At their feet, Violet was snoring, and the heat from the dog's body was warming his calf.

Maddie was staring at his stomach, but he knew she wasn't seeing it. Her mind was elsewhere, thinking.

He wanted to ask what was on her mind. He wanted to slide his hand along her jaw and kiss her, taking her away from her thoughts, and offering her a moment of peace and connection.

But he didn't.

Finally, she looked up at him. "My ex. His name's Adam."

Lucas settled down on his elbow so he was level with her. He moved his hand to her hip, lightly drawing circles. "I'm listening."

She pressed her lips together for a moment. "He was my high school boyfriend. We were together for four years before he graduated. He went to college to play football."

Lucas was going to have to have Dylan find this guy.

"I..." She stopped, and Lucas thought for sure she wasn't going to continue.

She'd shut him out.

Dammit.

He couldn't give up. Not yet. *Not yet.*

CHAPTER SIXTEEN

MADDIE ROLLED onto her back and stared at the ceiling, feeling the weight of her emotions. Lucas kept drawing little designs on her hip, and for some reason, that touch grounded her. Made her feel safe. Connected to him.

It was her connection to him, her need for him, her desire for him, that made her want to tell him the truth.

She wanted Lucas to understand why she was the way she was. Why she didn't want to try to connect with him. But she barely knew Lucas. Why would she pour all her secrets out to this stranger, simply because he seemed to get inside her soul and call to her?

She looked over at him, and then almost smiled. He was watching her intensely, but his shoulders were relaxed. She grinned. "You're dying to hear the story, aren't you?"

He flashed a grin. "I'm not going to lie, Maddie. I am. But I'm trying to play it cool. Not working?"

"No. I can feel your intensity."

"Shit. I suck at hiding my feelings." He paused. "From the first moment the Harts came together as kids, before we were a family, Brody had a rule that we never kept secrets from each other. We always shared what we were doing, how we felt, what was bothering us, no matter what. That honesty created a bond between us that never would have happened without it. We had to share everything, and the rest of us were never allowed to judge. Ever. It was hard as hell because none of us had ever trusted anyone before, but it was the best thing ever."

She felt the honesty of his words. "I trust Piper like that. I tell her almost everything."

"Almost isn't enough," Lucas said. "Not for the Harts. Those little secrets can fester. When we try to protect ourselves or our siblings by holding back truths, it's like a little wound that breaks our integrity with ourselves. Never works, at least not for what our family needs."

Envy flickered through Maddie. She couldn't imagine having that kind of space to be herself. "That sounds terrifying and amazing at the same time."

Lucas nodded. "That's about right." He studied her. "You want to talk about Adam?"

Her instinct was to say no, but a different word came out. "Yes."

"Then do it." He rolled onto his back, squeezing in beside her, so they were both staring at the ceiling. "I'll try not to gaze into your eyes and stun you with my empathy."

She grinned. "You overdeliver empathy?"

"I do. It's my fatal flaw. It's why I keep everyone except the Harts at a distance. It's easier that way."

"I get that." She sighed and took a breath. Adam. Where to start with him. "I've been scared my whole life. Afraid of the bogeyman coming to get me and rip me away from my dad and my life."

Lucas moved his hand slightly so that his fingers were touching hers.

The touch settled her, and she scooted closer to him, so her cheek was against his bare shoulder. "Adam was big, and tough, and I felt like no one could get through him. He was kind of...a bit much, but that was okay. I needed what he gave me."

"Makes sense." There was absolutely no judgment in Lucas's tone, and she relaxed.

Lucas and his siblings had survived hell, every one of them. Maybe they would understand making stupid, blind decisions in order to survive. "My dad loved him. Adam got recruited to play D1 college football. Before he left, he said he'd come back for me, and we'd get out of town and live a huge life."

Lucas tapped his fingers gently against her palm. "How'd that sound to you?"

She let out her breath. "Honestly? Wonderful. I felt trapped here. Trapped by my fear. I thought that if I left town as the wife of a huge, tough, wealthy man, then I could finally breathe. I could live again." As she said it, the guilt came rushing back. "I felt so guilty even thinking it. Leaving my dad after he gave up his career for me? I was torn."

"I feel you." Lucas shifted, moving closer to her. "I feel the same way. I'm bound to the Hart Ranch because of my family, but I sometimes find myself wondering what life could be like if I wasn't connected so tightly to them. The bonds with family are beautiful and fulfilling, but they can also be complicated."

She nodded, the pain around her heart easing ever so slightly. Lucas understood, and it made her feel better. Not ashamed of what she'd wanted.

"What happened with Adam?"

"I waited for him. He came back to see me, but he was changing in a way I didn't like. He wanted me to go with him, but I couldn't yet. I couldn't make myself leave my dad and the store." God, how she hated that. "He got drafted, and he proposed to me. I said yes, of course. All my dreams come true, right?"

"Except?"

Oh, how everything had spiraled. "I didn't go visit him because there was too much press. I didn't want to get caught on camera." How she'd hid from life.

"And?"

She took a breath. "Piper convinced me I had to go see him. That I couldn't stay here and hide. So I went. I surprised him." That night. God that night. "I arrived at his house. He was..." She paused. "He was having a party with a bunch of women. Not just one. A bunch. I got mad, and he..." She instinctively touched her cheek, and then Lucas's hand settled on top of hers.

"He hit you?" His voice was low, rough, tightly controlled.

She closed her eyes, focusing on the feel of Lucas's hand on top of hers, drawing the pain that her memories had put back in her cheek. "Yes. Knocked me out."

"Fucking bastard." Lucas shifted beside her, moving in tighter, and his strength seemed to encircle her, protecting her from the power of the past.

"When I woke up, the women were gone, and I was on the couch under a blanket. He apologized and cried and said he loved me. Said it was difficult because I wasn't there with him, but he would always love me. He asked me to move in that day and get married that weekend."

"What did you do?" Lucas's voice was low and tense.

"I walked out, sold the engagement ring, and used the money for a down payment on my house."

He smiled and put his hand on her belly. "Good girl."

"Right?" She took a breath. "I haven't told my dad what happened. He adored Adam. They were best friends. My dad was so proud of him, and he still watches all his games and tracks his stats every week. He'd be crushed to know that he trusted Adam with me, but he was wrong." She paused. "I'd known Adam since I was fifteen. How could I not know what he was capable of? Who he was? If I was wrong about him, then how would I trust my judgment with someone else?"

"Like someone you met only a couple days ago?"

She turned to look at Lucas. He was on his side again, propped up on his elbow, watching her. He looked so handsome, so kind. Her heart turned over. She touched his jaw. "I told Piper I was done with dating. I meant it. I didn't want a man. I didn't want to deal with anything ever again."

Lucas flashed her a grin. "And then you met this good-looking guy who used to be homeless, in prison, and broke, and you thought, 'now, *this* guy tempts me.'"

She smiled. "Exactly. My judgment is getting worse, apparently."

"I'm very untrustworthy."

She giggled. "I can see that." For some reason, the fact Lucas wasn't trying to convince her that he *was* worth trusting was making her feel lighter.

"I was betrayed by a girl when I was eighteen, and I'm apparently still not over it. So you have at least another ten to fifteen years where you can ride the Adam wave and be good to go."

She laughed then. "What if I stretch it to twenty?"

"Completely valid." Lucas leaned in and brushed a kiss over the tip of her nose. "Just a reminder, Maddie. You made it through this thing with Adam. You're tough, a badass, and sassy as hell. He didn't steal anything from you. You used it to become the woman you are today, who's pretty fucking fantastic."

Her smile faded, and she stared at Lucas.

He cocked an eyebrow at her. "I mean it. Our past is dependent on how we choose to define it, the story we tell ourselves about it. The facts are one thing, but you get to choose the story you tell yourself about them."

"Like?"

"Like you got a house out of that failed engagement. You're such a badass that you had a chance to marry an NFL player who comes with fame, money, and power, and you said, fuck it, I deserve better, and you hauled your ass out of there and started over. Impressive as hell, if you ask me." He paused. "And you do deserve better, Maddie."

Her heart turned over at his words. He meant each one. She knew he did.

How could this man be so kind? See her and make her feel like she was so much more than she believed she was? She felt so good about herself when she was around him. Not simply safe and protected, but capable, beautiful, and worth believing in.

She touched his jaw. "You make me want to try again," she whispered.

He smiled. "You do the same for me."

"Are you scared?" she whispered the question.

"Hell, yeah."

"Me, too."

His face softened. "I know, Maddie. I know you are." He paused. "I know that words mean nothing, and you have to choose what you believe, but know that I am a born protector. Before I even met you, my job was to protect you because of Jacob. That job will never end, regardless of what happens between you and me. I will always protect you, physically, mentally, and emotionally. *Always*. And so will my family. We couldn't do anything else. It's how we're made. It's what defines us. And that would never, could never, change."

Tears filled her eyes at his words. "So, I could just march onto the Hart Ranch, announce I'm there, and ask for help?"

"Any day, any time, for any reason. Yes." He paused, then pulled out his phone. "Hang on. I'm calling my brother."

"No." Panic hit her. "I don't want to talk to Jacob."

"Not Jacob. I wouldn't do that to you. It's Dylan." He put it on speaker phone and dialed a number.

"But—"

A man answered on the first ring, and she closed her mouth. "What's up, Lucas?" he said.

"Dylan. I'm here with Maddie. You're on speakerphone."

Dylan didn't hesitate. "Hi, Maddie. Nice to meet you."

Her heart tightened at how friendly his voice was. "Um, hi."

"Maddie asked me a question, and I wanted her to ask it to you."

"No problem. What's the question, Maddie?"

Maddie felt her cheeks heat up. "It's nothing—"

"It's never nothing," Dylan interrupted. "It doesn't matter what it is. If you thought it, it matters. Ask me."

Lucas raised his brows at her, and she couldn't help but roll her eyes. Dylan was proving true Lucas's claim that the Harts never kept anything from each other.

"Ask me, Maddie," Dylan said again. His voice was gentle and kind, but also unyielding.

She punched Lucas lightly in the shoulder and made a face at him. "Fine. Lucas gave me a speech that—"

"No," Lucas interrupted. "Don't give Dylan context. Ask him the question so you get his instinctive answer."

"Hell. Now I'm interested," Dylan said. "Spill it, Maddie. I'm not hanging up until you do." His voice was rumbling with amusement.

"Fine." She stuck her tongue out at Lucas. "What I said to Lucas was this: 'So, I could just march onto the Hart Ranch, announce I was there, and ask for help?'"

"Absolutely," Dylan said without hesitation. "Any day, any

time, anything you need. You're one of us, Maddie. You and your dad. The minute you crossed paths with Jacob and found your place in his soul, you were in."

She felt his earnestness, and she realized both men meant what they said one hundred percent. Suddenly, without warning, she had literally an entire posse in her life. Emotion clogged her throat, and she had no words.

Lucas wrapped his arm around her shoulder and pulled her against him, placing a kiss to the top of her head. She squeezed her eyes shut and pressed her face into Lucas's neck, trying to hold back her emotions. She'd been so alone and lost for so long, clinging to her dad, and recently Violet, as her only safety, her only family, her only home, her only roots.

And suddenly, she had more. It was overwhelming.

Dylan continued. "I'm sorry it took us this long to find you, Maddie."

He'd apologized. This stranger had apologized for not finding her sooner and giving her a family that she'd never asked for, didn't have a right to, and didn't belong with.

Except both these men believed she did.

Lucas kissed her again. "Maddie's feeling a little overwhelmed by the way the Harts do family," he said.

Dylan laughed. "Understandable. We're a lot to take. Especially Lucas. Hang in there, Maddie. You'll get used to Lucas. He's an acquired taste, but worth the effort."

A little smile broke through. "It sounds like he's a bottle of wine."

"He's my brother. I'd move the entire damn world for him, and you, too." He paused. "I got a couple leads on Les. It's possible he's in your area. Keep vigilant. I'll call the minute I can find him."

Les. She'd forgotten about Les for a minute.

"Right. Thanks," Lucas said. "Talk later."

"You bet. Maddie, it was great to talk to you. I look forward to meeting you someday. Drop into the Hart Ranch. We'd love to have you." Then, before she could answer, Dylan hung up.

Maddie flopped onto her back, staring at the ceiling as she processed what had just happened. She felt Lucas watching her.

"You all right?"

She nodded, but her throat was still thick. "I just... For my whole life, it's been just me and my dad. I've been so scared that if anything happened and I lost him, I'd be all alone. Even being with Adam didn't take away that fear. I was so afraid that if anyone came after me and my dad, we had no one to help us..."

"And now you have a bunch of anti-social cowboys willing to use all their resources to help you unconditionally."

She turned to look at him. "You all are so normal. The papers make you into this elusive image. And you're just... family guys."

Lucas shrugged. "We are elusive. And we give that image to make sure everyone knows we're powerful. It keeps us safe if people are afraid to mess with us."

"Safe? You guys worry about being safe?"

He met her gaze. "Maddie. The soul never forgets. We all have scars that make us look over our shoulders. Every single one of us. The more powerful we get, the safer we are."

She bit her lip. "I feel that when I'm with you. I feel... empowered. Not just protected, but also like I can protect myself."

He smiled. "No greater gift than to know you can handle yourself. That's fantastic, Maddie."

His smile was so warm. So beautiful. So honest. Suddenly, she wanted to lose herself in this man, in the family he represented, in the integrity he lived by. She couldn't offer herself, or long term, but he knew that.

Right now, she simply wanted him. "Kiss me, Lucas," she whispered.

The way his face lit up made her almost start to laugh, but then he kissed her, and she forgot about everything but the man in her arms.

The emotions from their conversation and the call with Dylan had erased her walls, leaving her raw and exposed. She needed to fall into the protection Lucas offered her, to lose herself in his strength.

He seemed to feel her need, because he rolled onto his side and dragged her against him, kissing her like a man made of passion and soul. His kisses were hot and intense, but there was a tenderness that made her want to cry.

Lucas made her feel like he was there *with her* completely. Like she was his entire existence, his complete focus. She felt seen, protected, and like she mattered.

And she loved it.

Lucas trailed kisses along her neck, and she sighed and leaned back, giving him access. His hand was still on her hip, claiming her as he kissed his way down her chest and across the swell of her breasts.

Her heart started to race as he eased aside her shirt and kissed her. She couldn't believe how good it felt to be with him. She focused on everywhere their bodies were touching, needing to feel that connection to him.

Lucas moved lower, spanning her hips with his hands as he kissed her belly, his tongue tracing the most tempting circles along her skin. She put her hands on his shoulders, and then grinned when she felt his muscles contract.

The man was built, and she loved it. She wasn't a tiny person, and she loved that he made her feel like she was.

Then Lucas flipped the front clasp of her bra, and she

sucked in her breath as the lace parted. He cupped her breasts immediately, pressing kisses to her body that seemed to wrap around her soul and pour warmth and light into it.

Maddie didn't feel vulnerable or scared with Lucas.

She felt like she was where she needed to be. Where she wanted to be. Where she'd always wanted to be, but had never known it.

So, when Lucas tugged her shirt over her head, she sat up and held her arms up to make it easier.

The moment her shirt was off, Lucas paused to look at her, his gaze sweeping across her body with an appreciation that made her giggle.

"I'm the luckiest guy on the entire planet right now, Maddie. There's no doubt in my mind."

She burst out laughing. "You're such a dork."

He shrugged, locked his arm around her waist, and pulled her onto his lap. "I'd never lie to you." He didn't wait for her answer. He just kissed her with an intensity that made her muscles clench.

Her nipples were hot where they were pressed against his bare chest, and her core was pulsing with need. She wrapped her legs around his waist, and he drew her tighter against him. She could feel his erection pressing against her core through their jeans, teasing them both in the most glorious way.

She locked her arms behind his neck, holding him tight as they kissed, as the intimacy coiled tighter and tighter. His hands were on her breasts, her hips, her lower back, sliding along her thighs. Touching and kissing her everywhere he could reach, until he finally leaned her back on the cot. "I need more skin, Maddie," he whispered, his voice low and rough and sexy.

"Me, too." She quickly wiggled out of her pants while he

did the same, and then he was back on top of her, kissing her as if he'd never stop.

Which was perfect, because she didn't want him to ever stop either.

He slid his hand between her legs, and then followed with his mouth, stirring her into a cascade of sparkles and need. "I don't have a condom," he said, "but if I did, I'd be making love to you—"

"I have some."

He lifted his head and cocked his brows, a slow grin spreading on his face.

She felt her cheeks heat up. "It's part of our girl pact. The four of us always have to have condoms with us so we never have to trust a man with our bodies."

"Girl power rules. I get it. Where are they?"

"In my purse. It's over by the—"

"I know where it is." He rolled off her and strode across the room. He was fully naked now, and she treated herself to a view of his backside. The muscles in his back were enviable, and his butt was curved and tight. He kicked the door to the front room shut and flipped the lock, even though they both knew the front door of the store was locked. He grabbed her purse. "Inside pocket?"

"Yes."

He found the condoms, and when he turned toward her, he got a wicked gleam in his eyes. "I love how you're looking at me."

"How am I looking at you?" Her heart started racing as he strode across the room toward her, moving with an athletic grace that was pure temptation.

"Like you enjoy what you see." He joined her on the cot and pulled her into a glorious kiss that was all about heat, seduction, and promises. "Which is great, because I'm loving every second of this, and I'd be shattered if you took one look at me and went running for the hills."

"I'm not running anywhere. Not today."

"Fantastic." He slipped the condom on, then kissed her a good long time.

The kisses were hot and intense, but there was an intimacy that was so much more, more than she wanted to think about, more than she was ready to acknowledge. "Make love to me, Lucas."

He didn't answer, but he shifted his body to slide into her, a fit that felt natural and perfect, as if her body had been preparing for this man and this moment her whole life.

Lucas let out a long, deep breath that sounded like pure heaven. "Perfection, Maddie. You've ruined me for life. Nothing I ever experience will live up to this moment."

She smiled, put her hands on his face, and kissed him. "You're making it so difficult for me to stay emotionally unattached right now."

"Just go with what you feel, Maddie." Lucas began to move inside her, a glorious rhythm that erased her walls. "I don't need any promises for the future. All I want is for you to be fully present right now. Trust whatever you feel and share it with me."

She searched his beautiful eyes, and found no guile. No attempt to control. Just a man who had learned how to live in each moment. "I feel like you're my forever," she whispered.

He smiled, a smile so tender that she felt like her heart would never recover. "Me, too." Then he moved his hips again, and she was swept away in the movement of his body, in the rising electricity between them.

Lucas controlled the moment, and she surrendered to him, allowing him to bring her to a stunning precipice of hope, desire, and intensity, before the touch of his hand brought her plummeting over the edge into his arms, shaking and whispering his name, while he did the same.

It was the moment Maddie hadn't known she wanted, but that her entire soul had burned for.

It was perfection, and she decided not to question it.

Instead, she closed her eyes, snuggled into his arms, and pretended that reality would never come back.

Ever.

Even though she knew it would.

And soon.

CHAPTER SEVENTEEN

Lucas pressed his face to Maddie's hair, while she dozed in his arms.

Dusk had fallen, and the flower shop was cast in shadows now. Maddie had been asleep for several hours, and he remembered how she hadn't been able to sleep the night before.

She was sleeping now, trusting him to keep her safe.

Violet was tucked between their legs, her chin resting on Maddie's calf. She opened her eyes and looked at him, and he grinned, shifting to pat her. "Good girl," he whispered. "I'm glad she has you."

Violet licked his hand, and then closed her eyes to go back to sleep.

Keeping Maddie tucked against him, Lucas looked around the back room of the shop. It was packed with flowers, and the room was filled with the vibrant scent of all the flowers mingling with each other. It reminded him of being out for a horse ride in the spring, when the wildflowers were everywhere, with water droplets glistening on their petals.

He suspected Maddie would appreciate the Oregon flowers.

As he thought it, his smile faded. Would she ever want to come to Oregon? Her home was here, with her friends, her dad, and her store.

His home was the ranch. He liked being here, but at the end of the day, home was with his family.

The thought was sobering. Was there a possibility for a real future with him and Maddie? It was easy enough to fly back and forth with the jet, but Maddie couldn't be bicoastal with her store, and he knew that he needed the anchor of his home.

He understood Maddie's need for roots and a foundation she could count on, because he needed it as well. And their roots were on opposite coasts.

Hell.

He tightened his arms around her, as if he could hold onto this moment forever and not have to deal with facts that he didn't like—

The hair on his arms suddenly prickled, and he lifted his head, searching the room again...this time for a threat.

Violet lifted her head and perked her ears, staring toward the front of the shop.

Swearing under his breath, Lucas quickly rolled off the cot and yanked on his clothes. "Maddie," he whispered. "Get dressed."

She bolted upright with a start, her gaze immediately alert. "What's happening?"

"Ssh. Violet and I both sense something. Get dressed." He got his boots on in record speed, then eased his gun out of his holster, which he'd stashed under the cot, within easy reach. "Keep the light off."

While Maddie got dressed, Lucas crept toward the door that led to the front of the store. Violet stayed with Maddie, but she was on her feet now, still watching the front of the store.

Lucas eased up next to the door, listening. At first, he heard nothing, but as he quieted his mind, he heard the muffled sound of footsteps.

He looked back at Maddie and gestured to the front of the store.

She nodded, grabbed Violet's collar, and pointed to the back door.

He shook his head, knowing that there could be someone on the other side of that entrance as well. He gestured to the corner, and she shook her head.

He got that. She didn't want to feel trapped.

But at the same time, it meant she didn't have to watch her back—

The door suddenly eased open, and he pressed his back up against the wall.

"Maddie? You in there?" Piper's voice echoed, and he let out his breath.

"Piper?" Maddie hurried over, relief evident in her voice. "What are you doing here?"

Piper walked into the room, walking right past Lucas without noticing him. She was wearing a navy pants suit and heels. "I went by your house and you weren't there, so I was worried. I thought maybe you fell asleep here again."

Lucas liked that Maddie had friends who checked on her. Maddie's friends were like the Harts—found family with ties as tight as blood.

"I did fall asleep here," Maddie said, not looking at Lucas.

Piper suddenly stopped, and then whirled around to face Lucas. "Good God, Lucas. You scared the heck out of me! Why are you lurking in corners?"

He grinned and put his gun behind his back. "I thought you were an intruder. I was protecting Maddie."

"Are you armed? Is that a gun behind your back?"

He shrugged. "Maybe."

"Did you almost *shoot* me?"

"Never. I'm very good at what I do."

Piper put her hands on her hips. "And what is that?"

"Among other things, protecting people I care about."

Maddie met his gaze, and Piper raised her eyebrows. "So, you care about Maddie now? Is that it?"

He paused. "I do."

Piper glanced at Maddie, then walked over to him, right up to him, and gave him a long look. "Do not betray her, or all the money in the world won't be able to protect you from me, Keira, and Tori."

He raised his brows, impressed by the vehemence in her voice. "I won't betray her. I'm not cut like that."

She continued to stare at him, and he realized she truly didn't trust him. Piper had her own issues, ones that ran deep on Maddie's behalf, but also her own. "You're part of Maddie's soul," he said softly. "That means that I'm here for you as well. Whatever you need."

Sudden emotion filled Piper's face, stark, raw vulnerability, then she turned away quickly to hide it.

Piper. Lucas felt her deep pain. She was sassy, bold, and loyal, but underneath the surface was a past that still had its grip on her. He recognized it, because he saw it in his family and in the mirror every day. "How can I help?" he asked.

Piper shook her head and walked toward Maddie, who was standing near the back door. "I'm good," she said. "No one is trying to hunt *me* down—"

At that moment, the back door flew open, and three men burst in. At the same moment, something hit Lucas hard between the shoulders. He fell forward as the men grabbed Piper and Maddie and dragged them out the back door.

CHAPTER EIGHTEEN

MADDIE TWISTED and slammed her elbow into her attacker's stomach. He bent over, and she jammed her elbow up into his throat. She hit again and tore away from him, but just as she got free, another man grabbed her. Move. React. Instinct. All her dad's training roared to the surface, and she moved without even thinking, terror screaming silently in her mind, galvanizing her.

Violet was scratching at the back door and howling, but she was trapped inside.

"Get off me, you asshole!" Piper fought back just as hard, and she hit her attacker in the balls. He fell, but dragged her down with him.

Maddie went for the shin, but he sidestepped.

Behind her was her flower delivery van, with the door open. Ready for her. She twisted and screamed, but his hand went over her mouth, cutting off her air.

He flung her at the van, but just as she hit it, the back door of her store burst open and Lucas and Violet bolted into the alley. Violet went right for the throat of the man who'd gotten her, and Maddie screamed when he pulled out a gun.

"Not my dog!" Adrenaline surged through her, and she launched herself desperately at him with strength she'd never had before. "Violet!" Maddie slammed into her attacker with her shoulder, knocking his gun aside as he pulled the trigger.

The bullet hit the side of her building harmlessly as Violet sank her teeth into his wrist and dragged him down. Maddie scrambled out of the way.

Lucas hit Piper's attacker in the head with his gun, then swung at the third man, taking him down in one lethal strike. He then spun and ran to the man who Violet was attacking. "Call her off, Maddie! Call her off!"

Maddie ran over to Piper as she called her dog. "Violet! Come!"

The hours of training worked, and Violet immediately released her attacker and ran over to Maddie while Lucas grabbed him and pinned him to the ground.

Seconds later, it was over.

Lucas looked over at Maddie and Piper, his knee still in the back of the man Violet had attacked. "You two all right?"

Maddie nodded, and Piper sat up. "We're good," Maddie said.

"Call the cops." Lucas felt the man's pockets, and pulled out zip ties. At the sight of them, Maddie went cold.

Piper grabbed her hand, and the two women looked at each other as Lucas put the zip ties to work on the men who'd planned to use them on her. Maddie quickly called 911, reporting the break-in as Lucas secured the men.

By the time he was finished, Maddie was shaking. The adrenaline was fading, and she was starting to freak out. "Piper and I will wait inside—"

"No." Lucas strode over to them, his back to them as he faced the store, his gun by his hip. "Someone hit me from behind. There's still someone else around."

Oh, God.

He pulled out his phone and made a call. "Declan. We got hit. You good?" He listened for a moment, then swore. "Get out of there. Tell your pals on the force that we're leaving the scene. Got it?"

Maddie bolted to her feet. "Is my dad okay?"

Lucas nodded at her as he continued to talk to Declan. He rattled off an address, then hung up. "My truck's in front. Let's go around, not through the store."

Maddie felt like she couldn't breathe. "Go around front? What if they're there?"

"They could be anywhere. I want you out of here. We need to take control." His attention was still focused on the shop. "Let's go. Maddie, hold Violet's collar. I don't want her taking off."

Lucas was pure focus, all business, and Maddie realized he hadn't been lying when he said he could handle this.

She took a breath. She could handle it, too. Her dad had trained her for this. She grabbed Piper's arm. "Let's go."

"You bet." Piper scrambled to her feet. Her face was pale, but she was maintaining her composure as well.

The four of them hurried around the building, staying close. Maddie kept looking over her shoulder, and she saw Lucas was doing the same. Violet was pressed up against her leg, and Piper was close.

Silently, they made their way around to the front. Lucas's truck was parked by the door, only a few yards away. They all scanned carefully as they headed toward the truck. "In fast," Lucas said, unlocking the passenger door only.

They all climbed in quickly, and he locked it behind them.

The minute they were inside, Maddie breathed a sigh of relief. *Almost there.* She watched Lucas as he hurried around the front of the truck, still looking around. He got in, and then locked the truck and started the engine.

As he pulled away from the curb, Maddie twisted around,

searching the streets for any sign they were being followed, but she saw no one. "You think the fourth person took off with their truck?"

"Looks like it, but I'm not counting on it," Lucas said.

Piper scanned the streets as well. "Do you see anyone following us?" she asked.

"No, but we'll make sure." He hit the gas and careened about a corner, then spent the next several minutes engaging in slightly terrifying driving as he made it impossible for anyone to follow them without exposing themselves.

Maddie braced herself and looked at Piper. "Are you all right?"

Piper managed a grin. "Anytime I don't get shot at during an altercation, I feel like I've won."

Maddie relaxed slightly, grateful for Piper's past, which made her a little more resilient than Keira or Tori might have been. "Fun night, huh?"

"Girl bonding is the best," Piper agreed.

As they spoke, Lucas hit the speakerphone on his dash.

This time, Maddie recognized Dylan's voice when he answered. "What's up?"

"Les found us."

"Shit. How?"

"I don't know. Four guys jumped us at Maddie's store, intending to kidnap her. Someone tried to kill her dad, but I had a man with him, so they're out and on the run."

"Where are you headed?"

Lucas glanced in the rearview mirror at Maddie. "The jet. We need to get out of here until we can figure out how Les found her, and how to track him."

"The jet?" Maddie sat up. "We're running away? I don't want to run away."

Lucas ignored her. "I'm bringing Maddie and her dad to the ranch."

"The ranch?" Maddie leaned over the seat. "We're not running away. The Vales don't run. We fight."

Dylan chuckled. "I'll let you deal with Maddie. I'll get everything set up. See you soon."

"Bring medical."

"Got it." Then Dylan hung up.

"I don't need medical." Maddie balled her fists. "Lucas, you don't get to control my life—"

"Your dad was shot, Maddie."

Maddie felt her gut plummet, and she grabbed Piper's arm. "Bad? Is he going to be okay?"

"Yeah, but he needs treatment. I don't want him in a hospital around here. They might find him, and he'll be defenseless."

Maddie felt like she was going to throw up. She'd stormed out on her dad, and now he'd been shot? Tears filled her eyes. "Lucas, is he—"

"He'll be fine, Maddie. Declan is a trained EMT. He handled it for the moment." Lucas was driving fast, skidding around corners. "Piper, we're going to meet up with Declan and Maddie's dad. Declan will drive you home and keep an eye on you, but I don't think they know who you are."

Piper took a breath. "I'm sure I'm fine. I was just in the wrong place at the wrong time." She squeezed Maddie's arm. "We'll clean up the store tomorrow and handle your flowers. You go be safe."

"No, you can't be at the store," Maddie protested. "What if they come after you?"

"They don't want me," Piper said. "But your store has to go on."

"No—"

"I'll send people to watch the store," Lucas said. "Piper, don't go there until I text you that we have coverage. Les's men may be watching the store for Maddie to come back."

Maddie and Piper looked at each other, then suddenly, Piper grinned. "At least now you get to face your demons. It's so satisfying. That dude probably will never use his wrist again." She patted Violet's head. "Good doggie."

Maddie managed a smile. "I've been waiting for a fun night like that my whole life."

"Right? Your dad taught you all those self-defense skills, and you had nowhere to use them. Until now. Yay, you."

"And you got to kick some butt, too."

"Right? Girl power is always awe-inspiring," Piper said.

"Totally." But even as they tried to lighten the mood, Maddie couldn't stop thinking about how much trouble she'd have been in if Lucas hadn't been there. Her attackers had managed to get Maddie away from her dog, and if she'd been alone, she wouldn't have been able to save herself.

But Lucas *had* been there. She hadn't been alone. It had all worked out. "Hopefully, the cops will get some answers from the three we left behind."

Piper nodded. "You don't have to wait and wonder. You have Lucas and his entire family plotting how to protect you. Les and his pals don't have a chance, and finally, after all this time, the threat will be over. When you're done with this, you'll be free, Maddie. Finally free."

Maddie's throat clogged and tears suddenly blurred her vision. To be free? Truly free of the past that had stalked her for so long? To no longer have to fear the shadows and the unknown?

She couldn't even imagine what that would be like.

But she wanted it. She wanted...her gaze went to Lucas. What *did* she want?

"There they are." Lucas whipped off the road into a busy parking lot. "Less than ten seconds to make the switch, ladies. Maddie, you and Violet stay in the car. Piper, with me."

As he swung into a parking spot beside a big, black pickup truck, Piper pulled Maddie into a hug. "Have fun," she whispered fiercely. "You're about to get an all-expenses paid vacation to a billionaire ranch with a hot guy."

"Fun?" Maddie laughed. "I'm running for my life."

Piper winked. "Not at all. You're running *to* your life. Big difference, sweetie. Huge!" Then she gave one last hug as Lucas put the truck in park. "Keep in touch!"

Maddie grinned as Piper jumped out of the SUV with Lucas, slamming the door shut behind her.

Maddie draped her arm around Violet's neck, suddenly nervous to be alone in the vehicle, even though Lucas and Declan were only a few feet from her.

Dammit.

She didn't want to fear being alone again. She wanted to be stronger. Not weaker.

Then she saw Lucas helping her dad out of Declan's pickup truck, and her heart seemed to freeze. "Dad!" She lunged for the door as they reached it.

Her dad gave her a gritty smile as Lucas guided him in. "Maddie—"

"Dad!" She threw her arms around him and hugged him, unable to stop the flood of tears. "I'm so sorry I left mad. I know we never do that. I'm so—"

"I'm sorry too, Peanut." Her dad held her tightly as Lucas got in the front and hit the gas.

Her dad grimaced in pain as he held her shoulders. "Maddie, girl, this is it. We can do this."

She nodded through the tears. "But you're a wimpy old man who can't even handle working at a flower store right now."

Her dad burst out laughing as she knew he would. "And you're a dreamy girl who can't function without her dog. What chance do we have?"

She grinned and leaned against his shoulder, hooking her pinkie through his, as they had so many times when she was growing up. "We don't need chances. We have us."

"And me," Lucas said. "I'm not just a good-looking chauffeur, you know."

Maddie and her dad looked at each other, then they both burst out laughing, even as her dad grimaced in pain, making her heart tighten. "You're not that good-looking," Huck said. "But as I always say, if they don't find you handsome, they better find you handy."

"Then I'm a double winner," Lucas said. "Because I'm both."

Maddie grinned. "Confidence is beautiful."

"It is," her dad agreed, putting his arm around her shoulder. He kissed the top of her head. "I love you, Mads."

"I love you, Dad." She frowned at him. "Were you really shot? How bad is it?"

He squeezed her arm and winked. "A little nick on my leg. Not as bad as I've been shot before. It's been a long time. Kind of nice to be back in the game."

She raised her brows. "Of being *shot?*"

"Of feeling alive."

"Oh." Her stomach tightened again, that little guilt demon who tried to tell her that it was her fault her dad had given up the life that made him shine. She refused to listen when it tried to whisper in her ear that she wasn't worthy, that she wasn't enough. Not when she'd come so close to losing him already.

She wasn't going to listen to the noise in her head.

Instead, she was going to ground herself in this moment, and the second chance she'd been given with her dad.

She closed her eyes and rested her head on his shoulder, one hand tucked through his arm and the other wrapped around Violet, holding tightly to the two most precious things in her life.

And she was putting them both, and herself, in the hands of a stranger.

A knight in shining armor?

Maddie opened her eyes and watched Lucas drive. He was speeding down the highway, his gaze constantly searching behind them, around them, ahead of them. This man, this stranger, was committed to keeping them safe.

Why? Because his brother had passed through her life briefly a long time ago?

That didn't even make sense.

But at the same time, it did. Maybe she was crazy. Or maybe she was starting to understand Lucas a little bit.

Maybe she was understanding him a little too much, because there was something about him that was making her want things she didn't want...like falling in love, like trusting a man, like giving it one more try.

She didn't want to try.

She wanted her life back, the freedom she'd never had before.

Freedom. And that included not being tied down to a man who would want her to be anything other than herself... because she hadn't found herself yet, either, and it was time.

CHAPTER NINETEEN

FORTY-MINUTES LATER, they were airborne, Maddie's dad was in the back of the plane being treated, and Lucas had time to breathe.

To sort out what had happened.

He'd talked to Dylan, who was still working on untangling what had happened. The people who'd shot Huck were unaccounted for, as was the fourth person at Maddie's store. None of the men he'd left zip tied at the store were Les, and none of them were talking.

They all had rap sheets, though. Long ones.

Les had connections with the underbelly of the criminal world, which although expected, gave them clarity on the level of threat that Les represented.

The threat was elusive, mobile, and dangerous.

Lucas was glad they were going to the Hart Ranch, even if Maddie didn't want it.

"Lucas?"

"Hi, Maddie." He looked up as Maddie walked into the front section of the plane, Violet by her side, as always. "How's your dad?"

"He's good. The bullet went through his thigh, but didn't hit anything vital. He was very lucky." She paused, looking awkward, so Lucas nodded at the two seats across from him. "For you and Violet."

"Thanks." She walked over and sank into the seat, pulling her knees to her chest, while Violet hopped up and curled herself into a ball.

Lucas leaned forward, his forearms braced on his thighs, watching her body language. She was tense and worried, as was natural. "How are you?"

She glanced at him, then shrugged. "Fine."

"We don't have much food on the plane because we left in such a hurry, but I put out a few bottles of water and some snacks." He nodded at the table between them.

She picked up the water. "I've never been in a plane like this before. It's like a castle in the air."

He looked around the plane, trying to look at it through Maddie's eyes. It was neutral tones, and everything was top quality. Big, plush seats of the finest leather that could be converted into beds. The bedroom in the rear. Elegant light fixtures. "Too much?"

She raised her brows. "It's gorgeous. If you can afford it, why not have the best?"

He narrowed his eyes, not sure if she was mocking him. "When you grow up sleeping under a bridge having to steal food to eat, there's a tendency to try to wipe that away with overcompensating."

She smiled. "Lucas. I do think it's beautiful. And you guys deserve it."

"All right." He relaxed slightly, but her comments about the plane made him realize that when they arrived at the Hart Ranch, she was going to be thrust right into their life of luxury and entitlement. With most women, he'd expect them to want more of him once they saw the ranch.

With Maddie, he was a little concerned that it would turn her off. Already, there was a wall and distance between them, which he didn't like. They'd bonded at the store before and while they'd made love, then chaos had ripped the moment apart.

He wanted it back with a fierceness that made him wary. He didn't want to push Maddie away, and he was still trying to process his reaction to her. But it was important that she knew she mattered. "We didn't have time to talk after we made love."

Her cheeks immediately turned pink. "We don't need to talk about that."

"I do."

She looked out the window. "I thought it was sex only. Nothing more."

He ground his jaw, tempted to give her the distance she wanted, but knowing that he couldn't. He owed her more. "I know you were burned recently, so it's important to me to make sure you understand where I am with our lovemaking."

She didn't take her gaze off the clouds. "I'm good."

Shit. She had completely withdrawn from him. Her defenses were in full force. Afraid of being hurt? He got that. So, he had to do what he could to take that fear away from her. She could still choose to reject him, but he didn't want it to be out of fear.

He took a breath. "I'm in, Maddie."

Her gaze shot to him. "What?"

"I'm in." He gestured to her, and then to himself. "Whatever it is that's happening between us, I'm in. That wasn't a quickie for me. I know you're not into anything serious, and I respect that. But if there's anything there, anything at all worth pursuing, I'm in. I'm not going anywhere." He let out his breath as he finished, surprised to find his heart racing a bit.

146

Maddie stared at him, her hand rubbing Violet's head. "All right."

All right. It was an acknowledgement of what he'd said, and no more, except it *was* more. She hadn't told him to back off. She hadn't announced her need for distance. Instead, she'd let him know she'd heard him, and she accepted what he'd said.

It was a start, and a good one...which was fantastic, because now came the challenging part.

"Maddie, we're going to need help for a little bit."

Her eyes narrowed. "What do you mean?"

"The threat we're facing is real, and it's legit. Les had at least five experienced people in play, all striking at the same time, in a very efficient manner. We thought he was going to be heavy-handed at best, but he's not. He has skill and connections."

She closed her eyes and took a breath, muttering a little curse under her breath that made him grin.

"Our ranch is very secure, because all of us have pasts that can come get us at any moment. Every member of my family is trained in every way we'd need them for help."

She met his gaze. "Lucas—"

"I know, baby." He reached out and took her hand, relieved when she didn't pull away. "I know that the Harts are connected to the ugly past that you want to leave behind. I'll make you two promises. First, you don't have to see Jacob. He'll stay away. Second, as a family, we all do our best to live in the present. When you meet any of my siblings, they'll be like Dylan: they'll accept you and move forward with what needs to be done. They won't bring up the past. It's about the present threat, not the past."

She looked down at their entwined hands and let out a breath. "If I had any choice, I wouldn't be going to the Hart Ranch."

"I know."

She looked up. "I think my dad is excited. I suspect he's going to try to sneak off and find Jacob as soon as we get there."

Lucas swore under his breath. "That's a very bad idea. Jacob doesn't handle people well. He would need time to process meeting your dad before actually doing so."

Maddie grimaced. "I think my dad is focused only on what *he* needs right now, but I'll talk to him."

Lucas nodded, then steeled himself for the final blow. "I've been trying to think of the best way to keep you safe once we get there."

She looked at him and cocked an eyebrow. "And?"

"You and your dad need to stay with me, in my house."

He half-expected her to protest, but instead, a smile quirked the corner of her mouth. "Why doesn't that surprise me?"

He relaxed. "Because you know how clever I am?"

"Because you've claimed us."

He thought about that. "No. I've taken responsibility for you. There's a difference. Claiming implies I'm taking away your choice and your independence. It implies that I have rights over you. I'd never do that."

She smiled then, the first real smile he'd seen since all hell had broken loose. "You're all right, Lucas Hart."

He smiled back. "I know."

She laughed then, as he'd hoped she would. "Let me guess. You have two bedrooms, so I'm going to have to sleep in yours?"

"I have plenty of bedrooms, but I still hope you'll sleep in mine."

"My dad will be there. I can't sleep with you while he's in the other room."

He cocked an eyebrow, noticing that she hadn't said she

didn't want to. "We're resourceful. I'm sure we could figure something out, if we want to."

"I don't want to." But the smile playing at her lips told him another story.

"That's fine. I don't want to sleep with you either," he teased. "I was simply being polite."

She watched him, then she leaned forward. "Lucas," she said quietly. "You've completely rattled me. I don't know what I want."

He mimicked her pose, so that their faces were inches apart. "Honesty is great. It's how I operate."

She searched his face, then brushed her finger along his cheek. "I've spent my life trapped in my past, and once this is over, I might be free for the first time in my life. I don't want—" she paused. "I don't want to trade one trap for another."

He swore under his breath. "You think I'm a trap?"

"Not that you'd try to trap me, but the effect would be the same."

He ground his jaw. "I would never trap you—"

"No, but I'd trap myself, and I don't want to take that chance—"

"Any food around here?" Huck limped into the cabin, and the connection was lost.

Lucas sat back as Maddie got up to tend to her dad, her face lighting up at the sight of him.

He'd lost everything once to a girl and her dad, and Maddie's relationship with her father was unbreakable.

Lucas didn't know how to do parents. He hadn't had any good ones. Neither had any Hart.

But Maddie came with a dad, a business on the East Coast, and walls designed to keep him out.

Everything that threatened all that mattered to him.

But as he watched her tuck her arm through her dad's and

help him toward the seat she'd been sitting in, all Lucas could see was the love and warmth shining from her eyes.

Maddie might have had a tough history, but the woman who had survived it had somehow managed to embrace love, laughter, family, and friends. And courage. She was so strong.

She was a light, a beautiful, shining light, and Lucas knew he wanted her to be in his life even after this incident was resolved.

He didn't know how it could work.

But he had to find a way.

A way that both brought them together and set her free.

An impossible task...but one he had to find a way to succeed at.

CHAPTER TWENTY

THE HART RANCH WAS STUNNING. Vast. Beautiful.

Maddie leaned forward, scanning the oasis as Lucas drove down a dirt road that wound through the property. There were numerous paddocks with horses. A gorgeous barn. Several beautiful houses perched on hills with scenic vistas. Acres and acres of pasture.

"I feel like I could run forever out there," she whispered.

"This is magnificent," Huck said.

Lucas smiled. "Thanks. We've worked hard on it. We're all a little different, so each house is unique, but we all agree on the horses, and keeping the land untouched as much as we can." He paused as a horse and rider approached from a nearby pasture.

Maddie instantly tensed, suddenly worried about facing Jacob. About what seeing him might trigger in her memories.

"It's my sister, Bella. She was very excited you were coming."

Maddie let out her breath. "You have a sister?" Maddie had forgotten that. Lucas and his brothers seemed to be all-encompassing with their maleness.

"Two of them." Lucas pulled the truck over and rolled down the window. "Hi, Bella."

"Is she here? Is she in there?" Bella leaned down, peering into the truck. Her face was friendly and warm, blue eyes glistening with delight when she saw Maddie. "Maddie! It's so great to meet you! We need more women over here. I'm Bella!"

Maddie smiled, feeling the warmth pouring off the woman. Her tension eased slightly. "Hi. Nice to meet you."

Bella's skin was a gorgeous medium brown that made her blue eyes seem even more vibrant. Her cowboy hat had a string of beautiful lace around the crown, and her chestnut horse was gorgeous. She looked like a dust-covered model, except that her smile was so radiant and full of life that Maddie felt an instant bond.

"Do you cook?" Bella asked.

Maddie raised her brows. "Cook what?"

"Anything. Do you like to cook?"

"I'm capable of keeping myself alive," she said. "Not much more than that."

Bella shrugged. "That's fine. I can teach you. Cooking is my super power."

"Bella," Lucas interrupted, amusement dancing in his voice. "She just got here. Don't put her to work already."

Bella rolled her eyes at her brother. "I need help, Lucas, so stay out of it. Maddie, I run a restaurant on the property. We host dude ranch vacations on the west side of our ranch, and I have one starting soon. I need help in the kitchen. You want in?"

Maddie was almost tempted to say yes. Bella's warmth reminded her of her friends, and she realized how much she already missed them. "I—"

"She needs to stay off the radar," Lucas said.

"I know, but she can't live locked up in your basement the

whole time." Bella patted her hip. "I'm always armed, Maddie. I don't get to shoot bad guys nearly as often as I'd like, but maybe we can shoot yours. Wouldn't that be fun?"

Maddie smiled. "I can shoot, too."

Bella brightened. "Really? Do you have a gun?"

"Yeah."

"That's amazing. Most women don't have guns. Definitely come over to the kitchen. We'll cook and shoot. It'll be great."

Maddie felt like Bella actually meant it, which felt good. She'd been worried that the Harts would trigger her, but Bella felt like home. "If I can dig Lucas's overprotective claws out of me, I'll come over."

"Claws? I have *claws?*" Lucas sounded amused.

Another rider came into view behind Bella, and this one was clearly a man. He was too far away to see any facial features, but his broad shoulders and tall stature made it clear.

Lucas swore under his breath. "That's Jacob. We gotta keep going."

Fear shot through Maddie, even as her dad bolted up. "Jacob? Where?"

Maddie sat back and closed her eyes. She didn't want to even see him.

"That's Jacob? I want to talk to him." There was a sudden scuffle, and then Maddie heard Lucas yelling at her dad.

Maddie opened her eyes to see her dad already out of the truck, limping hurriedly toward the approaching horse and rider. Crap! She leaned out the window. "Dad! Don't you dare approach him! You don't have that right!"

Her dad kept going, and Lucas bolted after him, shouting at her dad and Jacob.

Jacob reined in his horse, paused, then turned and rode off in the opposite direction in a fast gallop.

153

Maddie watched Jacob go, panic gripping her chest. That man was her past. He knew things about her that she couldn't remember. That man was the life that had tormented her for so long.

She didn't want to see Jacob's face. She was so scared that when she looked into his eyes, she'd suddenly remember everything, things she didn't want to know, unleashing emotions she couldn't handle, memories that would scar her in ways she'd never recover from.

Bella and Lucas had caught up to Huck now. Bella was chastising him, her voice strong and furious, but in control. Lucas had her dad's arm, and was speaking in low, terse tones, no doubt ordering him back to the truck.

Maddie felt her heart sink as she watched the Hart siblings deal with her dad.

Bella had made her feel so welcome. Lucas had taken them into his family sanctuary, and the very first thing her dad had done was violate the Harts' trust and seek out a damaged, traumatized man that they'd made very clear he could not approach.

Maddie put her arm around Violet. What if the Harts kicked them out? It would be their right. And why was her dad so obsessed with Jacob that he couldn't follow basic rules?

Lucas opened the back door. "Get in, Huck." His voice was terse and clipped, barely holding onto his anger.

Of course Lucas would be angry. The Harts protected each other, and the person he'd brought inside his family circle had just threatened his brother, at least that's how his brother might interpret it.

"I just wanted to talk to him," Huck grumbled.

"Get in." Lucas glanced at Maddie, but his face was inscrutable.

Bella hadn't come back to the truck. She was still on her

horse, but she'd pulled her phone out and she was talking on it. Calling Jacob? Calling his wife? Calling the rest of the family to tell them the Vales weren't welcome?

Huck got in the truck, scowling as he slammed the door shut.

Lucas climbed into the front. His jaw was hard, and he didn't look at Maddie as he started the truck again.

The tension in the truck was palpable, and Maddie felt it seep into her skin, unraveling all the good feelings Bella had given her. She took a breath, trying to stay calm. "Dad. Apologize."

Huck threw up his hands. "I didn't do anything wrong! I just wanted to talk to him."

Lucas gripped the steering wheel tighter. The truck was bounding over the ruts in the dirt road, and Maddie knew Lucas was driving too quickly.

He was visibly mad, and it was her dad's fault.

"Dad!" Maddie scowled at him. "The Harts brought us to this ranch to protect us. You know that Jacob is vulnerable. Lucas very clearly told you that you can't talk to him unless Jacob consents first."

Her dad looked at her, his eyes glistening. "I need to talk to him—"

"No, you don't." Anger coiled through Maddie, the same anger that had made her walk out on her dad earlier. "I don't understand why you have such issues with him, but they're yours to solve. It's not Jacob's job to make you feel better. It's not his job to forgive you or not forgive you. It's yours. Just because you're near him doesn't give you the right to put your baggage onto him."

Her dad narrowed his eyes at her. "Jacob wants to talk to you. The reason this Les bastard found you is because Jacob looked for you. Why is *that* okay, but it's not okay for me to talk to him?"

Maddie hadn't wanted to think of that, but now that her dad mentioned it, she couldn't deny the truth: it was possible that Les found her because the Harts had tracked her down. "The difference is that I don't want to talk to Jacob, so he isn't trying to get to me. He's respecting my boundaries. You're not respecting his."

"He tracked you down!" her dad shouted. "Why are you so obsessed with the Harts that you ignore that? These Harts are the reason we're in danger now! When they tracked you down, they exposed you!"

Maddie had to fight not to cover her ears. Her dad never yelled. Ever. Because she hated it. Even as a little girl, she'd hated it, and couldn't handle it. Adam had shouted at her before he'd hit her. "Don't yell," she whispered, her voice strangled. "Don't yell at me." Violet climbed onto her lap and licked her face, but Maddie was too tense to hold her.

Her dad grimaced. He lowered his voice, but the undercurrent of yelling was still there, already given life. "Jacob endangered you! The reason we're here now is because the Harts exposed you! And after that, he won't even speak to me?" Her dad's voice rose again.

She pressed her hands over her ears. She knew her dad was upset. He was having his own trauma, seeing Jacob again, and not being able to get to him yet again. Always elusive. She got that. She didn't blame her dad. But she didn't have to take it. "Lucas. I need you to stop the truck. Right now."

Lucas looked over at her, and immediately pulled over.

She didn't wait to explain herself. She just bolted from the truck, slammed the door behind her, and started walking, Violet pinned to her side. Her hands were shaking. She couldn't breathe. Her vision was blurry.

She didn't know where she was going. She just had to get away.

"Maddie!" Her dad shouted. "Come back! I'm sorry!"

"No!" She held up her hand, but didn't turn around. "I need a minute. Don't follow me."

"Maddie—"

"No, Dad! You'll make it worse!" She kept walking, her hands clenched as she fought not to lose the battle waging inside her.

"Maddie." Lucas's voice was soft, and she jumped as he came into view on her left side.

"Don't touch me," she snapped.

"I'm not going to. I'm just going to walk with you. Okay?"

"Yes, okay." She kept walking, fast, as fast as her legs would go, her right hand searching for her dog. Violet kept jumping up so she could touch her without bending down, but Maddie couldn't slow down enough to pat her.

"No, Huck." Lucas spoke in a low, but commanding, tone. "Stay in the truck."

"Maddie!" Her dad shouted.

Maddie covered her ears and kept walking. "I'm safe," she whispered. "I'm safe. I'm safe. I'm safe. I'm safe. I'm safe."

Lucas kept pace just off her left shoulder. "I'm going to make a call, Maddie. I'm with you, but I need to make a call."

She nodded, but she didn't answer. She had to keep talking. "I'm safe. I'm safe. I'm safe."

"Tristan," Lucas said. "I left Maddie's dad in my truck near the north stables. I need you to get him, take him back to your place, and lock him down for the moment. He was trying to get to Jacob."

Maddie kept walking. "Don't hurt him," she whispered. "Don't hurt my dad."

"Keep him safe," Lucas added. "But keep him away from the family. Someone might try to shoot him. Don't let them."

She nodded at Lucas's words. Her dad was safe. "I'm safe. I'm safe. I'm safe."

"Put eyes on me and Maddie, but no one approach,"

Lucas continued. "I want people nearby. Get Dylan's people on us, but again, no one approach."

No one approach. Lucas wasn't going to let anyone come near them. "No Jacob," she said. "I don't want to see him."

"No Jacob," Lucas added. He paused, then, "Thanks. I'll be in touch." He hung up the phone and shoved it in his pocket.

Silence fell as the three of them walked. She didn't even know where she was going. There was grass under her feet, not driveway. They were off the road, and she didn't care.

She just kept going. "I'm safe. I'm safe. I'm safe." It was the mantra that her therapist had helped her create. The words always worked for her. But they didn't right now.

"Maddie," Lucas said gently.

I'm safe. I'm safe. I'm safe. "What?"

"I'm right here with you." His voice was very soft and gentle. Soothing. It felt like a warm blanket settling over her skin. "How can I help you?"

She stopped suddenly and turned to face him. "It's not working." She felt panicked.

His expression was schooled into serenity and peace. "What's not working, sweetheart?" Again, his voice was gentle. Calm. Serene.

"My mantra. It's not working. It always works. I'm freaking out." She couldn't stop the tears that were streaming down her cheeks. "I can't breathe. Don't tell me to breathe and settle. I can't. I'm—" She bent over, bracing her hands on her thighs, fighting to breathe. "I feel like I'm going to die."

Lucas bent closer to her, but not so close, not too close. "Do you want to sit?"

"No. I'm trapped if I sit. I need to move."

"All right. Let's move."

"I can't walk. My legs feel frozen. I don't think I can stand up anymore." She squeezed her eyes shut, fighting not to spiral. Fighting to hold onto some semblance of sanity. She dug her fingers into her thighs, trying to feel pain from her fingernails, trying to feel anything that would draw her back from the vortex she was in.

Lucas paused for a moment. "How about a piggyback?"

"A piggyback?" *I'm safe. I'm safe. I'm safe.*

"Yeah. I'll carry you, but you're not trapped on my back. You can get off at any second, but we'll keep moving."

Piggyback. She nodded. "Okay. Yes. Okay."

"All right. I'll kneel in front of you, and you climb on when you're ready. Okay?"

She nodded, not looking up, still fighting for breath that felt dangerously elusive.

Lucas went down on one knee in front of her, his back toward her.

She stared at him, but didn't move.

"Put your hand on my shoulder. See if it feels all right." His voice was still so calm, no terror for her to grip onto. "One hand, Maddie. That's all."

She stared at his shoulder. She'd touched him before. She'd felt safe with him. She remembered that. Violet nudged her hand, jerking her back to the moment.

She lifted her hand, unable to stop it from shaking violently. But she put her hand on Lucas's shoulder. The moment she felt the heat from his body against her palm, her body shuddered, and she felt a wisp of calm in the storm fighting to consume her.

She immediately grabbed onto him, locking her arms around his neck. "Help," she whispered, her voice strangled.

Lucas reached back, helping her get her legs around his hips. The moment her feet were locked around his waist, he rose to his feet and started walking. "Come on, Violet," he said, snapping his fingers. "Let's go."

Knowing he would keep an eye on her dog, Maddie closed

her eyes and pressed her face to his back, trying to focus on the feel of his body against hers. On his muscles, flexing as he moved. Of his steady stride. His strength. She focused on grounding herself in him so that the panic had nothing to hold onto.

The heat from Lucas's body seemed to penetrate the chill that had gripped her, allowing her to breathe through the wall trying to suffocate her.

She gripped Lucas more tightly, afraid that the relief he was giving her would disappear. "Talk to me," she whispered. "I don't care what. Just say something."

"We have wolves on the ranch," he said, after a brief pause. "At night we can hear them howling. It's such a beautiful, eerie sound."

Wolves. "Do they attack the horses?"

"No. We bring all the animals in at night, though, just to be sure." He was still moving fast, his stride even and purposeful, his grip on her legs supportive and reassuring.

"How many horses do you have here?"

"It varies. We rescue horses. Sometimes they get adopted by someone, but often, this is their forever home."

Forever home. That sounded like an elusive dream. "You save them?"

"We do. We're a sanctuary."

A sanctuary. Suddenly, she felt like crying. "I feel like one of your horses. Broken."

"Not broken," Lucas said. "Alive, healing, beautiful."

"I can't even walk. I'm hanging onto you like a backpack."

"Backpacks are valid, contributing members of society."

She let out a snort of choked laughter. "Well, that's good to know."

He chuckled. "You can walk just fine. I have news for you, Maddie. The Harts are a family full of traumatic pasts. We all handle it differently. The fact that we're all alive and functioning is a victory every day."

She kept her cheek resting against his back, her feet swinging with the rhythm of his stride. "So I'm a winner, then?"

"Yep." He didn't elaborate or try to explain. It was simply such an unequivocal statement of her worth that she felt it deep in her gut.

She sighed, a shuddering deep breath that was the first sign that she was going to be all right. She stopped talking, this time, to focus on her own body. On her muscles starting to relax. On her mind beginning to settle.

They fell silent, not talking, but she felt connected to him.

Safe.

Worthy.

Like she could breathe again.

CHAPTER TWENTY-ONE

LUCAS WALKED FOR A LONG TIME, paying close attention to how Maddie's body felt against his. She was wrapped so tightly around him that he could feel the tension in her body ebbing away. He could feel her ribs expand as she was able to breathe deeper.

Most importantly, he could sense the change in her energy as the panic lost its grip and gave her back to herself.

He loved carrying her. He loved that she trusted him. He loved that she'd let him into her space when she'd been at her most vulnerable.

He was a born protector, and that instinct was especially high with Maddie.

And that instinct forced him to know when it was time to step aside and let her find her strength again. He had a lifetime dealing with his family, and he knew how important that was. He stopped. "Maddie." He kept his voice gentle, well aware of how she'd reacted to her dad yelling. The moment he'd seen her covering her ears, he'd made a promise to himself to never, ever, under any circumstance, raise his voice when he was around her.

The protector was at work.

"What?" she asked.

"Time for you to walk."

She stiffened. "Are you getting tired of carrying me?"

"Nope. I'd carry you all day. But you need to take your power back now. I'm going to let you down." He released her legs, and she slid down his body to her feet.

She put her hand on his arm, and he could see that her legs still felt shaky. "I'll escort you. Come on, my lady." He tucked her hand into the crook of his arm, then began to walk.

Maddie decided to keep up with him, and he smiled as she leaned against his side, keeping her hand tucked around his elbow as she walked beside him.

He knew the moment she looked around, because her little gasp was exactly what he'd expected. "Where are we?"

"We call it Hart Pond," he said. "It's fed by a river that runs through our property. It's small, but we take care of it to make it an oasis." Hart Pond was the reason his family had chosen this land to buy. It was rich with flowers and trees, and it had a little clearing with grass. The Harts had put out some seating, and planted an abundance of wildflowers. It was now a haven for wildlife, and most of the Harts spent time there to decompress.

He knew because he saw his siblings there when he went there for himself.

"Oh." Maddie's hand tightened on his arm. "It's like heaven."

"I thought you might like it." He gestured to several chairs set up along the shore. They were wooden Adirondack chairs, and he saw that someone, probably one of his sisters, had added thick cushions recently. "Want to sit for a moment?"

"I do." She hurried over to the chair closest to the water's edge and sank down like she was becoming a part of it. He could practically see her inhaling the energy of the pond.

Violet trotted down to the edge of the water and started playing. Lucas stood beside Maddie, scanning around them. He saw three guards on horses, and he nodded at them, relieved to see them.

It meant he could focus on Maddie.

He sat down in the chair beside her. "Maddie—"

"Can I sit with you?" she interrupted. "On your chair?"

Satisfaction pulsed through him. "Of course." He leaned back, holding out his hands to guide her as she sat on his lap and tucked her feet under her. She leaned back against his chest and let her head rest on his shoulder.

He locked his arms around her waist, and she rested her hands on his.

It was intimate and peaceful, and he felt like he could stay there for the rest of his life.

Maddie relaxed into him, and she took a deep breath. "Thank you for not making me feel like an idiot for falling apart."

He rested his chin on her shoulder. "Thank you for trusting me to stay with you."

She picked up his hand and began to play with his fingers, making him smile. "My dad's a good man. I love him completely."

His smile faded. "I know."

"He never yells. That's why I freaked out. I wasn't ready for it." She sat up suddenly. "I should go back to him. I completely bailed on him—"

"He's fine, sweetheart. Tristan picked him up." Lucas began to rub her back, and he smiled when Maddie settled back against him. "Your dad has his own trauma. I get that. I don't blame him." Well, he did a little, but he was trying his best to support Maddie. "But he doesn't get to put it on you.

You did the right thing to take your space." Hell, Jacob had spent much of his life at a distance from the rest of them... not that bringing up Jacob was a good call right now.

"I need to talk to him."

She pulled out her phone, but he interrupted. "I'll have Tristan bring him over to the house later."

She paused. "Your house?"

"Yep."

Maddie was quiet for a moment, then she looked down at her phone. He could see her warring with the decision of whether to call her dad. He'd instructed them to keep their phones off for the duration of their stay, in case they were being tracked.

If she chose to use it, they'd adjust. In a way, it would almost be better to have Les come after her there. They could catch him and end it sooner.

Finally, after a long moment, she put her phone on the armrest, leaned back, picked up Lucas's hand again, and began playing with his fingers. He loved her need to touch him, even absently. Their physical connection was real, and it went far beyond the amazing sex they'd had earlier. "Lucas?"

"Yeah?"

"What's your history? What's your story?"

He let out his breath. Fuck. He didn't like to talk about it, but he knew Maddie needed to hear it. She needed to know she wasn't the only one with the kind of past that could knock him on his ass.

"My mom was a drug addict," he said.

Her hand tightened around his. "I'm sorry."

He shrugged. "It is what it is. I don't blame her for that. She spent a lot of time in jail before she died of an overdose, and I lived with my aunt and uncle." He shifted, trying to ease the tension that crept up on him.

Even after all this time, he never forgot what it had been like.

"Were they bad?"

He reached around her and pulled up his sleeve. The round circles on his forearm were the same as many of the Stockton brothers had. The Stocktons had become the Harts' extended family after one of his sisters had married into the Stockton clan.

Maddie touched the scars. "Cigarettes?"

"Yep. There's more like that. And other stuff."

Maddie put her hand over his forearm, then she bent down and pressed a kiss to the old scars.

Lucas sucked in his breath, stunned by the gesture. "No one has ever done that," he said quietly.

"Sometimes the only way to heal is to fill the wound with so much love that it takes up all the space and crowds out the damage."

He leaned his forehead against her back as she went down his arm, kissing each little circle. "When I was twelve," he said, "my uncle stabbed me. I got out of the house and went on the run. It got infected, but I knew if I went to the doctor, they'd send me back or put me in foster care. I decided I'd rather die."

Maddie twisted around to look at him.

He slid his hand along her jaw, needing her touch to ground him. "Brody found me in an alley. I was almost dead. He took me to the hospital, and then, as soon as I was well enough, he snuck me out. He saved my life, and gave me a family. I owe him and my siblings everything."

Maddie frowned at him. "You've been on your own since you were twelve?"

He nodded. "It was better than being with my aunt and uncle, or in foster care. There aren't a lot of good options for kids with bad homes."

She searched his face. "I'm so sorry, Lucas."

He shook his head and put his finger on her lips. "Don't feel sorry for me. I have an incredible family. Every single morning, I wake up and remind myself how lucky I am. I'm grateful for my life every day..." He paused. "Even when it sucks."

She frowned. "How does it suck?"

He took a breath, but forced himself to abide by the Hart promise of honesty. "I still have nightmares from time to time. Sometimes, I feel like that little kid again, unable to defend myself, the memories are so vivid."

"What do you do when that happens?"

"Grab a horse and go out for a ride, usually. Call one of my siblings. Go take care of the horses." He shrugged. "Remind myself why I'm still alive."

She was watching him intently. "What do you do for a job?"

He shrugged. "I work on the ranch."

"Taking care of the family and the horses?"

He loved the way she was running her fingers over his forearms, as if her touch could erase the scars that his skin still carried. "Yeah."

"What do you do for yourself?"

He closed his eyes, focusing on the feel of her on his lap. It was an intimate connection, and he never wanted to move. "Take care of my family."

"But what do *you* want to do?"

"Take care of my family," he repeated, frowning, tensing a little bit at her questions. He opened his eyes to look at her, trying to get a read on what she was getting at. "Why?"

She shrugged. "It's just that working at the flower store helps me, because I'm involved with a cause bigger than myself. I love creating joy and giving joy. And now that I'm working with weddings through Piper, it really helps, too."

Her eyes lit up as she spoke, and the faintest hint of envy sparked through him, startling him. He didn't want more than what he had. His family was everything. He was complete. "It's great you have the flower store," he said, meaning it.

She bit her lip. "I hope it's all right. Did you text Piper that she could go there?"

"I did. She said she, Tori, and Keira are heading over there in the morning."

Emotion filled her face. "I wish I was there. I miss them."

Her love for them was etched on her face, making Lucas swear silently. He could never take Maddie away from her home. He could never ask her to move to Oregon and live on the ranch. Her world and her support system were in Boston.

His was in Oregon.

There was no way to fix facts like that. *Hell.*

Maddie frowned at him. "What's that anguished look for?"

He took a breath. "You won't ever leave Boston, will you?"

She shook her head. "No. Why?"

"I can't leave my family."

She stared at him for a second, confusion etched on her face, then understanding dawned. "Oh."

He leaned forward, caught her face in his, and kissed her. Hard. Intense. Needing to connect with her.

Maddie kissed him back just as fiercely, and the kiss went from desperate to searing hot instantaneously. He needed this woman. He needed her with every fiber of his soul. And there was no way to have her. Not for real. Not for beyond this moment in time.

He slid his hands through her hair, continuing to kiss her, to taste her, to breathe her in.

"Well," she whispered, between kisses. "At least that

makes you safe for me to be with. I never have to worry about you taking over my life."

"Just a one-night stand?" Fuck. He was surprised at how much he didn't like the sound of that.

"It's perfect for me." She kissed him before he could see her face and try to read her emotions as she spoke.

Perfect. Was it? No. It wasn't. But what else did they have?

This moment. That was it.

It wasn't going to be enough. He knew it already. This woman had gotten under his skin and inside his soul, and he'd just met her.

And he was going to lose her. Maybe not today. Maybe not tomorrow. But eventually?

Yes.

CHAPTER TWENTY-TWO

BY THE TIME Maddie and Lucas abandoned Hart Pond and arrived at Lucas's gorgeous house an hour later, she could think of only one thing: Lucas.

His home was huge and beautiful, with a western flair and an expansive wooden deck. His gardens were vibrant and flourishing, surprising her with how much time and attention he'd put into the flowers. The big picture windows promised an amazing view of the ranch.

His house was understated for a billionaire, but it was designed with a cozy ranch aesthetic. There were gorgeous wooden beams across the vaulted ceilings. A massive stone fireplace took up most of the south-facing wall, and the couches around it created the coziest living space.

It was gorgeous, inspiring, and cozy. She couldn't wait to explore it...later.

The minute Lucas shut the front door behind them, Maddie wrapped her arms around him and kissed him.

Her dad was going to be dropped off in an hour.

This was all they had.

This was her moment, with this man who was making her trust again. Want again. Feel alive again.

Lucas picked her up, and she locked her legs around his waist as he carried her across the floor and up the stairs. She didn't even bother to look around. She was desperate to focus on him as much as she could until time ran out.

Violet's toenails were clicking on the hardwood floors as Lucas strode into a bedroom and tackled her onto the bed. She laughed as she hit the plush comforter, barely able to catch her breath before they were both tearing off their clothes "I feel like a teenager in heat," she said as he grabbed her foot and untied her sneaker.

"Me, too." He ripped his shirt off, revealing a body that was even more sculpted than she'd noticed in the dim, evening light of the flower store. He was absolutely breathtaking, and she giggled when he gave her a cocky look. "My chick magnet abs are working on you. I can see it in the way you're gawking at me."

"I'm totally gawking." She propped herself up on her elbows, watching as he shed his jeans, tossing them aside before he climbed onto the bed, moving with predatory grace. He was sexy, ripped, and delicious.

On his side, she saw a scar, and she remembered that he'd been stabbed by the man who was supposed to keep him safe. Instinctively, she palmed it, then scooted down to kiss it. "A kiss makes the pain go away," she whispered.

Lucas caught her face as she looked up at him. "Thank you," he whispered. "You don't know what that does to me."

Violet hopped up on the bed and then laid down across the pillows, planting her back foot across Maddie's forehead. They both laughed, and Maddie reached up to grasp Violet's paw. "My baby girl," she said.

Lucas scratched Violet's ears. "Beautiful puppy."

Maddie's heart turned over. What man would let a giant

pit bull lie across the pillows when he was making love to her? Lucas did. He welcomed her dog completely. He accepted her panic attacks.

Damn the man.

He seemed like he was everything she needed. Everything she wanted. Everything that could make her want to trust again.

Except that he had to stay in Oregon, and she couldn't leave her home.

She'd done the long-distance relationship with Adam, and she knew it didn't work for her.

This moment with him might be all she'd ever have, and she would have to make the most of it.

So, she drew him down to her, kissing him. She let go of her reservations, of her fears, of all the old stories in her head that she used to hold back and protect herself.

She gave it all up, and let herself surrender completely to Lucas.

The moment she did, she felt him pause, as if he could sense that she'd dropped all her walls.

He searched her face, then he kissed her, a kiss that took her breath away with its tenderness. He was such a wonderful kisser, making her whole soul dance in response.

He palmed her hips, his hands holding her still as he kissed his way down her body, between her breasts, across her belly, and then between her legs.

"Lucas." She whispered his name, her body instinctively arching into him as he worked his magic on her with his mouth and his hands. His whiskers were rough across the inside of her thighs, his hands tantalizing perfection everywhere he touched.

She was his. Completely. She didn't want to overthink the moment. She just completely gave herself over to him, trusting him in a way she'd never trusted in her life. She didn't try to protect herself. She didn't watch her back. She didn't hold back.

She gave herself the gift of absolute surrender, of complete trust, of fully being in the moment, of letting go of every story she carried with her. She gave herself into the safekeeping of this amazing man, absolutely certain that he was her oasis.

By the time Lucas grabbed a condom from the nightstand and sheathed himself, Maddie was lost to him, and she loved it. She'd never felt so completely free to simply bask in the moment, in life.

Lucas moved over her, smiling down at her with a smile so tender that her heart turned over. "My beautiful Maddie," he whispered.

My beautiful Maddie. Habit made her want to protest that she wasn't his, that she belonged to no one, but in this moment, she *wanted* to be his, to be claimed by him. So she wrapped her arms around him and claimed him back. "My Lucas."

"All yours," he agreed as he slid inside her.

Her body and soul welcomed him, and she breathed in the moment their bodies connected. He began to move, and she was overwhelmed by the expression on his face, like he'd absolutely meant it when he'd called her his beautiful Maddie.

Her throat clogged with emotion, and she closed her eyes, needing to separate herself from the intensity of the moment. Instead, she focused on the feel of his body against hers, on his hands around her wrists, of his tender kisses on her forehead as Lucas continued to move inside her. Faster, slower, teasing her, making promises, until she was trembling, on the burning edge of absolute surrender.

Then he reached down, and his fingers brushed against her in just the right way, and a cry tore from her throat as he coaxed her over the precipice, sending her into the most delicious spiral. She clung to him, riding the wave of pure ecstasy, as he did the same, bucking against her in his own release, both of them fully giving themselves over to each other.

To this moment.

And this moment only.

Because there was no future.

Not unless one of them gave up the family and life that made them whole.

CHAPTER TWENTY-THREE

BASKING in the aftermath of their lovemaking, Lucas stared at the ceiling, his arm around Maddie, listening to her breathe.

They had only a few moments before they had to get up, but neither of them was moving.

They weren't talking.

They were simply lying there, tangled up in full pretzel-style. Maddie's face was pressed into his neck, and he was playing with her hair, while Violet breathed on them both.

It was a simple intimacy, a peace he'd never experienced before. "How do you feel right now, Maddie?"

"At peace."

He smiled and kissed the top of her head. "Same."

"How do two people who carry such shadows create peace when they're together?" She began to trace designs on his chest, which he loved. "Shouldn't it be worse when we're together? Like we feed off each other?"

"It depends on the people. I've known plenty of people who set me off."

"Me, too." She nestled closer. "After Adam, I truly

believed I would never want to be with a man again. All I wanted was to build myself up to be so strong and independent that I'd never want a man, so I'd never sacrifice for a man again. For anyone."

He swore silently. Her words were no doubt meant to express that she trusted him, but he read the subtext that she hadn't even intended: that knowing as he did how important her life in Boston was, even if she were to decide to leave it for him, he couldn't let that happen, because she'd be making a choice to honor someone else instead of herself. Again.

Dammit. His job was to protect her, not to tempt her into betraying herself.

Regret filled Lucas. Not regret that he'd met her, but that it hadn't been under different circumstances, ones that weren't so damned complicated.

THEY MADE IT DOWNSTAIRS, dressed, before her dad arrived, but it was only minutes before Maddie saw a pickup truck approaching Lucas's house.

She was sitting on the couch, watching out the picture window for her dad. Instinct made her tense when she saw a pickup truck approaching, even though she knew that Jacob wouldn't be driving up to the door.

Her dad got out of the passenger seat, stepping down gingerly, but with a fierceness and determination she hadn't seen in a long time. He limped to the house as a man in a cowboy hat got out of the driver's side and followed him.

Lucas was already opening the door by the time she got there. "Any problems, Tristan?"

He didn't greet her dad directly, and she could feel his tension.

"No one came after him," Tristan said, his voice equally

cool, clearly not discussing how her dad had behaved otherwise.

Crap. They weren't happy with her dad. Why would they be? He crossed the line with someone they loved.

Her dad limped in, and he looked angry as he looked for her. His gaze lit on Maddie. "We need to talk in private."

Maddie couldn't believe the tension between all the men. Her dad had loved Adam even though Adam was an ass. And now her dad had been the ass with Lucas and his family, even though they were trying to keep her and her dad safe.

Men were such pains in the butt. This was why she didn't want one.

She ignored her dad's request for privacy and walked over to Tristan. He was tall, taller than Lucas. The cowboy hat made him look rough and rugged, but his jeans were of a quality that most cowboys didn't wear. He wore more money than Lucas did, but he still looked like a man who'd get dirty for his horses on a regular basis.

He was handsome and attractive, but he didn't touch her soul the way Lucas did. "Hi," she said, extending her hand. "My name's Maddie Vale. Thank you for taking care of my dad and supporting Lucas in trying to keep me alive. I appreciate it very much."

Tristan's face morphed into a warm smile, and he shook her hand, his grip warm and reassuring. "Maddie. Great to meet you. We're all so glad that you're here."

She relaxed into his friendliness, and she felt Lucas put his hand on her lower back, providing even more welcome.

She saw Tristan notice Lucas's hand on her back, and his gaze shot to Lucas. He searched his brother's face, and then understanding flickered in his eyes as Tristan looked back at Maddie, speculation gleaming in his eyes. "You like the ranch?"

"It's beautiful," she said honestly. "I saw Hart Pond. I loved it."

Tristan nodded. "It's a healing energy. I swim there every morning."

"Maddie," her dad said again. "We need to talk."

Irritation tightened Maddie's shoulders. This was the man she loved with all of her soul, and yet she couldn't bring herself to deal with him. Was she a terrible person? Probably. "I'm sorry if my dad was a pain in the butt," she said to Tristan. "He's obsessed with Jacob. Guilt for leaving him there. It's been tearing him up all this time. He's desperate to look Jacob in the eye and apologize."

"Maddie!" Her dad spoke sharply, but his voice was low. Remembering now that raising his voice to Maddie was never allowed.

Tristan's gaze flicked to her dad. "Don't let your emotions make you do stupid things, Huck. Be better than that."

Maddie had to bite her lip to keep from laughing. Her dad was a freaking badass, and she found it hilarious that Tristan had just spoken to him like he was a teenage idiot.

But to her surprise, her dad didn't respond. He simply stared at Tristan silently. Plotting his revenge? Or listening to sage advice from a man who'd probably faced the same level of trauma that everyone else in the room had? Maybe he'd experienced even more.

Tristan turned his attention back to Maddie and Lucas. "You want people inside your house? Dylan has some posted outside and around the property. We're expecting Les to show up here. If he found you guys once, he'll find you again."

Maddie bit her lip. "Why does he want me?"

Tristan shook his head. "We don't know yet. We're guessing he's pissed because we killed his half-brother, but it could be more than that. If he knows Jacob cares about you, the best way to hurt Jacob is to hurt you. We have his family

178

under tight protection, and the rest of the Harts are all on alert. We're ready, but we don't know what he'll do or how strong an attack he'll mount."

Maddie stared at him. "You're very calm about this."

Tristan shrugged. "Many people would like to cause us harm. We're committed to keep living fully, regardless. Les might not come after us for months. Or ever. We can't hide just because he's out there."

His words sank deep. She'd spent her whole life being worried that a faceless bogeyman would come to get her, and the Harts just went about their normal business.

Maybe that was because the Harts were able to set up all the safeguards, and knew they could handle it.

But her dad had taught her to protect herself. She wasn't a victim.

"Maddie." Her dad came up behind her. "I need a word."

There was an edge to his voice that got her attention, and she turned to look at him. His eyes were focused and sharp, and he jerked his head toward the stairs. "Walk with me." He was acting like the FBI agent she'd once known. A man who would never stand down. The man she used to feel so safe with whenever she'd have a nightmare and crawl into his bed when she was a little girl.

"Dad," she whispered. "It's good to have you back."

He nodded at Lucas and Tristan. "I'm going to have a word with Maddie. We'll head upstairs."

Lucas waited for Maddie to give a nod before he agreed. "Fine. But stay inside." He looked at Maddie. "Give a shout if you need me."

She nodded.

"She won't," Huck said, taking her arm. "I'm her father, Lucas. Remember that."

Both Lucas and Tristan were frowning at Huck, and discomfort prickled through her. There was male posturing happening, and she didn't like it. "Let's just go to the living room," she said, not quite wanting to shove a spike between her dad and the Harts. "We'll stay in sight," she assured Lucas.

He nodded, and she saw the relief in his eyes. "Great."

She took her dad's arm and led him to the couch in the living room. Tristan came inside, and he and Lucas were in low conversation inside the entry way. She sat down and patted the couch for her dad.

He didn't sit. "I'd like to talk in private."

"I was attacked, and you were shot less than a day ago. We're not getting out of their sight."

"I can protect you!"

Ah...she finally understood now. "Dad. Sit."

After a long moment, he sat down on the coffee table, facing her. "Maddie." His voice was low. "We need to get out of here. We'll handle this ourselves."

She leaned forward and put her hands on his knees. "Dad," she said gently. "We need help."

"No, we don't. We've been fine all this time with just the two of us!" Again, his voice was low, despite his tension.

"Dad. What's going on?"

He shrugged. "What? It's fine. I'm just keeping you safe. It's my job."

"No." She moved to sit next to him on the table, and then she took his hand and leaned her head against his shoulder. "Daddy," she said softly. "I missed you. You're being a little crazy right now, but it's good to have you back."

He took a deep breath, and then he put his arm around her shoulder. "My baby girl," he said softly. "I'm so sorry I've let you down."

She didn't lift her head from his shoulder. "You could never let me down."

"Why won't you tell me what happened with Adam? Is it

because you think I won't support you? Because you'll always get my support. Always."

She bit her lip, but she knew it was time. There'd been too many walls between them for too long. "I didn't want you to feel sad or blame yourself."

"Blame *myself?*" Her dad's arm tightened around her shoulder. "What happened, Mads?"

She moved to the couch again, so she could face him. She took his hands and held them tightly. "I went to visit him, and I walked in on him getting naked with several women in his living room. I got mad, and he hit me and knocked me out."

Her dad's jaw dropped, and his eyes filled with pain. "*Maddie.*"

She kept going, refusing to stop now. "When I woke up, the women had left, and I was on the couch. He tried to convince me to stay, but I didn't. Obviously."

The sadness in his eyes was almost unbearable. "I've known him for seven years. I never saw that side of him. I never would have thought it was possible."

"I know. Me, too." She sighed. "I think I felt stupid, too. Not realizing it."

"I feel like I failed you." He bent his head and pressed his face to his hands, his shoulders slumping, as he transformed before her eyes back into the broken, worn-out man he'd been two days ago.

Panic hit her. "No, Dad, no! It's great. I kicked his ass, and it made me stronger. It's just one of those things that life gives us to make us more."

He lifted his head to look at her. "Are you happy, Mads? With the store? With our life? I never found you a mom. I tried, but no one was ever good enough for you. I wanted to give you a real family. A mom. Siblings. But I never found anyone. Every night, I wonder if I failed you. You deserved everything, and all you got was me."

Maddie's throat tightened. "Dad. I love you. I love our life. Our store is everything to me. I don't need a mom. I have *you*. That's all I need." She paused. "But if you found someone, that would be all right with me. I want you to be happy."

He shook his head. "It's too late for that, Mads. It's just us." He gripped her hands. "I'm sorry for my obsession with Jacob. I think...I felt he was supposed to be the brother that I couldn't give you. That if I'd gotten him out, then you would have had the family you were meant to have. Maybe he was your biological brother, and I left him there. What kind of father does that? If he was your brother, then I was supposed to be his dad."

She squeezed his hands. "I'm grateful to know about how you feel about Jacob, Dad. I don't want any more secrets between us."

He touched her face. "I didn't know if it would upset you. Or if you would be angry at me for leaving him."

This was the conversation she'd been wanting from her dad for so long. Truth. Honesty. Candor. For the first time, maybe ever, she felt like she saw her dad in a way she'd never seen him before. "I might get mad, but you're my dad. Nothing would ever change that."

He nodded and pressed a kiss to their joined hands, a tear trickling down his cheek. "I love you, Mads." His voice was raw and rough. "Before I adopted you, I was a guy who worked hard, played hard, and never thought I'd ever get married or have kids. I didn't want them."

She cocked her head, listening. "You never told me that."

"I wanted to be the Director of the FBI. I was in it for life. Nothing else mattered." He paused. "Until I saw this little girl hiding in the corner of this drug trafficker's house.

She was little, scrawny, and she was watching me with her big, scared eyes. Scared but curious. The moment I met you, that moment I saw you, everything inside me changed. I knew you were my daughter. I was your dad. There was no other possibility. After that, everything I did was to get you out of there."

Tears blurred Maddie's vision. "Dad—"

"I didn't tell you about my pre-Dad career aspirations because I was afraid you wouldn't believe me that I could change overnight like that. I didn't want you to feel guilty, like you'd taken my dreams from me."

She laughed through her tears. "I thought that anyway."

"Son of a bitch. Failed again."

"No dad can control his daughter's thoughts. You gotta give that up, Dad."

He cocked a half smile. "You can't blame a dad for trying."

"No, you can't." She took a breath. "Dad, I need to be honest with you. I feel like this life you chose for me is killing you."

"No." He sat back. "Absolutely not—"

"I know you love me." She squeezed his hands. "But there hasn't been a light in your eyes for a long time, not like there has been since someone tried to kill me."

He looked horrified. "I don't want anyone to try to kill you!"

She grinned. "No, but I don't think flowers are really enough for you."

"It is—"

"Dad. You were so angry today in the car. Where did that anger come from?"

He stared at her for a long moment. "You're my world, Maddie."

"I know." She took a breath. "But I'm a big girl now. You

don't need to stay small for me anymore. What would you do if you didn't have to watch over me?"

"I'm not going anywhere."

"What would you do, Dad?"

"Nothing else."

She sighed. "Well, think about it, okay? Because I like having a dad who feels like being alive is a good thing. I need you around for the next one hundred years, and that's not going to happen if your soul is slowly dying."

"It's not—"

"Listen to your heart, Dad. What if the best thing you can do for me is to get a passion for life again? *Your* passion, not choices that you think will serve me."

Her dad stared at her. "I wouldn't have any idea what that is. You're my world."

"I know, but you can have two worlds." She smiled. "Even though you were being a rude jerk earlier, I'd rather have that dad than the one who's dragging himself around."

He flexed his jaw. "I *was* a rude jerk. I apologize for that."

She smiled. "I know it was from the stress of Jacob and having someone try to kill me, so I forgive you and love you, but I do think an apology would be appropriate." She jerked her chin toward the door, and they both looked over.

She was startled to see that both Lucas and Tristen were silent, watching them. "Have you guys been listening the whole time?"

Lucas nodded without apology. "Neither of us ever had parents. Listening to the two of you was beautiful." He paused. "I didn't know it could be like that."

"Me either," Tristan said quietly. "Sorry I was rude to you earlier, Huck. I didn't realize how complicated it was."

Her dad rose to his feet and limped over to the Harts. "I would like to officially thank both of you for protecting my daughter and saving me. I'm sorry for being an ass about Jacob." He took a breath. "Seeing Maddie's reaction to him made me realize that the trauma from their time in that house was real, and that seeing me could bring back Jacob's." He paused. "I don't want that for him. I apologize for trying to force myself into his life."

"Apology accepted," Tristan said.

"Agreed," Lucas said.

Tears filled Maddie's eyes, and she hurried over and wrapped her arms around her dad's waist. She could feel his pain. "I love you, Dad."

Her dad put his arm around her shoulders. "Mads, I never understood the trauma you still carried. I didn't want to see it, so I didn't. I'm sorry for that."

She nodded. "I know." She took a breath. "We'll make it, Dad. Right?"

"Right. Always right." They hooked pinkie fingers, and then she threw her arms around him. The hug he gave her was strong and solid, and it made her feel like a little girl, safe in her dad's arms, always protected, always loved.

It had been a long time since she'd felt like that. Violet jumped on her, whining and wagging her tail. Maddie laughed and put her arm around her pup, bringing her into the hug. "And I love you, too, Vi."

Lucas's phone rang, and he turned away to answer it.

"Did Violet really rip your attacker's hand off?" her dad asked.

"Maybe. We left without checking—" Maddie paused when she saw Lucas hang up the phone and look at her. "What?"

"Jacob is willing to meet Huck."

Her dad stiffened beside her, but he turned to look at Maddie. "Only if that's all right with you, Mads. If it upsets you, I won't."

185

What was she supposed to say to that? Tell her dad no? "It's fine."

"He's outside right now," Lucas said. "That's how Jacob operates. He's here now. If you don't meet with him now, he might not come back."

"Outside? Now?" Maddie's dad stood taller.

"Yeah."

Huck looked at Maddie. "You sure?"

"Yes. Go." She stepped back and put her hand on Violet's head. "I'll wait here, though."

"I'll be right back." Huck moved toward the door, and Maddie saw Lucas watching him.

"Go with him, Lucas. Take care of my dad." She knew Lucas wanted to take care of Jacob, but it was her dad's heart she was worried about. What would happen to him when he saw the boy who had been haunting him for so long? She wanted to go with him, but she couldn't make herself do it.

Lucas didn't hesitate. "All right. Tristan, stay?"

Huck already had the front door open, and he was walking out, not waiting. Lucas shot Maddie a quick look, then he jogged out the door after her dad.

Tristan moved to the doorway to watch.

Maddie turned away.

CHAPTER TWENTY-FOUR

MADDIE SAT down on the couch and patted for Violet to sit on her lap.

She could hear the low murmur of men's voices, and her belly congealed. She tried not to listen, but she did, straining to see if she recognized Jacob's voice from some suppressed memory.

She didn't.

She'd been six when her dad had pulled her out of that house.

Six was old enough to have memories, but she had none.

How bad had her past been that she could recall absolutely nothing?

The door closed, and she looked up sharply, but it was simply Tristan closing it.

He raised his brows. "You all right?"

"How bad was it for Jacob? How bad was that place? I don't remember anything."

Tristan walked over and sat across from her. "You were there only for a short time. Jacob lived there for many years. It might not have been the same for you."

"How bad was it?"

"Bad."

"How is he doing?"

Tristan let out his breath. "Jacob is fragile. We all try to protect him. He's had the most difficult time of all of us. But he met a fantastic woman named Phoebe who has a daughter and a dog. They're healing each other. It's beautiful. Gives us all hope."

There was only kindness and love in Tristan's voice, giving truth to Lucas's statements about how the Harts were such a close family.

"How much does he remember about me?" she asked.

Tristan raised his brows. "You have haunted him every minute of his life since he came back from that run, and you were gone. He considers you his sister."

Tears burned at the corners of Maddie's eyes. She knew how her dad had suffered because of Jacob, and Jacob had done the same for her. "I'm scared that if I see him, I'll remember."

Tristan's gaze went to the therapy vest on Violet. "I think you do remember, Maddie. You just pretend you don't."

Her stomach was churning. "Can you go get Lucas for me?"

"You bet." Tristan stood quickly and headed for the door. He left it open, and Maddie could hear the men talking, including her dad's voice.

"Maddie?" Lucas walked in.

She looked up at him. "Will you go outside with me?"

Understanding dawned, and he held out his hand. "Come on."

"Okay." She patted Violet to get her off her lap, then she stood up. Her hands were shaking, and she felt icy cold. "I feel like I'm going to throw up."

"That's fine. No one cares if you vomit."

She put her hand in his, and he closed his fingers around hers, a solid, steady strength. He kissed her gently, a tender kiss that eased the tiniest bit of terror gripping her. "I don't know if I can do it."

"No problem. We'll find out. Whatever you choose is perfect."

"Okay. You go first."

Lucas smiled. "You got this, sweetheart."

She nodded, too tense to speak. She kept herself behind Lucas as he headed toward the front door. As they stepped outside, she used him to block her view of the men in front of her, gripping his forearm with her free hand. Violet was pinned to her leg, pressing so hard that Maddie had to fight to keep her balance so her dog didn't knock her over.

The conversation ceased, and she could feel the weight of their gazes, but she kept her focus on Lucas's back. *I'm safe. I'm safe. I'm safe.*

The frantic mantra did nothing to ease the panic clogging her throat, and she stopped. "I can't do this."

Lucas immediately turned to face her, using his body to block her view of the men. "Maddie. Look at me."

She looked up into his face, into those dark eyes that were so full of kindness and warmth.

"I know you don't want to hear this, but I'm telling you anyway."

Oh, God. "What?"

"I know it's fast, but when life has dragged you through hell and back, you get to know your soul in a hurry." He paused. "I'm falling in love with you, and I've got no chance of stopping myself."

She stared at him, her heart racing. "Lucas—"

"You don't need to answer, but I wanted you to know that. It doesn't matter if you talk to Jacob or not. If you walk away from me and never look back. But you deserve to know

189

you're loved, exactly as you are." Then he framed her face with his hands and kissed her.

It was a kiss of pure tenderness and love, and it settled inside her, grounding her.

He pulled back. "Don't listen to what your mind is telling you about what you can and can't do. What does your heart say?"

She paused, and she listened, and to her surprise, a sense of calmness settled over her. Maybe it was because of Lucas. Maybe it was because he'd said he loved her, and she believed him. Maybe it was because she was listening to something other than her crazy brain. But either way, she suddenly knew she could handle this.

That it was time.

She touched Lucas's wrist, took a breath, and then stepped around him to meet the boy she couldn't remember.

The *brother* she couldn't remember.

CHAPTER TWENTY-FIVE

LIKE LUCAS AND TRISTAN, Jacob was tall, muscled, and rugged. He was wearing jeans, cowboy boots, a cowboy hat, and sunglasses.

As Maddie stepped around Lucas, he pulled off his sunglasses and removed his hat, giving her a clear view of his face. His eyes were dark, intense, with long, dark lashes.

He was a man, not the fifteen-year-old boy she'd last seen so long ago...and she didn't recognize him at all.

Both relief and sadness rushed through her. Relief that no memories were triggered by him, but also a weird emptiness that this man who had loved her for so long was nothing to her.

His face morphed into emotion, and he took a step back. "*Sienna.*"

Sienna. The name went right to her core, right to her heart, and suddenly, she knew him. She'd heard him say Sienna before, laughing while he said it, crying while he said it, raging while he said it. "*Jacob.*"

They both suddenly reached for each other, and she flung her arms around his neck, holding him so close, while he did the same. His arms were locked around her back, and she buried her face in his neck. Memories came tumbling back, but they were memories of *him*.

Of him sitting with her when she couldn't sleep. Of him stealing food for her. Of him hiding her under the bed. Of him taking blows to protect her. Of him making her laugh when she didn't feel like laughing but desperately needed to.

She pulled back. "Jacob," she whispered. "Thank you for all the times you protected me. I remember now. Not the rest of it, but I remember you."

He nodded, tears forming on his cheeks. "Fuck, I'm so glad you got out of there, Sienna. I mean, Maddie." He gave a half smile. "You've always been Sienna to me, but I know that's not who you are."

"Using that name made me remember you." She didn't want to let him go. She couldn't pry her hands off his jacket, and he didn't release her. "I'm so sorry I was afraid to meet you. I just—"

He laughed softly. "Trust me, Maddie, I know that things like this take time. Whenever you were ready, if ever, was fine. I was just happy to know you were all right." He pulled her in for a fierce hug again, and she hugged him back.

The bond between them was so strong. She could feel it humming between them. A powerful connection of love and acceptance and survival. How had she forgotten him? How was it possible? "Thanks for not forgetting me," she whispered. "I'm glad to have you back."

"Hell, Maddie, I'd never forget you."

They held each other for what felt like forever. It reminded her of the countless times she'd sat in the corner on his lap, burying herself in his arms, hiding from the noises downstairs. "You were the reason I got through that time," she said slowly, knowing it was true.

Her whole body felt safe. Her soul felt safe. She felt like

she was home again, home in a way that she'd never felt before. "Are you my biological brother?" He must be. The way she felt with him was too strong.

"It doesn't matter," he said, pulling back. "You're my sister. Blood doesn't make a difference." His gaze went to her dad. "You know that, Maddie."

She smiled through her tears and looked back at her dad. "I do know that."

Huck was openly crying, and she held out her arm to him. "Dad. Come in."

He practically sprinted over and locked his arms around both of them, gripping them tightly and fiercely. "I love you both," he said, his voice gruff with emotion. "I will protect you both with my life for as long as I live."

Jacob's arms tightened around them in response, and Maddie realized that her dad and Jacob had solved their issues. Were they a family now, in a weird sort of way? "I want you guys to meet my wife and daughter," Jacob said. "I want this circle complete."

Maddie nodded, no longer afraid, her heart aching with emotion. "All right."

But her dad shook his head. "Not if it endangers them. We know Les is still out there."

Maddie smiled. Her dad was himself again. Meeting Jacob had healed a huge hole in his heart. She could see it in his eyes.

Jacob nodded. "I appreciate that, but we're good here. I'll bring them by later today." He hugged Maddie again, then her dad. "I'll see you later."

And then, without another word, he jogged off to his truck, hopped in, and drove down the dirt road, heading into the depths of the ranch.

Maddie let out her breath, watching him go. "Wow."

Her dad tucked his arm through hers.

They said nothing. Simply stood there watching until Jacob's truck vanished from sight.

After he was gone, Maddie looked around to find Lucas. He was standing with Tristan, and they were both frowning at her. "What?"

Lucas looked at her dad. "Did you see it?"

Her dad took a breath. "Yeah. I thought I was imagining it. No?"

"I saw it, too," Tristan said.

"What?" Maddie turned toward them and put her hands on her hips. "What are you talking about?"

Lucas eyed her cautiously. "I don't know how you'll feel about this, but you and Jacob look very similar. I think you could be biologically related to him."

She was stunned by the news. "Really?"

Lucas nodded. "That might mean you're biologically related to his dad, Ivan, or Ivan's half-brother, Les."

Understanding crept in. "Which would mean his hunting me is personal."

"Yeah." Lucas didn't say more, because he didn't need to.

They all knew that if it was about *her* specifically, and not just payback for Jacob killing Ivan, the stakes just went up. Way, way up.

Les might think he owned her, and that gave him license to think in ways that were terrifying.

But today, for the first time, fear didn't paralyze her. Meeting Jacob, the Harts, and having the frank discussion with her dad had unlocked the courage she'd been wanting her whole life.

Because instead of having a panic attack, she put her hands on her hips. "Well, then, we need a plan, don't we?"

CHAPTER TWENTY-SIX

A WEEK LATER, nothing had happened.

No sign of Les.

No sign of danger.

And they were all getting restless.

Lucas leaned on his kitchen counter, watching Maddie play with Jacob's daughter Annie while Jacob and Huck talked about Jacob's rescued horses. The bond between them was amazing. There were very few people Jacob could tolerate, but miraculously, Maddie and Huck fell into that zone.

Not too long ago, Jacob had been fully alone except for his horses, and the times he was able to handle being around his siblings. And now, he had a full family, because Huck had taken on the role of Jacob's dad and Annie's grandpa.

It was wonderful and amazing...but at the same time, Lucas felt like there wasn't a place for him. Maddie was discovering her new family, and she'd kept Lucas at a distance for the last week.

Ever since Lucas had told her he loved her, she'd been distant.

Lucas didn't regret saying it.

He knew she'd needed to hear it. And he'd needed to say it. And he'd known there was a chance it would push her away.

But knowing it might happen hadn't fully prepared him for experiencing it.

"Hey, Lucas."

He looked over his shoulder to see Bella walking into the kitchen. His home had become a gathering place for the Harts during the last week, everyone wanting to meet Maddie and her dad, welcoming her to the family. It was surreal, and he was amazed at how well Maddie and her dad fit.

Well, they fit everyone except him. Even her dad kept him at a distance.

What the hell was going on? "Hi, Bella."

She was wearing a green "Bella's Kitchen" tee shirt, jeans, and hiking boots. She gave him a look, then propped her hip against the fridge. "You look lonely over here."

"Do I?"

"Yep." She pulled up a bar stool and sat down. "Maddie's nice."

"Yeah."

"Where is she sleeping?"

He didn't bother to lie. There were no secrets in his family. "Guest room."

"How do you feel about that?"

He glanced over at his sister. "Not thrilled," he said honestly.

Bella laughed then. "You're just like Jacob. You men come on too strong and scare your women." She leaned on the counter and watched the gathering in the family room. "Have you really looked at her, Lucas? I mean, *really* looked at her?"

Lucas frowned and studied Maddie. "Yeah." But he was guessing he was missing something important.

"What do you see?" Bella asked as she helped herself to some of the nuts he had out on the counter for snacking.

"I see a strong, courageous woman full of love, resilience, and laughter," Lucas said. He didn't add that she was beautiful, compelling, and lit up every room she entered.

Bella tossed a nut in the air and caught it in her mouth. "Do you see a woman who wants to be small? Hidden? Stifled?"

"Hell, no."

"Then why do you have her stuffed in your house on our ranch, when her amazing flower store that's just coming to life is being neglected?"

Lucas looked sharply at his sister. "So she doesn't get kidnapped or attacked."

"It's been a week, Lucas. No one has seen or heard anything from Les. What if no one ever comes for her? How long until you set her free?"

"She is free—"

"Is she? You tossed her in a private jet and whisked her off to Oregon, without even giving her a chance to pack a toothbrush. She's awesome, but she has this great, wonderful life in Boston. You can't use the danger as an excuse to lock her up in the world you wish she lived in."

Lucas stared at Bella. "I'm not doing that."

Bella smiled gently. "You're doing exactly that, dear brother. Since when do the Harts hide from danger? We don't. We go into it. We decide what life we want to live, and then we do it."

"Yeah, but—"

"She's the daughter of an FBI agent. She knows how to defend herself and shoot. She's as good as I am, but you're sitting around disempowering her. Don't you see her anxiety? You think putting her in a safe house is going to help that? Do you?"

Lucas clenched his jaw as Bella's words sank in. Was she right?

His sister put her hand on his arm. "Lucas, I know you love Maddie. I can see it in your face. She is part of our family, and I'm sure she'll come visit, but she belongs in Boston. You have to let her go back. And then you have to figure out what's important to you."

Agony seemed to settle in his gut. "I can't leave our family."

"Leaving in what way?" Bella gave him a skeptical look. "Tatum goes on tour, and Brody goes with her. They're gone a lot, but that doesn't make them any less connected. We have two private jets, Lucas. The world is tiny for us." She sighed. "I look at Maddie sitting in your house, trapped in your living room, and it makes me realize that I've been doing that too. We've all made ourselves small living here, Lucas."

He stared at her. "You want to move away?"

"No. But I want to grow. I want to be more than simply running my restaurant for the dude ranch guests."

Lucas turned to look at her, completely surprised by what he was hearing from his sister. "What do you want to do?"

She shrugged. "I don't know. All I've ever thought of is being with you guys, and staying here in this oasis we've created. But at what cost? I don't have anxiety, but is that because I sit here in my safe little spot and never have to deal with anything?" She raised her brows. "The only men I know are my brothers, and my only friends are my family. I want more than that. Maddie already has it, and you're taking it from her because you love her and don't want to have to make a hard choice."

Lucas looked again at Maddie. Her face was full of laughter and joy as she played with Annie. She radiated life and joy. That was why he'd been so riveted by her in the first place. But her friends were amazing, and her store was fantastic. "You think she wants to go back?"

"Ask her. Give her the chance. Tell her you'll go with her to make sure that everything is safe. But offer her the chance." Bella put her hand on Lucas's shoulder. "What would you do if you weren't taking care of all of us, Lucas? Have you ever thought of that?"

"Maddie asked me that," he admitted.

Bella raised her brows. "What did you say?"

"I didn't have an answer."

She nodded. "I don't either, but I want to find one. Maybe you need to find one, too."

He ground his jaw. "I like being on the ranch."

"Me, too. But we can be that and more." Bella looked at her phone. "I gotta go. Talk to Maddie, Lucas. If you have any chance with her, you must set her free. You can't keep her caged forever, especially when there's no visible danger." She kissed his cheek, waved at the gang in his family room, then headed out the door, leaving him to stew in the bomb she'd dropped.

Lucas leaned on the counter, his jaw tense, as he mulled over Bella's comments.

He didn't want Maddie to go home.

He was afraid he'd lose her.

He'd offered her his family, in hopes that would be enough.

But Bella was right. He couldn't trap Maddie here. He had to let her be the woman who he'd fallen in love with.

Even if he lost her.

IT WAS after midnight by the time the house was quiet, and Huck had gone to sleep in the downstairs bedroom. He'd insisted on being downstairs so he could be the first line of defense if there was an intruder, not caring that the house was impenetrable.

Maddie was in her room upstairs, at the far end of the hall from Lucas's suite.

She'd never invited him to her bedroom, saying that she couldn't do that with her dad there.

So, he invited himself.

Restlessly, Lucas walked over to her door and tapped on it. "Maddie? You up?"

"Yes, come on in."

He opened the door, and Violet thumped her tail at him, not lifting her head from Maddie's legs.

Maddie was under the covers, curled up on her side, the comforter tucked up to her chin, clearly almost asleep.

Lucas sat down next to her on the bed, careful not to touch her, even though he wanted to. He cleared his throat. "It's been over a week."

She nodded. "I know."

"Les has gone underground again. We can't find him."

She sighed, and lightly punched the pillow. "What do we do, Lucas? I can't stay here forever. What if he got run over by a kid on a skateboard and died? What if we wait forever, and he never comes?"

Fuck. Bella had been right. "You're correct." He let out his breath. "If you want to go back home, I'll go with you. I can't promise it's safe, though."

She sat up, excitement dancing in her eyes. "*Yes.* I want to go back home. Piper just texted that she has a new bride for me, and asked when I was coming back. Hang on." She pulled out her phone and quickly texted. "When will I be back? Tomorrow? Can we leave in the morning? My dad's leg is healing. He'll come too."

Lucas grinned as he watched Maddie put plans in place

for her store and her dad, happy to see her fired up. Bella had been absolutely correct. "You want me to come with you? I can just send you in the jet. Dylan could send some guys."

She looked up at him, her brow furrowed. "You don't want to come?"

"I want to come, but Bella informed me that I was stifling you." He paused. "It's your life, Maddie. I don't need to be a part of it."

She bit her lip. "You don't need to come. I mean, that's fine. You have stuff to do, right?" Her chin went up, and she pulled her shoulders back. "I've already been enough of a burden. So, yeah, you know, my dad and I can fly commercial. We don't need your jet—"

He caught her wrist as she started to turn away. "Maddie."

"It's fine." She looked down. "I'm tired."

"I meant it when I said I love you."

She still didn't look up. "You don't need to mean it. You can take it back."

"Hell, Maddie, I don't want to take it back!"

She finally looked at him. "Then why haven't you talked to me all week? It's like this wall between us."

"Me?" He stared at her, then started to laugh. "Hell, Maddie, I thought you were putting up the wall. I was trying to give you space. I thought I freaked you out when I said I loved you."

Her mouth opened and shut, then she sighed. "You did freak me out," she admitted. "But it wasn't just that. It was a lot with Jacob and his family and my dad. I just—" She paused. "I don't know. I didn't know what to say to you. I didn't know—"

He leaned over and took her hand. "You don't need to say anything. You owe me nothing."

She stared at their entwined hands. "I don't think," she said slowly, "I can be the woman you want."

He hated that she felt that way. "How so?"

"This." She gestured to the house. "Your family. This ranch. I love being here. I love your family. I do. But it's not my home. My home is in Boston. I really tried this week to see if I could live here, move here, be who you need me to be, but I can't."

He was stunned. She had been thinking that all week? *Hell.* "I didn't expect you would feel any differently than you do," he said, forcing himself to speak the truth that had been weighing on him, especially since his conversation with Bella.

She raised her brows. "You didn't?"

"No. Your friends are amazing, and your passion for your store is clear." He paused. "I would like to go back to Boston with you, to protect you, but also...see what it's like for me. The way you did it this week."

She stared at him. "Really?"

"Really." He paused. "I can't make any promises, Maddie, other than that I love you. That won't change, but I am firmly planted here."

She sighed. "I know. I think...I think that's why I tried to keep my distance this week. I don't want my heart shattered again."

Hell. He took her hands and pressed a kiss to her knuckles. "I don't want to hurt you." He'd do whatever it took not to. "Want me to stay here?"

She took a breath. "If we have a chance, I would always regret not trying. I'd like you to come, but..." She paused. "I have to protect myself."

"I get it. We'll take it slow."

She nodded. "All right."

He didn't move. "I'll leave then. We'll depart in the morning."

"Great." She kept holding onto his hands. "Lucas?"

"Yeah."

"Stay here with me? Not to have sex. Just to be together." She looked at him, her gorgeous eyes searching his. "To hold each other?"

"Hell, yeah." He didn't hesitate. He crawled right onto the bed, dropped down beside her, and pulled her against him.

She sighed and snuggled against him. "I missed this."

"Me, too."

She laughed. "We've never spent the night together. How could I have missed it?"

"Because we haven't been touching much this week." He pressed his face to her hair, breathing her in. "I love touching you."

She wiggled more tightly against him. "Why does it feel so good?"

"Because we fit." He wrapped his leg over her hip, trying to get closer. Her body was so warm, and his entire soul seemed to settle. In all his time with his family, he'd never felt the way he felt in this moment.

His family was his everything, but Maddie filled a space in his soul that he hadn't realized was empty.

He closed his eyes. He'd spent his childhood empty, scared, angry, alone, which was why he treasured his family so much. How did Maddie fit into his world? How did he fit into hers?

He had no idea how this story could do anything but break his heart into a thousand pieces, because no matter what he chose, he would be giving up part of his soul.

CHAPTER TWENTY-SEVEN

MADDIE WAS SO happy to be home.

She threw open the doors to Vale's Flowers and inhaled the beautiful fragrances that had been a part of her heart for so long. "Welcome home!" she called out, throwing her arms out to the sides.

Lucas laughed and walked in, carefully checking all the corners, doors, and windows. "Do the flowers hear you?"

"They do. Can't you hear them?" She walked over and picked up a vase of white roses that her friends had put together in her absence. "Listen. They're saying that Piper, Tori, and Keira took such good care of them, but that they're so happy to have us back."

She crouched down and let Violet sniff them. "They're saying, welcome back, Vi."

Violet wagged her tail, licked Maddie's face, and then set about inspecting the store, just like Lucas was doing.

Her friends had done incredible work handling all the flowers arriving, but there was still so much to catch up on.

"Looks like the security system Dylan's team installed is working." Lucas checked out the controller by the back door, scrolling through the screen. "No one has tried to get in." His gun was on his hip, visible.

She was also armed, and she was wearing sneakers and leggings, giving her full mobility to fight or run if she needed to. "It's weird, coming into work ready for war. Flowers and guns. What a combo, right?"

He looked over at her and smiled, making her heart turn over. "Life puts together some funny combos sometimes."

"Like us? West coast boy and east coast girl?" She'd had the best sleep in his arms, better than she'd slept in years. Full and complete surrender, trust that she was safe.

She still felt safe with him there, even though she knew she might not be. Lucas settled her, and it was magical. She spun around, holding out her arms, her heart wanting to dance. "Meeting Jacob was amazing," she said. "I was so scared, but it was so healing for me. All this fear I had about my past turned into love and safety."

Lucas grinned. "I'm not going to lie. I was a little jealous of your bond with him."

"You were?" She stopped spinning, surprised. "Seriously?"

"Yep." He walked over to her, caught her hand, and then pulled her into his arms. He began dancing with her, to music that only he could hear.

She laughed and let him lead, loving that this man was one who would dance with her to music that wasn't playing. "Jacob's my brother. Not the same thing."

He spun her around. "Can you say that he's the brother of your heart? Since he's my brother, it doesn't feel right that he's your brother. That just gets weird when I start thinking about you naked."

She giggled. "I didn't even think of that. That's so funny. I don't care about biological ties when it comes to family, but now that you point it out, three cheers for Jacob not being blood related to either of us."

"Well...to me, at least."

Her amusement faded. "You really think I'm biologically related to him?"

"I don't know. There's some facial similarity." He spun her around, and then dipped her, his arm strong and supportive. "But we may never know, unless you want to do DNA testing."

"DNA testing? No way." She locked her hands around his neck. "I don't need to revisit my past, or this Les guy. I feel ready to live my life now, and to let that go."

"That sounds like a great idea." He dipped her, and Maddie giggled.

How they were having fun when they were both armed and a sociopath could be stalking them, she had no idea, but they were. Maybe it was because they'd both learned to live with shadows, that they both knew they had to decide to thrive in whatever moments they could find. Find joy in the darkness. Hear laughter in the silence. Be the light.

Lucas pulled her in for a slow dance, and her laughter faded into a sensation of peace as she tucked herself against him, resting her cheek against his chest. "Do you like flowers?" she asked.

"I do." He kissed her gently.

"I figured you did when I saw all the gardens around your house." She paused. "Want to run my flower store with me?"

Lucas tensed. "What?"

Oh...crap. She shouldn't have sprung the idea on him like that. It had just seemed like such a perfect fit when she'd had the idea earlier. She quickly moved on. "My dad told me this morning he's retiring." She still couldn't believe it. She was terribly sad not to have her dad involved with the store, but she was absolutely thrilled with what he was doing instead. "He asked Dylan if he could help out with his detective agency, and do some local work."

Lucas grinned. "Dylan told me. Your dad will love that."

"I know, right?"

"Dylan also asked me to tell you that he won't let your dad do anything dangerous."

Maddie laughed. "If Dylan doesn't let him do anything dangerous, my dad will get mad."

"Let him get mad. He's your dad. We have to keep him safe."

Maddie felt the sudden tension in Lucas's body, and she pulled back. "You're still not okay with my dad?"

Lucas shrugged. "We haven't really connected. He's focused on Jacob and his family, and on you."

Maddie sighed. Her dad was her world. It would work with Lucas only if he and her dad could connect. "Have you tried talking to him?"

Lucas shrugged. "We've been friendly."

That wasn't enough. She knew it. Lucas loved fiercely. He could never be all right being simply friendly with her dad. He wasn't built like that. And he knew how close she was with her dad. He'd always feel on the outside, and he deserved more than that.

Her dad was stubborn, and he'd been burned by Adam. Why would he trust Lucas?

Lucas had been burned by a dad a long time ago.

How did she bring them together? Because she had to do it, if there was any chance of Lucas wanting to stay.

A WEEK LATER, Maddie knew she was in trouble.

She was in love with Lucas. One hundred percent.

He'd fit perfectly into her life. He loved working with flowers, her friends loved him, and his presence in her life felt like home.

If he decided to leave, she would be crushed.

She'd tried a thousand times to imagine leaving home and moving to the Hart Ranch, and every time, she'd started crying.

It was impossible for her.

But Lucas spent a lot of time on the phone with his family, and she was beginning to suspect it would be impossible for him to give up his life for her.

Could they do a part-time relationship? What would that even mean?

She looked over at Lucas as he drove. They were on their way to her dad's for dinner, as she always did on Sunday nights. He was relaxed and singing along to a song by his brother-in-law, Travis Stockton, who was as famous as Tatum, his brother Brody's wife.

Lucas was so loyal to his family, both Hart and Stockton. He'd talked a lot about the Stockton clan, and how he wanted her to meet them. They were a family of nine brothers and one sister who lived in Wyoming on a ranch much like the Harts.

They, too, had had a shared traumatic childhood, and the bond they had as adults was like the Harts. They sounded like an amazing family, and she was sure she'd love them.

But first, she and Lucas had to figure out their own situation. "Lucas."

"Mmm...?"

She was going to ask how he liked being there with her. What he thought. But she swallowed her words, afraid to ask, afraid to get an end to the story that was just beginning.

She wanted a next chapter.

But before anything could happen, they had to be able to get back to living a normal life, and not hiding in the store or her house, always vigilant, always watchful, always on edge. "Any word on Les?"

"Nothing." He paused. "Dylan has to pull the guards tonight. He works with a woman named Eliana, who helps women escape from bad situations, usually domestic ones. She's got a big situation happening, and he had to give her resources. I told him we would be all right."

Maddie tensed, and put her hand on her hip, where her gun rested. Violet sat between them, wearing the bullet-proof therapy dog vest that Lucas had ordered for her. "We're ready."

But as she spoke, she felt her tension rise. Having Dylan's men watching out had given her the ability to relax. But suddenly, once again, it was just them.

"They've cleared all the areas around your house, your dad's, and the store. There's been no sign of anything since that first night."

"You think Les has moved on?"

"Honestly? No." Lucas looked over at her. "I think he's waiting. I think he'll move tonight."

Her heart started racing. "What's the plan?"

He pulled into her dad's driveway. "I have Declan outside watching. We'll hunker down inside and let them come in." He looked over at her. "You ready?"

She nodded. "Ready."

He leaned in to kiss her. "Maddie," he whispered. "I love you. I would ask you to go back to the ranch and let me handle this, but I know you need to be here."

She closed her eyes, breathing in his kiss. "I do. Thanks for understanding that."

"Let's end this tonight."

CHAPTER TWENTY-EIGHT

WHEN LUCAS and Maddie walked in, Lucas saw that Huck was waiting for them, armed and ready.

There was a steadiness emanating from Maddie's dad, a focus that made Lucas nod. Maddie's dad would be an asset, despite the still-healing injury.

There was no fear in his steely gaze, just focus. But, as always, and as would be expected, Huck had eyes only for Maddie. "How are you doing, Mads?"

"I'm ready."

The shades were already down, and the indoor lights were dimmed. "My guess is that Les's team will move in after we've had time to eat and drink. Right when we'd be relaxing." Lucas had gone over this with Dylan a bunch of times, and they had a plan.

A plan that had not included the three men who walked down the stairs, stunning him. "What the hell?" He had help. *His family had come.* On their own.

Maddie's eyes widened. "Tristan? Jacob? And who are you?"

Falcon was tall and imposing, in his jeans, black jacket,

and boots. He was a man who didn't socialize. A man who was about the battle and survival. He was an enigma who slid in and out of the Harts' lives, but he was always available in an emergency. He wasn't a Hart, technically, but he shared those teenage homeless roots with the Harts, and he was a part of their family...on the occasions he was around, which were less and less frequent.

But here today. Son of a bitch. *Yes.*

Falcon shook Maddie's hand. "Name's Falcon. Here to help."

"We are too!" To Lucas's surprise, Bella came jogging down the stairs, along with his other sister, Meg, who hadn't even met Maddie yet.

Meg was wearing pink camo pants, a pink bulletproof vest, and a black cowboy hat. "Hi, Maddie," she said cheerfully. "I'm Meg Hart. Nice to meet you."

Maddie's eyes were wide. "Um, nice to meet you, too. Why are you guys here?"

Bella flopped down on the couch. "We snuck in so Les's men wouldn't see us! It was super fun. I feel so badass."

"Right?" Meg beamed at them. "Bella told me how she was feeling the need to be more and do more, and we thought it was time that our brothers stopped having all the fun." She patted her hip. "We're both armed and dangerous."

"We couldn't stay home and let you be the only girl here!" Bella beamed at them. "I overheard Dylan telling Jacob that he was going to have to pull coverage. We're not idiots, right? We all figured that if Les was going to make a move, it would be when the coverage was off. Dylan's men have been visible, and Les knows that the Harts killed Ivan, so he's not going to take a chance by going for you when you were at the ranch. So, tonight's the night."

Tristan sat down at the kitchen table and stretched out

his legs. "Lucky for us, we have this thing called a private jet, so we got out here quickly."

Falcon grunted and remained standing. "I was in the area already."

Jacob wasn't smiling. He looked intense and focused. On edge. But committed. "I didn't get the chance to protect you when you were little, Maddie. This is my redemption."

Lucas felt the emotion in his brother's words, and he walked over and hugged him. Jacob didn't used to let family hug him often, but that had changed since he'd met Phoebe and Annie. A lot had changed.

Like the fact half his family was standing in Huck's living room. Lucas looked around, stunned by the sight of his family. "Thanks."

"Thanks?" Bella rolled her eyes. "You're thanking us for doing what we do? That's ridiculous. Take that back right now."

Lucas felt his tension ease. He'd thought he was alone out here, but he wasn't. Not at all. "I take it back."

"Good boy," Bella said. "You're so trainable, Lucas. It's so handy."

He started laughing. "Trainable?"

"Like every good man should be, right, Maddie?"

Maddie finally grinned, recovering from the shock of seeing everyone. "Absolutely."

"I have gear." A man's voice echoed from her dad's basement, and Lucas spun around to see Caleb Stockton walk up the stairs.

"Caleb?" Lucas was even more surprised. The Stockton clan was related to the Harts because a woman who had gone through the Hart camp, but never changed her name, had married a Stockton.

The Stocktons were like the Harts: family loyalty above

all. For both clans, family had nothing to do with blood and everything to do with heart, so the bond had been instant.

Now they had businesses together, pooled resources, and celebrated holidays together.

But having Caleb show up for this situation was next level. Of any Stockton, Caleb was the one for this assignment, though. Caleb had spent years in the military and then in private ops employ. He was a highly trained military expert, and an absolute badass. The Harts were all trained, but nothing like Caleb. He'd been missing for years, and when he'd come back, he'd shocked everyone.

"And me." Behind him, emerging from the basement was Logan Stockton, a former CIA agent. Like Caleb, he'd retired to focus on the Stockton horse business and his wife and family, but the skills were in his DNA.

Lucas grinned. "Son of a bitch." He walked over and hugged Logan and Caleb, then turned to introduce them to Maddie. "These guys are family to us," he explained.

"Always family," Logan agreed.

"Two private jets make things so easy," Bella said cheerfully.

Lucas looked around the small kitchen, and he couldn't believe it. So many members of his family, immediate and extended, had shown up at a moment's notice to help him. Unasked. They'd simply done it. It was how they operated, but out in Boston, he'd felt isolated. He'd expected to be on his own out here, except when he went home.

This kind of support was what he couldn't live without. He thought he'd have to give it up if he set up a life in Boston with Maddie.

Tonight showed him how wrong he'd been. He looked over at Maddie, who was now sitting at the table talking to Meg and Bella, and a sense of rightness settled over him.

The Harts had blended with the Stocktons. But he'd been

blind...driven by fear and loss...thinking the Harts wouldn't blend with Maddie and her dad, just because they didn't make up a massive clan. He'd believed he couldn't have it all, that he didn't deserve it all.

And his family had just made that so crystal clear that even he couldn't miss it: they were all together, no matter where he lived.

Maddie met his gaze, and he grinned at her, feeling lighter in his soul than he had in a very long time.

Her eyebrows went up, no doubt feeling the energy rolling through him. Then she smiled back, a private smile just for them, connecting them across the room.

"Let's make plans," Meg said, lightly smacking her palm on the table to get everyone's attention.

"I vote for pizza," Tristan said. "We'll order in, and when we open the door to get the food, they'll use that as an excuse to come in. We'll have to make sure the delivery guy is gone before we open the door. No one else gets sucked into our battle."

Our battle. Because his whole family and the Stocktons had taken on Maddie's safety as their own.

Lucas fucking loved that. *Loved it.* They accepted her, welcomed her, and that mattered to him.

"You think it's that easy?" Lucas asked.

"They've been waiting for two weeks to get to Maddie and Huck," Jacob said. "They have no idea how long until Dylan's guys come back. They'll move fast."

"Agreed," said Caleb. "They'll wait long enough to make sure it's not a trap, but then they'll take action. Maybe they won't wait for pizza."

"I have vests, night vision goggles, helmets, and gas masks for everyone." Logan unzipped his bag and started handing them out. "We don't know how sophisticated they are, but we'll be ready. Anyone need a gun?"

Lucas looked over at Maddie as everyone went for their gear, laughing and chatting, clearly at ease. Maddie's eyes were wide as she watched, so he walked over to her and leaned in close. "Maddie." He kept his voice low. "You okay?"

She looked over at him, and to his surprise, there were tears in her eyes. "All these people came to help me and my dad? They flew cross-country to get here as fast as they could."

He smiled. "Yeah, they did."

"What if one of them gets shot?"

"They won't, but if they do, that's part of the deal. It happens."

"I don't want it to happen."

Lucas grasped her shoulders and turned her toward him. "We make our own choices, Maddie. There are a lot of us now, and we're very good. We live for family, and doing this is part of what makes us whole. Allow everyone in this room the chance to do what they want to do."

She nodded, but her eyes were full of tears. "It's beautiful."

He smiled and put his arm around her shoulders. "I know it is."

"No wonder you don't want to leave the ranch."

"Yeah, but they made a good point that a couple of private jets makes the world very small. And they're willing to do some of the work to keep us connected. And I'm willing to do the rest."

Her eyes widened as she looked at him...and then the lights went out.

CHAPTER TWENTY-NINE

THE ROOM WENT SILENT, and then Lucas's phone lit up. He looked down to see a text from Declan, who was outside. *Eight men. Three coming in front. Two from the back. Two going in through the basement. One going in a second-floor bedroom.*

"Eight men," Lucas said quietly, into the darkness. Some of his family had the night vision goggles, but he hadn't grabbed any yet. He kept his hand on Maddie's shoulder. "They'll be going for Maddie, the dog, and Huck. I'll stay with them in the living room. Everyone, take them out as they enter." He relayed Declan's message, and then the room went into immediate action.

Someone shoved night vision goggles into his hand. He put them on, and saw that Maddie and her dad already had them. He grabbed Maddie's arm. "Both of you, come with me. Maddie, put a leash on Violet. They'll be ready to shoot her if they see her."

Maddie grabbed Violet's collar. "Where?"

"Living room. Behind the couch." He helped Huck to his feet, then the four of them raced across the downstairs. He pulled out the couch, shoved it to the corner, and then sent them all behind it. "You stay down," he said. "I'm covering you."

Maddie grabbed his arm. "I'm coming with you."

"Not today, my love. Today, you're the treasure we're protecting. If you move, you'll mess it up. We need to know where you are. You both have to stay, because you two are the targets tonight." He looked at Huck. "Got it?"

Her dad had been in battle enough times, and he nodded. "We're ready. Mads, come on."

Maddie looked at Lucas once more then, gave him a look of impatience, pulled out her gun, and then ducked behind the couch with her dad.

Lucas let out a breath, then he went down on his knee beside the couch, watching. Ready.

Game on.

~

MADDIE KEPT a tight grip on Violet's collar as she crouched next to her dad.

He was crouching, his gun and his body ready. He wasn't looking at Maddie. His head was cocked, and he was fully focused on listening.

He looked fierce and focused, the dad she'd counted on as a kid.

How many times had they played games like this? Pretending the bad guys were coming. Figuring out strategies to escape. To defend.

She realized now that it hadn't been just games.

He'd been preparing her for this moment.

Thanks, Dad.

He looked over at her, as if he'd heard her thoughts. He gave her a grin, then turned his head again to listen.

She wanted to peek over the edge of the couch, but she'd

played enough games with her dad to know that being hidden was her best choice right now. She had a whole bunch of Harts and Stocktons who were her eyes right now.

As long as the bad guys didn't know where she was, they would have to keep looking, and that gave the Harts and Stocktons a chance to take them out.

Maddie was worried about all the people out there trying to save her, but at the same time, she was inspired by them. Especially Meg and Bella. Those were women she wanted in her life. Sassy, fun, and refusing to live life in fear.

Violet's head was cocked, and she was listening as well.

Maddie heard a thump from upstairs, and she instinctively inspected the ceiling. Had a Hart gone down? Or a bad guy?

There was another thump from the direction of the kitchen, and then another. Maddie's heart started to race. How would they know if it was Harts and Stocktons who had gotten hurt?

No. It wouldn't be.

There were so many of the Harts and Stocktons, and they were ready. Waiting. Skilled.

Les's men wouldn't be prepared.

Another thump.

Then another.

Still no shots fired.

She laid down on the floor to see if she could see under the couch, but there was no gap.

She just had to wait in the dark, trusting that she would be safe, trapped in her little corner behind the couch. Trapped. She was trapped, but it made her feel safe. How amazing was that? Maybe because it wasn't a trap when she was surrounded by love.

She waited, listening for each thump. Counting them. Five. Six.

Then, suddenly, she realized that she wasn't panicking. She was calm. Listening. Trusting.

Her hands weren't shaking or clammy. Her heart was full of adrenaline, but not the panic that would make her incapable of reacting.

Triumph filled her, the most exhilarating feeling.

Two weeks ago, she couldn't have sat behind the couch, trapped in a little dark hole, while evil raged only a few yards from her.

But now, tonight, she'd done it without even thinking about it.

Because of Lucas, his family, Jacob, her dad.

But most especially Lucas. He'd given her strength and confidence, and acceptance, and he'd unlocked the doors with her dad, Jacob, and the rest of his family.

Maddie closed her eyes, as the most immense sense of gratitude swept over her.

She had her power back. Power that she'd given away when she was a little tiny girl, before she'd even known what she was doing. Of course, she'd still have her moments, but the core of her, the core deep in her soul, was healing, becoming whole, becoming her authentic self.

Lucas suddenly leaned over the couch, grinning. "It's over. Les came. We got him. Night vision goggles off. Declan's turning the power back on."

She ripped the goggles off, and launched herself to her feet, throwing her arms around Lucas, holding onto him with all she had. "Thank you," she whispered, her voice raw with emotion.

Lucas wrapped her up in a big hug, laughing. "I didn't take anyone out. I just sat here."

She pulled back. "You gave me my heart back. I love you, Lucas. I do. Let's make this work. I can do a long-distance relationship. I'll go back and forth. Whatever. I love you."

He grinned and looked over her shoulder at her dad. "Huck, I'm going to marry your daughter. Maybe not today, maybe not tomorrow, but she's the one."

Her heart turned over. "Aren't you going to ask me first?"

"No. I need to work this out with your dad. He needs to understand and accept me." Lucas hopped over the back of the couch, landing with a foot on either side of Violet, who jumped up and started wagging her tail fiercely.

The lights came on, and Maddie covered her eyes to adjust. As she did, she saw the Harts and Stocktons appearing, dragging inert figures with them, and putting zip ties on them, laughing and clearly enjoying themselves, and she grinned. These were her people.

But first, she had to manage the men in her life.

She turned to her dad as he stood up, drawing his shoulders back to full height, making him almost as tall as Lucas.

He held out his hand to shake Lucas's hand, and Maddie's heart tightened.

Lucas grinned and shook his hand.

"You're a good man, Lucas," her dad said. "Your family is loyal, honorable, and courageous. We're lucky to have you." He paused. "I consider Jacob my son, and if you marry my daughter, I'll get another one."

Maddie's throat clogged with emotion at the expression of raw vulnerability on Lucas's face. She threw her arms around both of them and dragged them into a hug. Both men wrapped their arms around her, and each other, holding on as if they'd never let go.

They stayed that way for a long moment, until Violet barked and jumped up on her, knocking her off balance. She burst out in tearful laughter and crouched down. "And you, too, Violet. We're a foursome."

Lucas knelt beside her. "Maddie, I'm in. For flowers, for you, for your dad, your friends, for a new start here."

"You're sure?" Her heart was pounding, pure joy, pure love.

He grinned. "Yeah. It's time for this billionaire slacker to get an actual business that he cares about. I'm starting with the flowers, but I'm guessing it might become something else. Gotta feel my way."

She nodded. "That sounds perfect."

"But I do know one thing I want." He slid his hand under her chin and leaned in, a mischievous sparkle in his eye.

She grinned. "What's that?"

"You." Then he kissed her, and she knew that a new adventure was about to begin. An adventure that included a world that had suddenly become so much bigger, in so many ways.

And she was ready.

CHAPTER THIRTY

"YOU'RE a braver woman than I am," Piper said, raising her glass of champagne. "Hooray for Maddie finding love again."

Maddie grinned as Tori and Keira echoed the cheer. They were having a girls' night at the store to put together flowers for Maddie's engagement party, which she was hosting at the house she and Lucas had bought. The guest list was limited to the Harts, the Stocktons, Falcon, her dad, and her friends. Even the currently long-distance members of their squad, Ellie Kent and Brie Jenkins, were going to come back for it, which made her so happy. Maddie missed Ellie and Brie, and having them back would be amazing.

She wanted to be surrounded by those she loved, both new and old, and no one else, and Lucas was delighted with her decision. Neither the Harts nor the Stocktons were particularly social, so both families were delighted with her choice Everyone was coming, including spouses and kids.

As it turned out, that made for a lot of people. Maddie had gone from a family of two and a friend group of five, to an entire village of love...and she loved it.

Les was back in jail. It turned out that he wasn't her

biological dad, but he'd been a drug supplier to her mother, who had been an addict. When her mom had died, Les had decided Maddie might be useful to him, so he'd kept her. He'd come after her as payback for the Harts killing Ivan, wanting to punish Jacob.

She knew she'd never know who her biological father was, but that was fine with her. Maddie had the only dad she needed.

Finding out who her mother was had been life-changing for her, though. Maddie now had a past, answers, and clarity, freeing her to move forward with her life.

Maddie had decided to do her own flowers for her engagement party, and she'd hired Piper to do the rest. Piper was still trying to make it in the wedding planner industry, but she was amazing, and Maddie wanted no one else to help her.

"It's not so bad, falling in love," she teased her friends. "You might try it."

Maddie patted Violet with her feet, joy bubbling in her heart. She was so happy. Happier than she'd ever imagined she could be. Her diamond ring glittered on her left hand. It was, of course, gorgeous, enormous, and custom designed for her. Lucas had put many special touches into the ring that made it just between them, personal and beautiful.

She'd decided to lean into being engaged to a billionaire, and she wore the ring and loved every second of it. No guilt or shame for the life she got to live. It had taken her a lot of work over many years to realize she deserved it, and she was owning that self-worth now.

"Fall in love?" Piper rolled her eyes. "Good heavens, girl. Don't you think I've been down that road enough?"

"I don't know," Tori said. "We heard how your hot landlord saved Maddie's dad. Ex-cop, right?"

Piper snorted. "He may be somewhat attractive, but Declan is cranky, anti-social, and a recluse. There's no chance

223

of anything romantic happening with Declan. I think we spoke about ten words the whole car ride home. If I'm going to fall in love, it wouldn't be with Declan."

Maddie exchanged glances with Tori. There didn't seem to be any secret pining for Declan under the surface. Piper had zero interest in Declan, which was too bad, because he seemed like a good guy. The Harts liked him, and the Harts were very selective about who they chose to accept.

But Maddie knew from her own experience that if the man wasn't right, the best choice was to stay away. "That's probably good that Declan isn't your guy. It would get complicated in a hurry since he's your landlord."

Piper rolled her eyes. "Can you imagine? He already has the key to my place. I'd invite him over to fix my sink, and he'd arrive naked because he would think it was code for sexy playtime."

They all burst out laughing at the thought of Declan showing up naked to fix a leaky faucet.

"You could do worse than Declan when it comes to naked landlords," Tori said. "The man is insanely ripped."

"Remember that day he was in his pool, helping his dog learn to swim?" Keira said. "I don't know which was better, him or the dog."

"The dog," Piper and Maddie said at the same time, and then they both laughed.

"Seriously, though," Maddie said. "Declan's not your guy, but maybe someone else is. You never know. I planned to be single forever, and then..." She waved her left hand in the air and wiggled it. "It can happen when you least expect it."

Piper shook her head. "No," she said emphatically. "I can't. I'm happy for you, Mads, I really am, but my true love fix is coming from my clients and you guys from now on. End of story."

"I second that," Keira said. "I'll be an auntie to all the little Maddies that run around this store."

"Ooh, yes, Aunt Tori. That's perfect," Tori said. "We'll be those eccentric spinster ladies that your kids call auntie, because we're wild, independent women with long, gray hair, freedom, and fabulousness."

"Gray?" Piper rolled her eyes. "Speak for yourself. I'm never going gray. I think I'm going fire-engine red. What do you think?"

Maddie sat back, bubbling over with joy as she listened to her friends. She might be getting married, but her friends were hers forever. Lucas adored all of them, and they treated him like one of their besties.

Everyone she loved got along, which was amazing, but at the same time, she still had her girl time, the roots that had given her courage and life all along her journey.

While she'd been hanging out with her friends, Lucas had taken her dad out to dinner, and they were stopping by the shop on their way home to load up the flowers and take them to the house. The engagement party was tomorrow, and the Harts and Stocktons would be arriving in the next few hours as well. Everyone was staying at the house. They had a big house, but they didn't have twenty bedrooms, so people would be crashing wherever they could. Kids would be in sleeping bags. Adults on couches, in bedrooms, in the guest house, everywhere.

It would be chaos, confusion, and awesomeness.

The front doorbell rang, and Bella walked in with Meg. "We're here to help with the flowers," she announced. "Girl time!"

Piper let out a whoop. "Grab a glass! We're talking about love, sex, and men."

"Perfect!" Bella and Meg hurried over, hugs went all around, and more champagne was poured.

Maddie had just settled down with a smile when Violet jumped up, and ran to the front door, barking and wagging. Maddie looked over to see Lucas and her dad walk in, both of them grinning.

Lucas was carrying a huge vase of long-stemmed red roses. He held them out as conversation stopped and everyone turned to look at him. "I had to go to a competitor to surprise you, so I apologize for that. Happy engagement, Maddie. I love you always, forever, and with all my heart."

Her friends let out little whispers of "aww..." while Maddie jumped off her stool, ran across the store, and threw her arms around the man she loved.

He'd never let her forget she was loved. Not ever. And she intended to do the same for him.

Because they'd waited a very long time to find love, and neither of them would ever take it for granted.

She'd found her home.

∼

WANT to know what happens with Declan and Piper? Or when Bella meets the cowboy who challenges everything she believes in? Order your copies now of *When We Least Expect It* (Declan & Piper), and *A Rogue Cowboy's Kiss* (Bella & the absolute *last* cowboy she would ever want to fall for!).

OR, you can keep reading for a sneak peek of *When We Least Expect It!*

THINGS GET sassy and spicy in *When We Least Expect It!* If you can't stand the heat, get out of the wedding! Except that the chemistry between wedding planner Piper Sheridan and her fake fiancé, ex-cop Declan Jones, is scorching hot...and in danger of combusting into something more real than either of them wants. Sparks fly when the sassy runaway bride recruits her reclusive landlord into her world of romance, tuxedoes, and happily-ever-after when she and Declan make a deal to fake an engagement for twenty-one scorching hot days. Treat yourself to *When We Least Expect It* today or keep reading for a sneak peek!

CHAPTER ONE

THERE WAS A SHIRTLESS, MUSCLED MAN in Piper Townsend's shower, and that was just not going to work for her today.

Or ever, quite honestly.

But especially today.

She put her hands on her hips as her landlord, Declan Jones, reared back with a freaking sledgehammer and aimed it at her still-intact shower wall. "Declan, don't—"

Her grumpy, ex-cop demolition squad slammed his sledgehammer into the tile, shattering the wall and eviscerating the last vestiges of composure she'd been clinging to when she'd walked in.

"Declan!" She strode into the bathroom and poked him in his shoulder.

He spun around so fast that he bumped into her, knocking her off balance. She tripped on his toolbox, and he grabbed her arm, swearing as he averted her certain death and hauled her upright again.

Of course he could toss her effortlessly to her feet. That was so irritatingly attractive in a man, and she didn't have time for irritatingly attractive men.

He pulled his earbuds out and scowled at her. "Don't sneak up on me when I have a sledgehammer. It's not safe."

"I literally shouted your name twice."

He frowned. "You did?"

She pointed to his earbuds. "Noise-cancelling?"

He looked down at his hand, then swore. "Sorry." He shoved the earbuds in his pocket. "You okay?"

Okay was such a vague term. "Technically, yes."

His brows went up. "You're not okay?"

"You didn't hurt me," she clarified, because did she want to have to explain to him what had happened to her in the last twenty-four hours? No, she didn't. Home was her oasis, and Declan was probably the only human within a few hundred miles who didn't know what had happened.

Or maybe that was an exaggeration, but that's what it felt like, so she was going with it.

"All right." He picked up the sledgehammer. "What do you need?"

"My bathroom, but that feels like a reach right now." Normally, a glimpse of Declan's gorgeous shoulders was enough to boost Piper's mood in an art-appreciation kind of way, but today his royal hotness was simply a big mass of muscles and man in her way. She did not have time for her bathroom to be in a pile of rubble.

Declan glanced over at her with those bright blue eyes

that always startled her with their intensity. "I told you I was starting the renovation today." He sounded cranky and tired.

Well, that was great for him that he was cranky and tired. So was she, and it was her bathroom that he'd just punctured a hole in. "Wednesday. You said you were starting Wednesday."

He frowned. "I said today."

"No, you said that you had to finish the molding in your kitchen, so you weren't going to start until Wednesday." It was currently Monday afternoon at five, which was not the time for Declan to be in her shower.

Well, in an alternate life, maybe any time would be the perfect time for Declan to be in her shower, but in this life? Never.

He narrowed his eyes, staring at her.

"Hello?"

"I think I did say Wednesday," he finally said.

Piper blinked. "I don't think I've ever heard you admit you were wrong about anything."

He flashed her a grin as he rested the sledgehammer against his leg. "I'm not that stubborn."

"You are, but I'm used to it." She waved her hand at her bathroom. "But about this—"

He'd offered to pay for a hotel while he redid her bathroom, but this was her oasis, and she'd needed the comfort of being there. She had a tiny powder room that had a toilet and a sink, and she could shower at her gym, so she'd decided it would work. "I didn't plan for this tonight. I need a shower."

And a miracle, but first things first.

Declan sighed and ran his hand over his short hair, his chiseled bicep flexing like God's gift to women. His hotness had never dawned on her prior to the last few weeks, but her trio of besties had recently been on a mission to get Piper back into the dating game, and they'd fixated on Declan as a good start.

She disagreed, but their constant harping on his physical attributes was working its way into her subconscious, which was incredibly distracting and annoying, especially when he was shirtless and sweaty.

Fortunately, she had a will of steel and enough relationship trauma to withstand any temptation, so it was all good.

"It was my mistake," Declan said, "so you can shower at my place."

"Your place?" Piper had never been in his gorgeous house that shared a gravel driveway with her little carriage house. She'd never even peeked through those beautiful French doors or tiptoed past his gorgeous, landscaped pool. Declan was private, closed-off. Almost a loner, from what she'd observed from her little vantage point in his guest house. He kept people away, except for the occasional visit by his parents, brother, and sister, whom she'd met a couple times.

Declan was a reclusive ex-cop who spent his life in jeans, boots, T-shirts, and a five o'clock shadow. His sole existence appeared to be working on his house, playing ball with his dog, and bartending part-time at a neighborhood bar.

His family was well-dressed, sociable, and always looked like they knew what a shower was for. She had no idea how they were related.

"Yeah. Back door is unlocked." Declan looked at his watch. "I'll be working until six, so you'll have privacy. Use the guest bath to the left at the top of the stairs. It's the blue bathroom."

Piper stared at him. "You're inviting me unattended into your sanctuary?"

He cocked a brow. "Why? Should I not trust you?"

"No. I'm very trustworthy." Well, apparently she was also demon spawn cursed to destroy love and romance in all its earthly forms, but she doubted Declan would be worried about that apparent flaw in her character. He didn't seem the type.

He grinned. "I know you're trustworthy. I ran a background check on you before I rented you the carriage house. You have an hour. Once I'm finished in here for the night, I'm kicking you out, so make it quick."

A background check? Sudden alarm gripped her. Did he know about her past? He was an ex-cop. If he'd decided to dig deep, his tentacles would have gone far. "What did you check?"

His smile faded. "Credit. Prison record."

"That's it?"

He leaned on his sledgehammer, studying her with open curiosity now. "What else is there to find, Piper?"

"Nothing." She shook out her shoulders. If Declan had uncovered her past, he wouldn't have rented her the carriage house. It was fine. Her past was still hidden. No one except her friend Maddie Vale knew. Relax, Piper. She ducked past him and grabbed her shampoo and conditioner off the sink where he'd moved it. "I'll be on my way—"

"You getting married?" he asked.

"What?" Alarm leapt through her, then she saw he was looking toward her left hand. Where there was no longer an engagement ring. Had he heard what happened?

He pointed. "The magazine."

She looked down and saw that her copy of the June issue of Elite Bride was facing him. Relief rushed through her. He didn't know. "No. I'm a wedding planner."

Or rather, a wedding killer, according to Kathryn Vespa, one of her bridal clients.

Kathryn had also called her cursed.

And bad luck.

And, most significantly, fired.

A second bride had also fired her today. And social media had embraced the new, viral hashtag #weddingkillerpiper.

And a third bride, the biggest client her firm had ever acquired, had left Piper three voicemails today, demanding that Piper call her back. She wasn't going to do that until she figured things out, since bride #3, April Hunsaker, was definitely going to fire her.

April was her last chance. If April fired her, Piper's career would be over.

Everything she'd worked for...destroyed.

Which meant she had to figure out how to regain April's trust tonight.

As in, within the next few hours.

Tomorrow, it would be too late.

Game over.

Piper had twelve hours to fix the unfixable. Hence the need for a miracle.

She'd find a way, but right now, she had no idea what that path was. She was worried that there wasn't an out, and that scared her more than she wanted to admit.

"Wedding planner?" Declan looked amused. "That job title brings fear into every man's heart."

"What? Why? I make dreams come true. And very well, I might add." Well, except for the string of bad luck over the last ten months...beginning with her own. But that wasn't bad luck so much as a nightmare of her own creating. Either way, same result, though.

"The bride's dreams, maybe, but that poor groom?" Declan chuckled. "Now he's got two women to complicate his life. All he wants is to get married, and now he has to deal with things like tablecloths, seating charts, and table centerpieces."

Piper rolled her eyes. "That's so unromantic! Just wait until you fall in love. You'll realize that your greatest joy is seeing your bride's face light up as her dream day comes to life."

His amusement faded, and his jaw got hard. "No chance. No wedding in my future."

It was her turn to be curious. His reaction had been intense and unyielding, far beyond a typical marriage-averse manly-man reaction. "Really? Why not?"

Something flashed across Declan's face, an emotion so raw and ragged that she sucked in her breath. "Because it's not." He turned away, picked up his construction assault weapon, and slammed it into the wall of her shower again.

Piper didn't move for a moment, stunned by the expression she'd seen on his face. Declan was always so reserved, so controlled, so grumpy, but that had been pure, raw emotion raking across his face for that brief second.

Declan had secrets, she realized. Secrets that would probably rip him to shreds if he let them out.

Wow. Just...wow. She'd had no idea that her reserved, solitary landlord was a boiling cauldron of secrets.

He looked over his shoulder at her. "You're down to fifty-eight minutes."

"Right. I'm going." She grabbed the rest of her toiletries and bolted.

Declan had just gone from annoyingly attractive on a physical level to maddeningly intriguing on an human level.

Which didn't fit into her life.

At all.

Piper was standing on the ruins of a promise she'd made to her mother before she'd passed away. If she failed to fix things in the next twelve hours, the dream she and her mom had created together would be shattered.

She needed miracles right now, not mistakes.

And Declan would be a mistake.

A huge, irrecoverable mistake.

Which meant she was keeping her distance from him.

In every way.

Because she was a woman on a mission, and she wasn't going to mess it up with romantic dreams of knights in shining armor.

She'd done that twice already, and the scars still burned.

Never, ever again.

～

DECLAN COULD STILL SMELL the flowers.

Piper was gone, and yet, he could still smell the flowers. Was it her shampoo? Her soap? Some sort of body lotion?

The thought of body lotion put a visual in his head that made him swear.

He set his sledgehammer down and stepped back, trying to focus on the carnage around him. Demolition was always satisfying. He knew damn well that he'd told Piper he was starting on Wednesday, but a few hours ago, he'd run into someone he used to know, and his past had been triggered.

He'd had to do something to distract himself. From the memories. From the pain in his gut. From the truth that wouldn't stop haunting him.

Declan had grabbed his tools and almost sprinted to the guest house, ignoring the instability in his knee. That first swing of the sledgehammer had reverberated through his body, jerking him back from the grips of the past and returning him to the present.

Now? He felt back in control again, locked down, focused...except for the fact he could still smell the scent of flowers that seemed to follow Piper wherever she went.

He fucking loved how she smelled.

He was going to have to find a way to get over it.

Because he wasn't ready for a woman, and he never would be.

That part of his life was over, and he was never going

back.

At that moment, his phone rang. He pulled it out and looked at the caller. When he saw who it was, he had to take a breath before answering it. "Declan here."

He listened for a moment, his gut tightening the longer they spoke. "Yeah, I can come in on Friday at eleven. Thanks."

He hung up and let his hand fall to his side, stunned.

He'd passed the physical to return to police work.

Interview on Friday.

After three years on the sidelines, fighting to get his body to work again, he'd done it.

It was all he'd been focused on. The only thing that mattered.

But now that he was going back there on Friday... Fuck.

It was only for an interview, but the nightmares were going to start again. He could already feel it.

He took a breath. Nightmares were fine. He was fine. He had a bathroom to destroy and that would get him right.

But as he picked up the sledgehammer, he caught a whiff of flowers again.

This time, he closed his eyes, paused, and inhaled, using that light, delicate scent to steady himself.

Piper was freaking sunshine, and she had no idea how she grounded him every time he saw her.

And she never would know, because he was never going there with her.

But would he take a minute to breathe in the flowers and let it settle him?

Yeah. He would.

Because he had only a few days to figure out how to make himself walk back into that station, and the life that had nearly destroyed him.

What happens when Declan and Piper decide to fake an engagement? Everything they aren't expecting, and think they don't want! Get *When We Least Expect It* now, and hunker down for some sassy, steamy romance with all the feels!

~

MORE HARTS ARE COMING! *A Rogue Cowboy's Kiss* is next! Order now so you don't forget!

WANT to know when Stephanie's next book is coming out, or when she's having a sale? Join her newsletter here on www.stephanierowe.com.

~

CHECK out Stephanie's other series below, or keep scrolling for excerpts of other Stephanie Rowe books!

WHAT ABOUT HEART-MELTING, fun, small-town romance? A new *Birch Crossing* is available! Leila Kerrigan is back in town with no time for the rebel who stole her heart long ago...but now he's playing for keeps. Treat yourself to *Secretly Mine* today or skip ahead to a sneak peek! It's a connected standalone, so you can enjoy it without reading any of the other *Birch Crossing* books (but you'll probably want to go back and read the others when you're done)!

NEW TO STEPHANIE'S cowboy world, and want more heart-melting cowboys? If so, you *have* to try her *Wyoming*

Rebels series about nine cowboy brothers who find love in the most romantic, most heartwarming, most sigh-worthy ways you can imagine. Get started with *A Real Cowboy Never Says No* right now. You will be sooo glad you did, I promise!

IF YOU WANT MORE SMALL-TOWN, emotional feel-good romances like the *Hart Ranch Billionaires*, you'd love my *Birch Crossing* series! Get started with *Unexpectedly Mine* today! Or jump in with the brand-new Birch Crossing book, *Secretly Mine*, or skip ahead to a sneak peek here!

ARE you in the mood for some feel-good, cozy mystery fun that's chock full of murder, mayhem, and women you'll wish were your best friends? If so, you'll fall in love with *Double Twist!*

ARE YOU A FAN OF MAGIC, love, and laughter? If so, dive into my paranormal romantic comedy *Immortally Sexy* series, starting with the first book, *To Date an Immortal*.

IS DARK, steamy paranormal romance your jam? If so, definitely try my award-winning *Order of the Blade* series, starting with book one, *Darkness Awakened*.

KEEP SCROLLING for sneak peeks of Stephanie Rowe books! You might find your next binge-read right here!

SNEAK PEEK: TRIPLE TROUBLE

A Mia Murphy Mystery

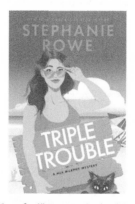

"So much darn fun!" Five-star Goodreads Review (Penny)

CHAPTER ONE

X.

I stared at my phone, stunned at the text that had just come in from an unfamiliar number. My brain immediately shouted at me that the *X* meant bad things, bad, bad things.

Then I remembered that I wasn't ten years old in the middle of a con with my mom. She wasn't standing on the other side of a luxurious room crowded with celebrities, holding up two crossed fingers, giving me the X sign that meant "abandon the con right now because it's going south."

I was, in fact, a grown woman who had walked away from that life and my mom ten years ago. I was currently standing on my dock in the gorgeous morning sunlight on a beautiful Maine lake, going over my list of all the must-do items still undone prior to the grand reopening of my new marina.

Not a celebrity or con in sight. And definitely no mom.

I took a breath. Wow. My head had gone to old places in an alarming hurry.

I grinned at my massive rescue cat, who was perched on the end of the dock, his tail twitching in anticipation of the next unsuspecting fish to swim past. "It's all good, King Tut."

He ignored me, but I knew that the love was still there.

My life was great. I had friends, a home, and a marina that I was determined to turn into a success. I looked down at my phone again, studying my list. The landscapers were due to finish today, and—

A second *X* popped up.

My heart sped up, and I sucked in my breath. *What the fudge?*

Tentatively, almost terrified of getting a response, I texted back. *Mom?*

I got an immediate, automated reply stating that the phone number was not in service.

I felt both relieved and weirdly sad. Of course it wouldn't be my mom. I hadn't had any contact with her since I'd left her when I was seventeen. Granted, I'd always felt that she knew exactly where I was and what I was doing, but even if that were true, why would she be texting me *XX* after all these years?

One *X* had meant abandon the con. XX had meant that it was getting dangerous and to get out as soon as possible. Get out? From my own home? That made no sense. But I couldn't help but take a more careful look around me.

The lake was relatively quiet, but there were a few boats around. Across the cove was Jake's Yacht Club, with its upscale blue and white awnings. Staff in their navy shirts and khaki shorts were strolling around helping customers. Everyone was calm. No danger that I could see.

I studied each driver of the boats that were near me, but I recognized everyone. No one new.

I turned around to examine my marina. The painters were working, the landscapers were making things beautiful. The front window that had been shot out my first week, almost killing one of my new besties, had been replaced, so the big plywood board was gone.

Everything was coming along well.

But despite all the warm fuzzies surrounding me, I could feel panic starting to build in my chest. I'd been relaxed for days, so the sudden descent into panic was throwing me. I was out of practice being on guard for my life.

I looked at King Tut again. He was my gold-star surveillance system. He'd sacrificed morals, pride, and common decency to save me more than once. "King Tut!"

He didn't take his gaze off the lake.

I took a breath, trying to get my head back into focus. The fact King Tut wasn't concerned meant there wasn't a threat. Granted, it could also mean that he was so deeply immersed in predator mode that he had no mental space for anything else...

My phone dinged again. My heart jumped, and I looked down.

X.

Three Xs.

Three Xs meant *get out fast, no matter what it takes.*

I looked around again, the hair on the back of my neck

prickling even as I tried to talk myself out of freaking out. It was a few Xs. There was nothing special about an X. Anyone could type an X. Glitches could produce Xs with zero effort.

I was at home at my marina. What could possibly be so dangerous that I needed to get out as fast as I could? My mom's messes hadn't been mine for a very long time.

Then my gaze settled on Vinnie, the sometime-gang-leader-ish guy who was currently acting as my unofficial bodyguard, due to the fact that my real one had been murdered (by a person unrelated to me and my life). The feds still couldn't figure out who had put surveillance cameras in my marina, so Vinnie had taken over keep-Mia-alive duty.

It had never once occurred to me that the spying had anything to do with my mother. I'd assumed it was connected to my ex-husband, who was currently in federal prison for being a drug kingpin. I'd put him there, and his mom had tried to kill me for it.

Vinnie was standing in the parking lot, his arms folded as he scanned the area. He looked dangerous and armed, despite the fact he had already admitted he would never shoot anyone for me, due to his aversion to a life of guilt and trauma, and things like that.

But at six-foot four, muscular, and wearing just the right amount of bling for a gang leader, he looked like a deadly force, so I doubted anyone would try while he was around. Plus, honestly, after spending so long looking over my shoulder, I'd gotten used to the possibility of being a target.

I was chill now.

Except, apparently, when being triggered by my past.

I looked down at my phone again, trying to think of a reply that might help me figure out if the sender was my mom.

My mom had been a code person, because living a life of

crime had taught her that paper trails were never good for the criminal.

I tried to remember something from the code we'd used, but all I could think of were the made-up symbols that we'd created, none of which were on the keyboard of my phone (go figure, right?). I couldn't quite recall how any of them went together anyway.

I did remember the symbol for my name, though.

I quickly knelt on the dock, dipped my finger in the water, and then drew the symbol on the wood. I took a picture of it then texted it to the number.

Again, an immediate reply that the number was not in service.

Then, right after that, another text came through. *XXX*.

Alarm shot through me, the kind that she'd triggered in me so many times as a kid. *Run, Mia, run!*

"King Tut," I shouted. "Let's go. Now." I didn't know where to go, but I had to get out, and get out fast. I had no idea what was happening, but I liked my life too much to be willing to die. "Vinnie," I shouted. "We gotta go!"

Vinnie started running toward me, but King Tut ignored me. I ran to the edge of the dock to get him. Leaving my cat behind didn't qualify as "no matter what." He was my family, and there was no way I was leaving him. "King Tut! We gotta go—"

He shot off the dock and dove into the water, disappearing under the surface. "Hey!"

I immediately jumped in after him, knowing that sometimes King Tut vanished for hours once he got under the water. I didn't know where he went, but wherever he came up for air was out of my sight. It used to freak me out, but I'd gotten used to it.

But now was not the time to lose my cat for hours. The late June water was warming, but still a shock to my system as

I hit the lake. I immediately ducked under, searching the crystalline water for my black cat.

I didn't see him.

I stood up, water dripping off me. Vinnie was already at the end of the dock. "What's happening?" He looked alarmed.

"Where's King Tut? Can you see him? We need to get out of here, but I need to get him first!"

"King Tut?" Vinnie pulled off his sunglasses and scanned the water.

At that moment, I heard the roar of the lake patrol boat. I whirled around and waved my hands at Devlin Hunt, the too-handsome-for-anyone's-good cop who was driving it. "Stop!" I shouted. "King Tut's under the water! Turn off your propeller!"

Because we'd done this drill many times since I'd bought the marina a few months ago and discovered that my cat was an avid underwater hunter, Devlin immediately shut his boat off and leaned over the edge to search the water.

For a long moment, there was silence as the three of us scanned the water for my baby.

"There!" Devlin pointed close to the beach, and I sloshed through the water toward where he was pointing, my heart pounding.

"Something's wrong!" I shouted as I hurried after King Tut. "I'm in danger!"

"What?" Devlin stood up and put his hand on his gun. "What's going on?"

"I don't know!" I saw a black shadow under the water, and I lunged for him. My hands wrapped around King Tut's waist, and I dragged the yowling beast out of the water. "I need to go!" I started running toward the shore. I had no idea what the danger was or where it was coming from, which made me even more alarmed.

Just as I reached the shore, fighting to hold into a sodden ball of long-haired anger, an extended-cab pickup truck shot into the parking lot. I knew that black truck. It belonged to one of my two best friends, Hattie Lawless, a seventy-something chef who ran a café in my marina and raced cars on the side. "Hattie!"

She hit the brakes and the truck skidded to a stop. She jumped out, grabbing my shoulders as I ran up. "What's going on? Why do you look like you're freaking out?"

"A triple X! I think my mom sent me a triple X!"

"Is that porn?" Hattie looked intrigued. "I had no idea your mom was into porn. I mean, not surprising because she's a wild card, but porn? Can I see it? I assume it's girl power porn, right? She seems empowered."

"Porn?" I stared at her. "No. It's our signal that the con has gone south, and we need to run."

"A con?" Her eyebrows shot up. "You're running a con with your mom? What con?"

"I'm not. I mean, that I know of. But I got this text from this random number, and it could have been her, and—"

"Wait a minute." Hattie put her hands on her hips. "Mia Murphy. Pull yourself together. You're not running a con. You own a marina in the charming town of Bass Derby. You don't engage in illegal activities, except to help others. And you haven't heard from your mom in over a decade. Whatever you think is going on, isn't."

I grabbed my phone and handed it to her as Vinnie ran up. "See?"

Hattie took the phone, and the two of them peered at it. "This?" Hattie frowned at me. "Some random text from a number that doesn't even work? You're freaking out about *this?* How do you know it's her?"

"I don't *know* it's her, but what if it is? What if there's something going on and she's trying to warn me and—"

"Hey!" Hattie cut me off. "Take a breath, girlfriend." She held up her hands palm up and inhaled. "Deep breath. Channel your inner river."

I blinked. "My river?"

"Yes. A calm, scenic river. Tranquility. Peace. Serenity. Imagine chiseled, charming men lined up on the banks, singing about how wonderful you are."

I stared at her. "Seriously?"

"Yes. Imagine their deep voices, singing 'Mia is a badass. She rules the world!' Maybe they're even dancing for you, some manly, synchronized beauty. How can that not feel good? Breathe in. Breathe out."

Devlin finally caught up to us. "What's going on?"

"Keep channeling your river, Mia. I got this." Hattie held up my phone. "Mia thinks this text is from her mom, signaling that the end of the world is upon us, and she must run away. To where? She doesn't know. From what? Also unknown."

Devlin took the phone and frowned at it. As he studied it, I found my pulse slowing and my panic easing. Devlin was a local cop in the small town of Bass Derby, but I was pretty certain he had a black ops background.

His buddy, Agent Hawk Straus, who I called Griselda to reclaim my personal power, was the FBI agent who had coerced me into a two-year-undercover sting against my ex. When I'd moved to Bass Derby, Griselda had asked Devlin to make sure no one from my ex's life assassinated me. He trusted Devlin with my life, which means I did, too. With Devlin standing by my side, no one would be able to get to me.

Plus, the river visualization had been surprisingly helpful.

I took the deep breath Hattie had wanted for me, and she nodded her approval as she studied me. "It's not like you to freak out like that," she observed. "You're very unflappable

when it comes to danger like assassins, guns, and other immi-
nent threats to your life. Why are you having a fit over this?"

Devlin looked over at me. "Hattie's right. This could
easily just be some random text."

They were right. I usually was pretty calm. A childhood of
crime had inured me to the small dangers in life. In fact, it
had instilled in me an affinity for a high-risk life, which I tried
to suppress as much as possible. "I know. It's just...well...it's
my *mom*."

"It's probably *not* your mom," Hattie said.

"I know. I just meant that she triggers me." I let out my
breath again. "The purpose of the triple X code was to get my
attention when I wasn't taking things seriously. She would use
it to freak me out and get me to do what she needed me to."

Hattie cocked her brow. "That sounds a little manipulative."

"When you're a criminal, sometimes you can't mess
around." I looked over at Devlin, who was frowning at me.
"What?"

He held up my phone. "I'm going to have Griselda, I
mean Hawk, track this number and see what he can figure
out."

I nodded. "Okay, great. Thanks."

"But in the meantime, I agree with Hattie," he said.
"Keep an eye out, but we're already on alert, so I don't think
we raise the alarm any higher. Unless you know something
else?"

I looked at the three of them, and buried my chin in King
Tut's soggy head. "You know, I think you guys are right. It
makes no sense that my mom would be telling me to run
from here." My tension eased even more. "It was an old trigger, I guess."

"We all have those," Devlin said softly.

I knew he understood. He'd been in a gang when he was a

kid, so I imagined he had his own share of childhood land mines that came up from time to time. "Thanks."

He nodded. "It's all good, Mia." But he continued to study me. "You do look like hell, though."

"Thanks." Not too long ago, Devlin had declared his interest in dating me. On the same day, Griselda had made the same announcement. They were besties. Griselda had warned me off Devlin. Devlin had warned me off Griselda. I didn't want to ever date anyone again.

It was awkward.

And yet somehow, I'd agreed to have dinner with Devlin tomorrow night. Umm...

Hattie peered at me. "You know, you do look haggard. It can't all be from that text."

"Mia was up all night working on the marina," Vinnie offered. "She's freaking out about having it ready in time for her grand reopening."

Empathy flashed across Hattie's face. "Sweetie, it looks amazing. It's going great."

"I know, but it's just that I have to overcome the marina's reputation and mine. Do you know that the sheriff came over here with some woman a couple days ago? She'd lost her diamond ring and accused me of taking it, due to my criminal history and all."

Devlin narrowed his eyes. "I didn't know about that." No one in the entire town was impressed with our sheriff, not even the mayor, who had hired him. She also happened to be his mom.

"Well, the lady found it under her own bed," I said.

"Which you could have put there," Hattie said. "It doesn't exonerate you."

I looked at her. "How is that helpful?"

"Just wanted to remind you of your awesomeness. Just because someone doesn't appreciate your specialness or sees it as a threat doesn't make you any less awesome." She put her arm around my shoulders. "You need a vacation."

I sighed. She'd offered this trip about forty times in the last two weeks. "I can't take a vacation. I'm opening my marina in ten days."

"And yet, you were ready to abandon it all forever, because of a random text," she said.

I grimaced. "So I freaked out a little."

"A lot," Vinnie said. "You dove in after your cat like he was about to be murdered."

I tightened my arms around my soggy cat, who was now purring and happy to be snuggled. "I thought he was in danger."

Hattie put her hands on her hips. "As I have told you repeatedly, I'm going to visit my cousin Thelma for a couple days to celebrate her birthday. Come with me. It's a five-star island resort on the coast of Maine. You'll come back rested, refreshed, and ready to receive all texts with a clear mind."

I wanted to go so badly, because having friends was a precious new treasure, and I loved every second of it. But setting down roots in my new town was critical for me, and getting accepted by the town was more difficult than I'd expected. I had a lot riding on this grand opening, and I needed to be here working, not on vacation. "I already told you I can't. I have the grand opening—"

"If the triple X *was* from your mom, then leaving for a couple days seems like a great idea as well," Hattie interrupted.

Huh. "You're not wrong about that," I admitted slowly.

"And Lucy's coming on the trip," Hattie said. "Girl bonding. You know you love it."

Aw...Lucy was going, too? Now I really wanted to go. The three of us had become such a tight trio since I'd moved to Bass Derby.

"I think it's a good idea to go," Devlin said. "Get off the grid for a few days while we figure this out."

I looked at him, both disappointed and relieved at the idea of missing our date. "Our dinner?"

He grinned, looking pleased that I'd even remembered we had plans. "I don't know about you, but I'll still live in this town when you get back. We'll figure it out."

I bit my lip. The idea of stepping away from the marina for a couple days did sound good. I was drained, I loved Hattie and Lucy, and a little part of me was worried that the text really had been from mom. "Is the resort cat-friendly?"

"I don't think so, but hang on." She pulled out her phone and made a call. "Beau. It's Hattie."

Beau Hammersley was a reclusive, wealthy mystery writer who claimed to hate the world, except for me, my mom, and Hattie. I suspected he liked people a lot more than he claimed, but I adored him either way.

"Mia needs to leave town for a couple days because her mom might have just sent her a cryptic text about danger. Can you come over and grab King Tut and watch him?"

I grinned. Beau was obsessed with my mom. He'd run across a documentary on the infamous Tatum Murphy when he'd been researching one of his books, and the obsession had been born.

Hattie hung up the phone. "He'll be here in a few seconds. He's around the corner. He's out boating."

My arms tightened around King Tut. "I don't want to leave King Tut behind—"

"Yo! I'm here!" Beau came flying around the corner in his boat, shouting and waving his arms. He sped up to the beach and ran his boat right onto the sand. He leapt out and came racing up. He was wearing his bejeweled sandals, denim shorts, and his tee shirt with the bloody dagger on it. His hair was ratty from the wind, and the only sign of wealth on him was the brand of his sunglasses. "Your mom's in danger?"

I almost started laughing at his delight about my mom being involved. "I don't know. Maybe."

Hattie pointed to King Tut. "Mia needs King Tut safe."

Beau eyed the cat. "Tatum might come to check on him?"

"She might," I agreed. Who knew what my mom might do? No one. Checking on my cat was as possible as anything else.

"Then he's safe with me." Beau held out his arms. "Come on, King Tut. Let's go." The reclusive mystery writer liked to put on a tough persona, but in his heart, he was a good man. If he said he'd keep King Tut safe, he would. He'd do whatever it took. After decades as a mystery writer, the man had ideas about danger, death, and murder that no one wanted to know.

King Tut gazed at Beau and didn't budge from my arms.

Beau met his steely gaze. "I have caviar."

King Tut immediately leapt out of my arms, raced down the sand, then jumped into Beau's boat. He sat down on the bow, flicked his tail, and gave us all a sullen, serious glare with his unblinking yellow eyes. Even with his black fur still dripping with water, he looked huge, menacing, and dangerous.

"Damn, girl." Hattie grinned. "If you decide not to go and deprive that cat of Beau's caviar, you will never be safe from that feline again."

"I need to channel King Tut's attitude for my next villain," Beau said. "Look at that threat. It's brilliant. Subtle. Unyielding. And yet disarming in that kitty-cat ball of soggy fluff. It's almost diabolical. I love it! He's my new muse. Get me his life jacket, and we're off."

I bit my lip. "I've never been without King Tut since I rescued him."

Hattie put her arm around my shoulder. "King Tut will be

safe away from the marina, and you'll be safe too. Plus, both of you will have fun."

"I think it's the best call," Devlin said. "Give me a couple days to figure out what's going on." He looked over at me. "I'll keep an eye on the marina."

"I will, too. I know what the contractors are supposed to be doing, and I'll manage it," Vinnie said. "I'll sleep in the spare storefront. It'll cost you, but I'm worth it."

I looked at the three of them, and my heart got all mushy. These were my friends, people who cared if I died, cared if my cat was safe, and cared about my marina. I might not have had my breakthrough with the rest of the town yet, but I'd found a little niche of home, and I appreciated it with all my heart.

The truth was, I did want to go with Hattie and Lucy. I wanted to go with every fiber in my being. "How long's the trip?"

"Three days and two nights," Hattie said. "The ferry leaves in four hours, though. We need to hurry. How fast can you pack?"

I looked over at her, and suddenly, I knew she was right. They were all right. Those texts might not be from my mom, but they were the impetus I needed. I was supposed to go on this trip, and I wasn't going to miss it. "Fast."

◦∼◦

Get Triple Trouble today!

SNEAK PEEK: SECRETLY MINE

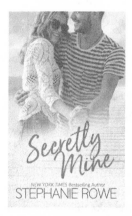

"Exquisitely beautiful!! All the feels. This is a do not pass up book. Perfectly written :)." -Five-star Goodreads Review (Jann)

She's back in town with no time for the rebel who stole her heart long ago...but now he's playing for keeps.

∼

Dash Stratton had just picked up his welder when he heard his name hollered from the front of the house.

Recognition flooded him, and he swore, spinning around. That voice sounded familiar, but there was no way Leila Sheridan would be at his house, bellowing his name.

But he'd thought he'd seen her in that car outside Wright's.

That was twice in the span of an hour.

What the hell was going on?

She, whoever it was, shouted his name again, and something prickled along his skin. He would have sworn it was Leila.

He set down the welder and strode out of his studio. He jerked his sunglasses down over his face, and headed across the lawn around the side of his house, moving with an instinctive urgency.

He practically sprinted around the side of the house, and then stopped dead, stunned.

Leila Kerrigan was in front of the house, her hands on her hips, staring right at him.

Emotions flooded him, so many emotions he couldn't sort them out. He couldn't take his gaze off her. She was a woman now, not a scrawny, scared eighteen-year-old. She was wearing shorts and sneakers, and a blue tank top, looking like she was ready for a day on the lake, like the old days.

She had curves now she hadn't had before, the curves of a woman. Her sunglasses were on top of her head, revealing those glorious blue eyes and dark lashes that he'd begun to think he'd imagined.

She sucked in her breath. "Dash."

"Fuck." He grimaced. That was all he could think of to say after all this time. "I mean, what the fuck are you doing here?"

Her eyes widened. and he swore under his breath. "Sorry.

254

I'm just stunned to see you in my front yard. You look great." Suddenly, he realized why she was there.

She wanted a divorce. The time had come.

Fuck. This time, he meant it.

A cute little frown furrowed between her eyebrows. "You don't know why I'm here?"

Double fuck. Had her lawyer served him? Had he missed an email? "No."

"You don't know about Bea's will?"

He narrowed his eyes. Bea's will? Not a divorce? He was annoyed by the relief that shuddered through him. "What about it? I know I got the house, because she told me many times that's what she was doing." He frowned. "What did she put in there for you?" Was there something at the house that was for Leila? He hadn't seen anything with her name on it, but Bea might have hidden it well. "Do you need me to find something for you?"

Leila stared at him, then understanding dawned on her face, and she burst out laughing. "I swear to God, I'm going to kill Eppie. And Clare!"

Ah...Eppie. He knew what kind of chaos she could cause. "What did they do?" Eppie was as much trouble as Bea had been.

"Clare gave me a letter for you." She fished around in her back pocket, then held up a folded envelope. "I suspect she explains it here."

He didn't move. If it was a letter from Bea, he didn't want to read it, hear her words, feel her presence. It was too soon for him. "You explain it."

Leila waved the letter at him. "No, thanks. Here."

Swearing under his breath, Dash walked over to her to take it, but as he neared, he felt like his world was spinning. Leila Sheridan was back, and she was unfinished business. *His* unfinished business.

He took the envelope, and his fingers brushed against hers, sending a shock reverberating through his system. Yeah, the attraction was still there, but this time, she wasn't an eighteen-year-old he had to protect from a piece-of-shit stepfather.

She was a woman, and their age difference no longer mattered like it had when she was barely eighteen and he'd been twenty-five.

When his hand touched hers, she sucked her in breath and jerked her hand back. "Letter," she mumbled.

"Letter," he agreed, as he took a step back, folded it, and put it in his pocket. "I'll read it later."

Leila's brows went up. "You need to read it now."

"I'm good. You need anything from me?"

She stared at him. "You're as stubborn and difficult as you were back then."

"Probably."

She folded her arms over her chest. "Read the letter, Dash."

"Nope." There was no chance he was reading Bea's words right now. He missed her like hell, and he wasn't in a place to read a letter she wrote to him in front of Leila. Or anyone. Or even himself. "Anything else you need?"

She stared at him. "Really?"

"Yeah. Whatever you need." This conversation felt awkward and distant, nothing like how he'd envisioned it might be all the times he'd thought about her over the years. "Want a drink? I have water and beer." And other stuff he didn't feel like mentioning.

"Water?"

"Yeah."

She put her hands on her hips. "Dash."

"Leila."

She sighed in aggravation. "Bea didn't leave you the house. She left *us* the house."

Dash stared at her. "Us?"

"Yes." She pointed back and forth between them. "You and me. Co-heirs. We have to both live in the house together for thirty consecutive nights before either of us can do anything with it. I'm moving in now."

"No." His amusement fled. Oh, wait, he hadn't been amused by anything about her sudden appearance. "It's my house. I've been living here for the last six months. She told me it was mine, repeatedly." He'd been counting on this house, and not just for himself.

"Well, it's also half mine. I need the money from selling it, and we can't sell it until we both live here together for thirty days."

Sell it? No one was selling this house. He couldn't afford to buy out Leila. He swore under his breath, then pulled out his phone and called Clare.

She answered on the first ring. "You read the letter?"

"I'm co-heirs with Leila, and we have to live in the house together for thirty consecutive nights before we can do anything with it?" It had to be wrong. It didn't make sense.

Clare sighed. "Yes, look, I'm sorry I didn't tell you, but Bea's will specifically said Leila had to be the one to tell you."

All thoughts of his attraction to Leila vanished in a surge of irritation. He ground his jaw. "So it's true?"

"Yes, it is."

He glanced at Leila, who was watching him, chewing on her lower lip. Why did she look so damned adorable chewing on her lip like that? Why did he care? He didn't have time for this. "I need this house. You know I do."

"Thirty days, Dash. You can have it in thirty days, as long as Leila agrees to give up her share."

Fuck. He couldn't afford to buy her out. "What else is in

the will that you didn't tell me? There's more, isn't there? More games that Bea put in there?"

Clare cleared her throat. "It's a rather complicated will, but that's the gist of it."

He swore under his breath. "Clare—"

"Look. You could probably contest some of the provisions, but it's *Bea*," Clare said softly. "You loved her. She loved you. Don't you want to let her do this her way? Would you deprive her of that joy?"

"No." Dash rubbed his forehead and cursed again. Bea had changed his life in many ways, standing by him when his parents disowned him. He'd spent the rest of his life giving back to her, and he couldn't stop now just because she was gone. "I'd never let her down," he admitted grudgingly.

"Bea spent a lot of time planning this," Clare said. "It's her gift to you. Not just the house, but all of it."

Dash looked at Leila. Was Leila a gift that Bea had decided to hand him? Another chance at the woman he'd let go? He ground his jaw. A year ago, cohabitating with Leila to compete for the house would have been very different than now.

Now, it didn't work for him. "Clare, she wrote the will before—"

"No, she didn't. She updated it afterwards."

That stunned Dash into silent. "She wrote it *after*?" After his whole life had changed. Rocked to its foundation. Shattered into a thousand pieces that he was still struggling to put back together. She wrote the will *after* that had happened? *What the hell, Bea?*

"Yes," Clare said. "It's your choice, Dash. You can contest it, and drag Bea's last moments of joy into question, or go with it."

He sighed. "You're very manipulative."

Clare laughed. "I know. You're welcome. Eppie and I have to confirm every night's sleepover, so you'll see a lot of us."

Roomie. Living with Leila Sheridan for thirty days. Thirty days in which to convince her to give him her half of the house. Not sell it to him. *Give* it to him.

Fuck. He didn't like needing charity from her. Bea's promise to give him the house had been his key to getting free. To have that compromised... *What the hell were you thinking, Bea?*

He didn't have a backup plan. He'd put everything into this house on the assumption he would get it.

And in those thirty days, he also had to avoid having Leila ask for a divorce. And...he to resist the temptation that she'd been to him for a long time.

Three bedrooms.

One and a half bathrooms.

One shower.

Hell. This was going to get rough fast.

And a part of him was looking forward to every minute of it.

How hot does it get when Leila moves in? And what secret is Dash hiding? Treat yourself today to *Secretly Mine*, and fall in love with Dash and Leila!

ABOUT THE AUTHOR

NEW YORK TIMES AND USA TODAY bestselling author Stephanie Rowe is the author of more than sixty published novels. She is a Vivian® Award nominee, a RITA® Award winner and a five-time nominee, and a Golden Heart® Award winner and two-time nominee. She has written for Grand Central Publishing, Harlequin, HarperCollins, Sourcebooks, and Dorchester Publishing. She loves her puppies, tennis, and trying to live her best, truest life. For info on Stephanie's newest releases, join her newsletter today! by going to her website: www.stephanierowe.com.

ACKNOWLEDGMENTS

Special thanks to my beta readers. You guys are the best! Thanks to Alyssa Bird, Anette Taylor, Ashlee Murphy, Brenda Wasnock, Bridget Koan, Britannia Hill, Carolena Emer, Cindy Abbott, Deb Julienne, Denise Fluhr, Diana Kassman, Dottie Jones, Elizabeth Barnes, Heidi Hoffman, Helen Loyal, Jackie Moore Kranz, Jeanne Stone, Jeanie Jackson, Jessica Hayden, Jodi Bobbett, Jodi Moore, Judi Pflughoeft, Kasey Richardson, Linda Rogers, Linda Watson, Nichole Reed, Regina Thomas, Summer Steelman, Suzanne Mayer, Shell Bryce, Susan Parker, and Trish Douglas. Special thanks to my family, who I love with every fiber of my heart and soul. And to AER, who is my world. Love you so much, baby girl! I am so proud of you! You're going to rock this world! And to Joe, who keeps me believing myself. I love you all!

Made in the USA
Coppell, TX
17 October 2024

38730950R00156